"You're getting the works."

Crosby gulped, and terror crossed his face. "What's the works?"

Sami waggled her finger at him. "I'm not giving anything away. Otherwise you won't show up." She pointed to his coat pocket. "Give me your phone, and I'll set an alarm and program a reminder for you to come by the salon."

He grumbled but pulled out his phone and let her do just that. "I'm getting better. I'm only late when something's not important."

"I'm important." She held her head up high. "I'm going to make a swan out of you yet, Crosby Virtue. On New Year's Day, you'll be the toast of the town and have so many admirers, you'll have to create one of those special files of yours to keep them all organized."

She caught the wobble in her voice as she'd said those words. The cold must be getting to her. For the first time, the thought of Crosby hanging out with another woman sent a tiny ping of alarm through her. To recover, she tried to focus on the makeover she planned for Crosby, but that only led to more thoughts of, well...Crosby.

Dear Reader,

Several years ago, I booked last-minute tickets for a holiday train excursion. After my family boarded the train, it became apparent why I'd received such a great deal. Our seats were located in the open-air compartment, away from the heated warmth of the interior. Thanks to hot cocoa and my husband's foresight to pack hand warmers, the three-hour trip across two states became a cherished memory, accented by a fun visit with Santa, who gifted us sleigh bells.

When it came time to write the youngest Virtue sibling's story, that train ride popped into mind as the perfect vehicle for Crosby and Sami. Crosby is the town historian who loves renovating the Violet Ridge Express almost as much as he loves his best friend and secret crush, Sami Fleming. Even though Sami wants to experience life's adventures and see the world, she is determined to help Crosby find his true love and holiday match before she departs Violet Ridge.

I hope you enjoy this trip to Violet Ridge for the holidays! I love hearing from readers. Please visit my website, tanyaagler.com, for ways to keep in touch!

Happy reading!

Tanya

THE COWBOY'S CHRISTMAS MATCH

TANYA AGLER

Harlequin
HEARTWARMING

If you purchased this book without a cover you should be aware that this book is stolen property. It was reported as "unsold and destroyed" to the publisher, and neither the author nor the publisher has received any payment for this "stripped book."

Harlequin®
HEARTWARMING™

ISBN-13: 978-1-335-46025-7

The Cowboy's Christmas Match

Copyright © 2025 by Tanya Agler

All rights reserved. No part of this book may be used or reproduced in any manner whatsoever without written permission.

Without limiting the author's and publisher's exclusive rights, any unauthorized use of this publication to train generative artificial intelligence (AI) technologies is expressly prohibited.

This is a work of fiction. Names, characters, places and incidents are either the product of the author's imagination or are used fictitiously. Any resemblance to actual persons, living or dead, businesses, companies, events or locales is entirely coincidental.

For questions and comments about the quality of this book, please contact us at CustomerService@Harlequin.com.

TM and ® are trademarks of Harlequin Enterprises ULC.

Harlequin Enterprises ULC
22 Adelaide St. West, 41st Floor
Toronto, Ontario M5H 4E3, Canada
www.Harlequin.com

HarperCollins Publishers
Macken House, 39/40 Mayor Street Upper
Dublin 1, D01 C9W8, Ireland
www.HarperCollins.com

Recycling programs for this product may not exist in your area.

Printed in U.S.A.

Tanya Agler remembers the first set of Harlequin books her grandmother gifted her, and she's been in love with romance novels ever since. An award-winning author, Tanya makes her home in Georgia with her wonderful husband, their four children and a lovable basset, who really rules the roost. When she's not writing, Tanya loves classic movies and a good cup of tea. Visit her at tanyaagler.com or email her at tanya.agler@tanyaagler.com.

Books by Tanya Agler

Harlequin Heartwarming

The Single Dad's Holiday Match
The Soldier's Unexpected Family
The Sheriff's Second Chance
A Ranger for the Twins

Smoky Mountain First Responders

The Firefighter's Christmas Promise
The Paramedic's Forever Family

Rodeo Stars of Violet Ridge

Caught by the Cowgirl
Snowbound with the Rodeo Star
Her Temporary Cowboy

A Violet Ridge Novel

The Triplets' Holiday Miracle
Saving the Rancher
A Family for the Cowboy Cop

Visit the Author Profile page
at Harlequin.com for more titles.

For my father-in-law, Dave,
who was a model railroad expert and loved all
things to do with trains, with my love and gratitude
for being such a great father and Papa.

CHAPTER ONE

COMMITTEE MEETINGS WERE the bane of Crosby Virtue's existence. Crosby bolted up the stairs of the Violet Ridge train depot and opened the office door as every face turned toward him. He nodded and slipped into his seat, silently chastising himself for forgetting to set his alarm. Not that he could help staying up half the night. He'd been engrossed in reading Linus Irwin's diary, a fascinating story about the opening of the very same train depot in the nineteenth century—now, a beloved landmark. Sometime toward the end of the account, Crosby had fallen asleep in front of his pet iguana Sundance's heated terrarium. Already late, he threw on what was once his father's favorite beige cardigan sweater over yesterday's black T-shirt and jeans and rushed over here. His brother-in-law, Mayor Ben Irwin, raised an eyebrow at Crosby's late entrance but called the meeting to order with a bang of his gavel.

An hour later, Crosby would have preferred to be anywhere but here, listening to the town accountant, Phillip, drone on about ticket sales when there was so much to do to get the depot and the Violet Ridge Thunderbolt into shape over the next three weeks. Still, enduring this would be worth it on Christmas Eve when the train operated for the first time in fifty years and the depot would be packed with passengers traveling to and from Gunnison with Santa making a surprise appearance. Unlike its original purpose of traversing the country, the Thunderbolt would now promote tourism and take sightseers on scenic tours of the region. Best of all, it would be financially self-sufficient.

Phillip switched slides to the next screenshot and started updating the committee on the Midnight Express New Year's Eve Celebration.

Zelda Baker, the former mayor, raised her hand. "Did we decide on formal or semi-formal dress for the gathering?"

"Semi-formal." Crosby fielded this one. "The event is a thank-you to the volunteers for their contribution to restoring the Thunderbolt."

Phillip nodded and continued, "There are a good number of choices we have to make today for the celebration." He launched into a price comparison of chicken versus salmon for the sit-down dinner.

A heated discussion about the merits of each ensued. After voting for chicken, Crosby started doodling in his notebook. When Phillip kept elaborating about his spreadsheet, line by line, Crosby studied the tree he'd drawn in the margin. Wrinkling his nose, he erased a stray mark and shaded the leaves with his pencil point. He loved that scratchy sound almost as much as he loved the smell of old books. There was nothing like a whiff of tannin. Being surrounded by old items and artifacts at the Miners' Cottage, the longest-surviving intact structure in Violet Ridge, was the highlight of serving as town historian.

Books were Crosby's safe space, and he cherished each volume at the Miners' Cottage. Soon, the site would need sprucing up for the holidays. Where had he stored the antique decorations? Certainly not at the cottage, which was open to the public. Space was tight, and the back room served as a storage area and his office. He definitely hadn't toted them to his house. As it was, whenever weather permitted, he walked the two blocks to his workplace with his pet iguana, Sundance, in a portable carrier. Then he remembered. He had dropped the decorations off at the Lazy River Dude Ranch, owned and operated by his family.

Once he located the garland and lights and such, he'd enlist his best friend, Sami Fleming, who possessed a flair for color and design, to help him decorate. When she had arrived at the Lazy River Dude Ranch this past May, she promptly took one look at him and asked if he'd lost a pair of glasses. There, at the duck pond, she'd plucked the ones off the top of his head and tapped the edge of his spare pair, which were adorning his face. He'd never forget that first encounter with her.

Sami was the most beautiful woman he'd ever seen. She'd been wearing a red silk blouse and white pants with her long blond hair loose and flowing over her shoulders. Taking him in hand, she had appointed herself his "new bestie" and he had fallen head over heels in love with her.

Shortly thereafter, Sami and her sister, Amanda, decided to move to the ranch. Amanda had arrived with only a temporary assignment—hired by his grandmother to create a new marketing campaign for the dude ranch—but ended up staying permanently after she and Crosby's brother Seth fell in love. They were now engaged with the wedding scheduled for Valentine's Day.

Meanwhile, back in California, Sami had also been looking for new opportunities. With her sister in love not just with Seth but Violet Ridge, she opted to give the town a try. Since she'd been here, Crosby had blown numerous opportunities to share his feelings. Like the family picnic when he had accidentally fallen into the duck pond. Or the hayride, where Amanda lost her engagement ring. Everyone combed the site until Sami found it. Somehow, the right time always came and went without him seizing the moment.

As much as he'd like to express his true feelings, he'd decided the best way to keep Sami in his life was as his friend. The pencil lead snapped. Crosby looked up and found five sets of eyes trained on him. Once again, his woolgathering had set him apart from everyone else.

Crosby delivered a small smile in their direction and laid down his pencil. "Sounds great. You're on the right track."

He laughed at his own pun until he saw Ben arch his eyebrow. "Thanks for agreeing to be the keynote speaker at the Midnight Express New Year's Eve Celebration."

"What?" Crosby moved so suddenly that he almost fell off the hard wooden chair he was sitting on, but he steadied himself just in time to keep from toppling over. "Surely there's someone else up to the task." As a dedicated lifelong introvert, talking to large groups in a public setting was the last thing he ever wanted to do.

Put together to officially mark the beginning of the train's return to Violet Ridge, the Midnight Express New Year's Eve Celebration was going to be the social event of the season. Anybody else would be a better choice. The last thing the organizing committee needed was for their keynote speaker to sleep through the event.

Everyone started talking over each other until Mayor Ben banged his gavel on the table. "Let's review our options one more time," Ben said.

"Why? Crosby fits the bill. He's a resident of Violet Ridge and has a connection to the train via the cottage. Otherwise, I'd nominate my favorite rodeo star, Ty Darling." Zelda Baker grew more animated when discussing Ty, although her Kelly green pixie cut stayed perfectly in place. "Crosby has helmed the Thunderbolt's restoration and will be overseeing the Miners' Cottage renovation, when we get to that next. He's a shoo-in."

But Crosby still wasn't convinced. He was a man destined for behind-the-scenes action. "What about my brother Seth?" he suggested, hopeful a senior Virtue would seem more official, if not, worthy.

Ben shook his head. "This is the first season there will be guests at the dude ranch from Thanksgiving straight through to Christmas. Seth is booked, literally and figuratively."

Crosby felt sick. He reached for more names. "What about Jase or his fiancée, Cassie?"

After returning to town to recapture an escaped criminal, Jase switched from the Denver to the Violet Ridge police force to lay down some roots of his own, having fallen for the convict's half-sister Cassie. His brother had not only met his soulmate during the case but also fell in love with her cool kids.

That was all fine and dandy for Jase, but Crosby had never hoped to nor intended on falling in love with anyone, so it was for the best he'd never expressed his feelings to Sami.

"They're not as close to the project, and—"

"What about Gordon? He owns the train and is one of the main sponsors of the renovation." Crosby grasped at straws.

If only he'd been paying attention.

"He's already saying a few words. But we need someone who's passionate about this project. That's you, Crosby. Besides, you made the town so proud this year by becoming *Dr.* Virtue when you completed your doctorate." Ben grinned and sent him a thumbs-up, not knowing how close Crosby had come to missing out on the designation. His fear of public speaking was fierce. Sami's presence outside the university room where he'd given his oral dissertation before the adjudication board had calmed him enough to succeed.

"And Zelda's right. You may be our second choice, but you're the perfect choice," Ben added.

Zelda raised her hand. "I motion that Dr. Crosby Virtue is the keynote speaker at our Midnight Express New Year's Eve bash."

Before Crosby could object, the motion was seconded and passed almost unanimously. Crosby was the lone holdout, but his nay was drowned out when Ben banged his gavel on the wooden table.

"Congratulations, Dr. Virtue. You're our keynote speaker."

IN HER SALON at the Lazy River Dude Ranch main lodge, Sami Fleming stepped back and checked her work. Were the ends of her client's hair even? There was nothing like a haircut and fresh color palette to enhance one's natural beauty. She wanted each client to walk out of the Porcupine Suite, the quarters for the Lazy River Spa and Salon, happy with their new hairstyle or feeling dewy after a facial. The Virtue family entrusted her with their guests, and she took that responsibility seriously.

That was why it would be so hard to leave after Amanda's Valentine's Day wedding. The Virtues had been wonderful to her, converting the Porcupine Suite into a first-rate spa and salon. Bridget and Martin had opened up their lodge and lives to her, letting her stay and paying her a generous salary. It almost felt like a betrayal leaving them, but Colorado had never been her ultimate destination.

When her friend Asia from the beauty pageant circuit had called with an offer to move in with her, Sami couldn't say no. Especially not after Asia's family had taken her on several trips, which Sami had used as an escape from her mother's constant scrutiny. Asia had been a lifesaver, and her family had never accepted a dime in return for luxury accommodations and cruises to Alaska and Austria.

For once, Sami had full control over her destiny, free of her mother's influence. And while Amanda had also done so much for her, saving her after their parents had drained Sami's checking account, this lodge was Amanda's success.

There was something else waiting around the bend for her, and Sami couldn't wait to explore all the delicious possibilities. Suddenly, a metal snowflake she'd suspended from the ceiling fell on her head. Ouch!

"Are you okay?" Betsy asked.

Sami plastered on the smile that won her the title of Miss San Fernando Valley. "Of course." She pulled down Betsy's hair on each side and double-checked the layers. *Perfect.* "You're going to love your new hairstyle."

"It's my holiday present to myself." Betsy's hands fluttered under the giant lavender cape with the Lazy River Dude Ranch logo. Betsy had lost her husband a year ago, and her daughter had planned this trip to coincide with the anniversary of their loss. "It's the first time…"

"A new beginning is scary at first." And yet there was nothing like visiting new places and seeing what was around the next bend. Sami reached for a dab of natural oils and rubbed it into Betsy's scalp for some needed moisture and frizz protection. "Especially after you lose someone you love. How long were you married?"

Her job involved listening to clients as much as styling their hair. Sami loved hearing stories and had heard quite a few since she discovered her true calling as a cosmetologist. This suited her far better than the acting career her mother had foisted on her.

"Almost forty years."

Sami glanced at the mirror in time to catch Betsy's wistful smile and dreamy expression. Sami was floored. Here she was not even forty weeks in the same place and she was all ready to take off. Being married for forty years? To the same person? How could anyone do that?

Still, Sami urged Betsy to tell her more. "What was his name?"

"Mark."

Sami's question was the floodgate Betsy needed. While she styled Betsy's hair, hearing the love in her client's voice, the same glowing tone she heard whenever her sister, Amanda, talked about Seth, Betsy highlighted Mark's attributes. Love was fine for Betsy and Amanda, but once was enough for Sami. She shuddered at the awful experience with her ex-boyfriend Aaron. The final straw was how jealous Aaron had been of her friend Jeremy Haralson. Goodness, she hadn't thought of Jeremy in some time. Last she had heard, he was singing to sold-out shows in Europe.

Sami's nimble fingers never stopped moving until she was done snipping the ends of Betsy's hair. "It sounds like a true love match," Sami said. "Now I'm about ready to cry, too."

"Is it that bad?" Fear entered Betsy's voice. "Oh no."

Sami reassured Betsy her hair was fine, better than fine, actually, and reached for the dryer and her favorite rolling brush. She turned the swivel chair away from the mirror so Betsy would be surprised at the final reveal. The hum of the dryer filled the room, drowning out the instrumental holiday music. This season was usually Sami's favorite time of the year, filled with surprises and happy outings.

This year, however, she dreaded two conversations on the horizon. She didn't know whom she should tell first about her impending move: her sister or her best friend, Crosby.

While Amanda would probably accept her decision with a stiff upper lip, especially now that she had Seth, Sami was more worried about Crosby's reaction. She wasn't sure he believed she would really ever leave Violet Ridge. A soft smile came over her face at the mere thought of Crosby. When she competed on the beauty pageant circuit, who would ever have guessed that she'd have a best friend like Crosby, the absent-minded historian who didn't care about his appearance? And why should he? His heart was in the right place, tied to the community with roots deeper than a walnut tree.

Yet his mind was always in the clouds, thinking about books and stories. He was always notoriously late for everything. Like that time they agreed to meet for dinner downtown. Crosby had been twenty minutes late wearing one black loafer and one brown moccasin. Then there was the time he was a day late to rock climbing.

Crosby would be devastated at her announcement. If only he had a girlfriend to distract him...

The heat from the dryer penetrated her hand, and she stared at Betsy's finished look. She flipped off the dryer and fluffed Betsy's hair with a critical eye. After a minute, Sami selected her blending scissors and clipped one stray strand. Then she reached for the hairspray and finished the job.

With a flourish, Sami turned Betsy toward the mirror and waited for her reaction. Betsy sat stony-faced. Butterflies welled in Sami's stomach. Perhaps cutting off eight inches of hair was too much although the new layered style flattered Betsy's face.

Betsy burst into tears. Sami plucked several tissues from the nearby box and passed them to her client.

"I'll talk to Seth and Bridget and Martin." Sami used all her resolve to keep calm, seeking a resolution that might appeal to Betsy. "I won't charge you for today."

Whether they'd give Betsy's family a partial

credit for their stay would be up to Seth, who co-managed the dude ranch with his grandparents. They were hands-on when it came to the lodge's daily operations. Or maybe she could offer Betsy a complimentary basket with Sami's favorite spa goodies, including loofahs, facial masks and a soothing lavender-scented candle.

It wasn't often that Sami had a dissatisfied client.

Betsy sniffed and blew into the tissue. She threw it in the wastebasket and plucked another to dab at the corners of her eyes. "You'll do no such thing. I love my new hairstyle." She wadded up the tissue in the palm of her hand. "I just wish Mark could see me. Thirty-nine years wasn't enough time with him."

Having that type of partnership would be something special indeed.

Sami unsnapped the back of the cloak and patted Betsy's shoulder. "You look beautiful." She reached for her business card and handed it to Betsy. "I want to find out what the new year has in store for you. Keep in touch."

Betsy beamed and placed the card in her purse before extracting an envelope. "This is for you."

"This service is included in your resort package." Sami objected and tried to return the tip.

Betsy laid the envelope on the counter next to a holiday gnome family. "Thank you for making me feel better about myself today."

With a wave, Betsy sailed out of the room. Sami switched the music from the instrumental background playlist to something more lively and contemporary. There was so much to love about Christmas. The best songs, the liveliest parties, the joy of seeing everything at its best.

Although the Porcupine Suite was the perfect size for her spa services, this was the only time of year she wished she had a little more room since every inch of the salon was resplendent with her gnome collection. She'd augmented that with fresh natural pinecones and draped sparkly garland around her salon mirror. With permission, she'd also snagged extra Virtue family decorations. Over the fireplace mantel she'd hung stockings, one for Amanda, one for Seth, one for Crosby and Sundance although she still was contemplating what one bought for an iguana, and then one for herself. Red ceramic cowboy boots occupied space on the mantel along with a jar of red and green Christmas balls below, around which she had twisted silver garland with white lights, plaid bows and several smaller gnomes.

She might have gone overboard with the gnomes this year, but who could resist their pointy hats and long beards? They were so cute. She had even placed a larger one at her workstation and another by the fluffy towels and still another in the pocket of the replica gift shop robe hanging in the bathroom. There was even a gnome wreath on the door to the Porcupine Suite.

Sami grabbed the broom stashed behind the Christmas tree and took a long whiff of pine. The scent from the fresh tree tickled her nose.

As soon as they had finished eating Thanksgiving dinner, she had dragged Crosby to a grove at the far end of the ranch. She deliberated for quite a while before selecting three trees, one for the Porcupine Suite, one for her private suite and another for Crosby's house near the Miners' Cottage. Crosby had chopped all three, barely breaking a sweat in his thick jacket while she'd bundled up in one of Martin's parkas.

While the tree in the Porcupine Suite was more sedate with strands of white lights, red ribbons and long clear crystal icicle drops, the one in her living space was bedecked with colorful twinkling lights and chintzy ornaments, including several gnomes.

Despite living in Texas, California and a host of other states, Sami had never experienced a white Christmas before. The prospect of crossing something else off her huge bucket list sent a thrill through her. Eager to head to the dining hall for Ingrid's pot roast, she started sweeping the floor.

One of her favorite holiday songs started playing. She grasped the handle of the broom like a microphone, singing along with the tune at the top of her lungs.

She got to the part about what she wanted for Christmas, whirled around and stopped cold. Crosby stood propped against the doorway. Their gazes met, and they finished the rest of the line together.

Sami held the last note as long as possible before they both burst out laughing.

What would she do when she didn't see him every day? She was so accustomed to his dirty blond hair that was too long, a shame considering those strong cheekbones, and those black-rimmed glasses, which hid eyes that changed color depending on his mood. Now, as always, those glasses were falling down his nose. She counted backward from three. When she arrived at one, he pushed them back to the bridge exactly on cue.

Sami rested her chin on the broom. "Was I supposed to meet you before dinner? Am I late? Have we switched bodies?"

Crosby entered the salon, his tall rangy frame filling the room, before he stumbled over the aluminum snowflake that had fallen from the ceiling earlier. He reached out for the salon chair and steadied himself at the same time she grabbed his muscular arm. The broom fell to the floor with a clatter. His cheeks grew red under a slight layer of stubble. "I'm okay."

Of course he was. Crosby always landed on his feet.

His resilience was something she envied. She

switched off the music. "I never doubted that for a second."

She grinned, feeling better with him nearby. Even after she left Colorado to see the world, she knew Crosby would read each text and make time for her video calls. He was solid and dependable, the type of person you knew would bail you out of any situation. What was the phrase from that song he loved to sing? Crosby was a huckleberry friend.

He reached into his pocket and pulled out something. "Glad I didn't buy the glass one." She drew closer and squealed. In his palm was the cutest plush gnome with a pointy red snowflake hat, holding a candy cane.

"For me?" Sami accepted the gift and then hugged the gnome close to her chest. She glanced around the room for the perfect resting spot and then shook her head. "This little fellow is going in my room, but I thought we agreed not to give each other presents this year. Only experiences."

Crosby needed more oomph in his life. That was why he needed her around, at least for a little longer.

"It's not a Christmas present. It's… It's friendship celebration day." He touched an ornament and the tree wobbled. He backed away, and the tree was still once more.

Sami grabbed her coat off the hook and squeezed his arm, still encased in his black jacket. "Something is bothering you. How about going for a walk? You can tell me what's wrong."

Moments later, they exited the lodge. The early December chill cut right through her. She pulled green fleece gloves and a knit red-and-green hat with snowflakes from her pocket. After Sami donned the gloves, her hands warmed up considerably.

"Are those new?" Crosby asked. The cold never seemed to bother him, perhaps because he was born in Violet Ridge. Colorado was as much a part of him as wanderlust was a part of her.

"They're on temporary loan from Cassie. My wardrobe is more suited for Southern California than the Rockies." Yet another reason to accept Asia's kind offer as she lived near the San Diego airport. Still, Sami adored the snow-capped mountains surrounding them. Slush from last week's snowfall still dotted the bushes outside the seven cabins that were the mainstay of the dude ranch. "A shopping trip to downtown Violet Ridge is in my future."

"I'd like to go with you if you don't mind helping me shop for my family. I have quite an extensive list. My grandparents. My siblings. My nieces and nephew." Crosby stopped at the fork in their pathway. "Duck pond or the horses?"

Sami loved seeing them both, but it seemed as though something more than his usual cluttered brilliance was weighing down Crosby. "Duck pond. Less interruptions."

Crosby stuck his hands in his pockets and tilted his head toward the pond. "After you."

Maybe he'd finally spit out whatever was bothering him. Over the past month, the comfortable ease between them had been punctuated with moments of edgy silence. As hard as she tried, she couldn't understand why.

Moments later, they approached the duck pond, which was a misnomer since the ducks had migrated to Texas or Louisiana or other Southern climes. Sami related too well to that internal pull.

Mounds of snow banked near the shore, and Sami took care where she stepped.

"What's on your mind, Crosby?" She maneuvered around a patch of ice. "Or better yet, what's the most pressing thing on your mind?"

He led her over to a black wrought iron bench decked out with garland and red bows. They sat side by side while she allowed him time to gather his thoughts. After a while, Crosby pulled a wool cap out of his pocket and placed it on his head, his long hair peeking out of the bottom. Then he let out a deep breath. "How do you change someone's mind about something?" He yanked the cap over his ears. "How can you show them that their plan is wrong and you know best?"

"Oh, Crosby, you don't realize what you're asking me."

Sami rose and walked over to the pond's edge. His question brought back too many memories of her mother always insisting her plans about the next big beauty pageant were in Sami's best interests. Never mind what Sami herself wanted.

Crosby joined her and laid his hand on her arm. Somehow, with him close by, she stopped shivering. "I think the world of you, Sami. You make everything brighter by being your wonderful self."

She offered a weak smile as relief coursed through her that Crosby was just being his dear sweet self. "You have to trust people and their decisions sometimes, Crosby."

"You're right, Sami. As always. That's why I think you can help me find a way out of something that has disaster written all over it." The tenderness in Crosby's voice gave her pause. He was telling the truth, but why? Unlike her, he always followed through and met people's expectations.

They settled on the bench once more. Her best friend was actually the nicest person she knew. "What's bothering you?"

Crosby took a deep breath and exhaled. "I was asked to be the keynote speaker for the Midnight Express New Year's Eve Celebration today…"

"What an honor!" She squealed and threw her arms around him. He stiffened, and she separated from him. His cheeks were as red as Rudolph's nose. Maybe the cold was starting to impact the Colorado native after all. "How marvelous."

"Except it's not." Crosby jumped off the bench and paced in front of her until she was almost dizzy. He stopped and stared right at her. "I have a confession. I dread public speaking."

"How is that possible?" She scoffed. "You completed your doctoral dissertation, Dr. Virtue."

He jammed his hands in his pockets and started prowling like a bobcat guarding the area. "You were there. In the hallway." He growled, a most un-Crosby noise, and then settled beside her once more. "You're creative and smart. Between the two of us we can come up with an excuse to get me out of this."

She examined his face, his yearning to rid himself of this albatross clear. And yet? If she learned one thing from her time on the beauty pageant circuit, it was that you have to face your fears. The first part, though, was acknowledging the fear. Personally, she dreaded stagnation. "It's okay to be scared of speaking in public. I've done it so often it's second nature to me."

"You don't understand. I've put people to sleep before. People yawn when I enter a room." Crosby kept pacing until she was most definitely dizzy.

"Sit down, and we'll figure out a solution to your problem." She patted the bench and was relieved when he did so.

He faced her, his eyes as bright as a child's on Christmas morning. "Great. What's my excuse?"

She steepled her fingers together, the fleece fabric of the gloves bending easily. An inkling of a plan popped in her head. "I was wondering what to do for you for Christmas, since we're doing something other than regular gifts, and this has given me the perfect idea."

Excitement shone on his face, replacing the look of an elk caught in the headlights. "Great. What is it?"

Her stomach tied up in knots. There was only one way to get rid of this antsy feeling. She had to tell him the truth about San Diego and Asia since that tied into her plan. She screwed up her courage and blurted out the dreaded revelation. "I'm moving, Crosby."

Now it was his turn to blink and that glow left his eyes. "What?" Then he waggled his finger in her direction and chuckled. "You're a genius, Sami. That's the perfect excuse. Helping you move to your own place in Violet Ridge is a much stronger priority. Thanks."

She gripped his hands in hers. "It's not an excuse. I'm moving to San Diego after Amanda's wedding."

His mouth slackened. "But your job is here..." He let go of her hands, and she folded them in her lap. "What did your sister say?"

"I haven't told Amanda yet. You're the first to

know." Other than Asia, that was. "I'm leaving right after Valentine's Day, the Virtue family will have plenty of time to find a new cosmetologist before the summer season ramps up."

He scrubbed his jaw and then walked to the water's edge. She joined him, taking care of icy slush. He licked his lips and then swallowed, a puff of vapor vanishing in the wind. "Public speaking and losing my best friend in one day." His chest rose and fell as he continued looking out at the pond. "Any chance you'll reconsider?"

While it would be easy to stay longer, if she postponed her adventures until after Jase and Cassie's wedding, she'd just find other excuses to stay. Then one day she'd wake up only to find she had never seen the Statue of Liberty or the Eiffel Tower or the Colosseum. "You're not losing me. I'll be back for important family events and arrivals." She nudged his side. "And I'll send you postcards."

"Sundance will eat them."

He finally met her gaze, and they both laughed at the image of his iguana nibbling at her scribbled notes. One last chuckle wrested out of him before sadness lurked in his eyes once more. "At least you'll be here for the holidays. Sundance would be devastated if you don't wish him Merry Christmas."

She raised her eyebrows. "Do iguanas celebrate Christmas?"

"Of course. I bought him a present and everything." Crosby was halfway to sounding like his old self again.

She tapped the end of Crosby's nose with her gloved index finger. "You'd best send me pictures of Sundance and the Miners' Cottage every day. No matter where I go, I'm still your best friend." And someday she'd be back in Violet Ridge for Crosby's wedding. If he ever let her style his hair and swap those glasses for the contacts she'd been encouraging him to try, he'd be snapped up in two seconds. A tingle of anticipation buzzed her fingertips. "Better yet, my Christmas present to you will be far better than anything you buy for Sundance."

Crosby wrinkled his nose. "I don't know. He asked Santa for a companion iguana."

There was some of that Crosby humor she took for granted. "This is better." She stepped back and assessed him with a critical eye. "I'm going to make a polished public speaker of you."

His blustery laugh carried in the stiff wind. "That's more than a present. That's a miracle."

She snuggled into the warmth of her coat, wishing they were inside by a crackling fire with a mug of hot apple cider. Still, this setting suited her proposition. Keeping Crosby on his toes was a full-time endeavor. She'd do more than help him deliver that keynote; she'd give him a makeover so he'd overcome his fear of public speaking, once and for all. An added bonus would come when he met the woman of his dreams on New Year's Eve, perhaps. He might even kiss her at midnight.

"Not a miracle." She assessed what was in front of her. Crosby possessed great bone structure and a dry but potent sense of humor. He was kind and compassionate, and from a practical point of view, he also had job security and lived in his own house. The raw material was there, but it was hidden beneath layers of protective wrap placed there by none other than Crosby himself. "A makeover!"

A tic in his jaw popped out. "What's wrong with me the way I am?"

She moved forward and peeked under his coat. She knew it. He was wearing that old beige clunky cardigan, the one with a belt that went out of style last century. "That sweater is at least twenty years old," she said and plucked his glasses off his face. "And these frames aren't flattering. Do you even need them?"

Sami donned his glasses and winced, handing the necessary item back to him.

Crosby pushed the frames into place once more. "Yes, I need these, but I don't need a makeover."

She removed her right glove and his wool cap, rubbing his hair in her fingers. Thick and curly, it would be a dream to style. "If we work on your outward appearance, you'll gain the confidence you need to give your speech." She grinned and donned her glove once more. "And once the new and improved Crosby is on that podium, the single women of Violet Ridge will all clamor for a chance to go on a date with the town's most eligible bachelor."

"No." Crosby reached for his cap and put it back on his head. Then he took another look at her. "Will this really make me a better public speaker?"

"Yes." Sami sensed victory was within her reach. "And land you a girlfriend."

By the time she left Violet Ridge, she'd see Crosby nail his keynote and take charge of his love life. Maybe she'd be coming back to town next year for three weddings: Amanda and Seth's, Cassie and Jase's and Crosby and some lucky woman who didn't know her life was about to change for the better.

Operation Crosby 2.0 would be Sami's biggest success to date, even more than wearing the tiara of Miss San Fernando Valley.

CHAPTER TWO

THE TRAIN DEPOT would be a bustling place on Christmas Eve for the inaugural Santa ride, but for today, except for Crosby, it was empty. He measured the wall for photographs and other memorabilia and frowned. There was less space than he remembered. He crossed over to his pile of treasures. Which should he discard?

He regarded each photo one by one. There was the framed original ledger page with the departure times and destinations. That had to stay. Then there was the photograph of the first freight crew with the engineer, conductor and brakemen solemn and austere. He had to keep that one. What about the picture of Violet Ridge from the early 1920s with the train pulling into the station? He had a dozen more and couldn't decide which one wouldn't make the cut. Each added to the ambience he wanted to capture, combining the past and the future for an experience like no other. Still, there was only so much wall space.

"Oh, Crosby, it's just you," Zelda Baker called

out from the archway. "We saw a light in the window and came to investigate."

Crosby placed the framed documents and photos back in the box and faced her. It wasn't a big surprise that she wasn't alone since she and her twin, Nelda, were usually seen in Violet Ridge together. Zelda wore a bright green coat that matched her pixie haircut while Nelda's ugly Christmas sweater was a sight to behold with real silver garland and colorful knitted ornaments attached.

"I just arrived a couple of minutes ago myself." Crosby nodded at the sisters. "The depot has my full attention this week."

And it was the perfect excuse to get out of Sami's ridiculous makeover idea. It was fine to be swept up in her excitement at the dude ranch, but in the light of day, Operation Crosby 2.0 struck him as a bad idea. There was no way Sami could change him, and he wouldn't want her to waste her valuable time trying.

Besides, he'd rather spend the time he did have with her, enjoying the holidays, before she moved in February. Well, when he wasn't prepping the depot and train for Christmas Eve, getting estimates from Gunther and Sons for the cottage roof repair and writing a book on the history of Violet Ridge.

Nelda nodded back at him. "As long as it's you."

"Who else would be here in the afternoon?"

Crosby chuckled, and then his eyes widened. "Oh, did I forget a meeting?"

He tended to do that.

Zelda looked at her watch and frowned. "It's almost seven."

That late? Why did seven strike a bell? Crosby gasped. "I was supposed to meet Sami for dinner at six thirty."

He'd best hurry to Mi Casa Mexican Restaurant, where he'd let Sami down gently about the makeover. He was an old soul at twenty-eight and far too set in his ways.

He started for the door before remembering his coat and keys. Turning around, he found Zelda kneeling beside the box of photos and documents. She placed her massive purse alongside it and rifled through the items.

"I like this one." She picked up the framed picture from the early twentieth century with women wearing big-brimmed hats and long dresses.

Nelda joined her and selected a different one. "Look at the Christmas decorations from yesteryear." Then they swapped photos, oohing and aahing at the details.

Although he shared their sentiments, he was already late. "Please come back another time, but I need to leave now. I'll lock up behind you."

Zelda rose and then reached out a hand to Nelda. "How's your hip doing?"

Nelda accepted the hand. "Much better after

the replacement. You really should consider having the surgery. It's made such a difference. I can keep up with my grandson now."

"My hips are just fine, thank you very much," said Zelda, her consternation clear. "Sofia and I have a date for ice skating at the downtown rink next week."

Crosby glanced at his watch, wondering if Sami was still waiting for him or if she'd given up and gone home. "Ladies..."

"Coming." Nelda brushed off her red leggings. "If you see him in the next day or two, thank Jase for us, won't you?"

With little chance of arriving on time, anyway, Crosby had to ask the question. "Okay, but why?"

"That Jase is such a sweetheart," Zelda said.

This might be the first time anyone referred to his no-nonsense detective brother as a sweetheart. While Crosby was plenty proud of Jase's accomplishments, he wouldn't refer to his brother like that. Determined, maybe, even fierce.

Nelda beamed. "He did the nicest thing today when he brought his new dog, Cookie, to the vet's office. You wouldn't recognize her with her coat all shiny. Her sweet personality is just bubbling through. Those two are just devoted to each other. Jase delivered a thank-you basket to the staff. It was full to brimming with vegetables and goodies from Cassie's farm."

"And her new Christmas jam, a mixture of

strawberries, cranberries and oranges." Zelda licked her lips. "We already tried it, and it's delicious."

Nelda nudged Zelda's side. "Don't forget. I snagged that cranberry tart, too. That Jase is definitely an asset to our community." With that, the twins hurried past Crosby wishing him a Merry Christmas.

Crosby hurried to lock up the depot and rushed south along Main Street. He was almost at Mi Casa when Valerie Kaminski, the owner of Lavender and Lace, waved him over.

"Crosby, can you pass on a message to your sister, Daisy, from me?" Valerie had a habit of getting straight to the point.

It seemed as if he was in kindergarten all over again. His teacher, Mrs. Calloway, had reached Crosby's name on the roster and made glowing remarks about Seth. Then his art teacher had delivered high praise about Daisy, while the librarian handed Crosby a new mystery to give to Jase. Always proud to be a Virtue, Crosby had shared each kind comment at dinner while an expanding pressure weighed on his chest. He couldn't let down his teachers or family by being any less of a student than his siblings. For weeks, he had fought sleep and searched for a way not to disappoint them.

Books were his solution.

Valerie cleared her throat, and he faced her with

that same guilty feeling as whenever Mrs. Calloway caught him dawdling. "I need ten more pairs of the silver snowflake earrings as soon as possible. Daisy's jewelry has been flying off the shelves. Her technique with silver is quite unique."

Crosby listened as Valerie raved about Daisy's newest jewelry collection. "Got it."

Crosby wished her happy holidays and sighed as the town clock chimed half past seven. So much for being not too late. Finally, he entered Mi Casa and admired the festive decorations adorning the cozy restaurant. He approached Luz Flores, a former classmate of Seth's, who lowered her phone and reached for a menu off the maître d' stand. "Crosby Virtue! Sami has been waiting for you. By the way, I'm so excited because my babysitter just confirmed she's available on Valentine's Day. My husband and I are looking forward to attending Seth and Amanda's wedding."

That day would be a double celebration for the Virtue family—it was also his grandparents' sixtieth anniversary.

"Seth will be happy to have you and Javier there," Crosby said.

"They're just the sweetest couple. Seth helped us with the finishing touches on our food truck last month, and Amanda designed our new logo." Luz held up a menu and pointed to the front image. "They're such good friends to Javier and me."

Crosby kept his smile intact and nodded. He

loved his siblings, but it had never been easy living up to their ideals. That might be why he preferred books. They never judged him.

He caught sight of Sami, who was standing near a booth talking to someone. Sami tilted her head back and laughed.

Almost an hour late, he glanced down at his dusty jeans and scuffed boots. While he'd had every intention of coming here tonight and ending any future discussion of Operation Crosby 2.0, perhaps he'd hear Sami out and consider what she had in store for him.

With a little polish, he might have the town talking about him in the same glowing way as his siblings.

THAT AFTERNOON, SAMI HAD given several facials at the ranch and brainstormed every aspect of Operation Crosby 2.0 until it was foolproof. Now it was time to relax. The noise level at Mi Casa on Mariachi Night precluded any deep conversation, and Sami relished the atmosphere. She found herself swaying in time to "Feliz Navidad," while sitting across from Crosby at a four-topper.

Sami scooped a tortilla chip into the guacamole and crunched the first bite. She almost moaned with pleasure. "Oh, this is so good." She shook her finger at Crosby. "How can you call yourself a Coloradoan without having tried guacamole before?"

He stared at the chip and his nose smooshed in that cute way of his. "Their salsa is the best in town."

Taking the biggest chip from the basket, she heaped it full of guacamole. While his face was resolute, she kept holding the chip in front of his nose. "It won't hurt you to try something new."

He crooked his ear toward her. "What did you say? It's really loud in here."

"One bite." She waved the chip under his nose. "Nothing ventured, nothing gained."

"You're impossible to resist."

Crosby popped the tortilla chip in his mouth while she dipped one in his favorite salsa. The garlic and tomatoes exploded in her mouth just as she sipped her margarita. Before she could ask him for his verdict, he was reaching for the guac bowl and downing more. She sat back with a satisfied smile.

"If that's so, you have no reason to refuse this makeover. My intent is to enhance your best characteristics, so public speaking comes more easily to you."

His face turned almost as green as the guac. "We're really going through with this?" His black-rimmed glasses fell down his nose before he pushed them back in place.

"I'm going to knock your socks off." He leaned toward her again. She raised her voice. "Seth,

Daisy and Jase won't recognize you once I'm done."

"Then I'm putty in your hands." Crosby sipped his beer and then loaded more guacamole onto another chip. "I'll wipe my mind blank so you can mold me into a better version of myself."

"You couldn't wipe your mind blank even if you tried." She took a sip of her margarita, savoring the citrusy flavor. "You always have fifteen projects running through that brain of yours."

His response was lost as the occupants at the next table burst into raucous laughter while a quartet of servers started singing "Happy Birthday" to a young boy. Sami sang along, drawing out the final syllable before clapping with everyone else.

There was something about a birthday celebration that always filled her with cheer. Maybe it was the possibility of everything good the upcoming year would bring.

Crosby waved his phone around. "I almost feel like texting you."

She shrugged. "Still can't hear you."

"What's your plan?" Crosby shouted.

Just then, the applause faded away, and everyone turned toward him. Crosby's cheeks reddened at the attention. Her project might be harder than she first envisioned, but she loved a challenge almost as much as she loved guacamole.

Besides, Crosby was worth it, and the benefits would stick around long after she moved to San Diego, and beyond. Someday he'd invite her to his wedding and they'd have a big laugh about his reluctance to venture outside his comfort zone, before taking her seat on the groom's side.

She opened her mouth to elaborate on her plan right as the server appeared with their orders: a Chile Colorado burrito for Crosby and fish tacos for her.

They thanked the server and ordered water. Then Sami squeezed the lemon over the halibut. "There's no reason to look so worried. I designed every step with you in mind."

"So, you wrote a book and I'll study it?" He sounded so hopeful that she felt like she was bursting his bubble.

"Ah, why didn't I come up with that solution?" Some salsa spilled onto her sweater, and she winced. "I'm going to the bathroom to blot this stain, but don't think you're getting off that easy. When I get back, we'll review Operation Crosby 2.0."

Sami headed for the bathroom but glanced over her shoulder at Crosby, who pulled out his book before dipping another chip in guacamole. She gave him credit for trying something new. By this time next month, he would hardly recognize himself.

Crosby laid his fork and knife over the empty plate, his burrito as outstanding as always. Now that they were through eating, he might as well broach the *M* word.

"What's the first step in my makeover?" He winced. A makeover conjured up images of those television shows where home contractors undertook a huge task. In his opinion, the original house usually had character and charm. All of that would go by the wayside at the grand reveal where the new space would be bland and formulaic.

"Crosby Virtue, it won't be that bad. Give me a chance."

She arched her eyebrow, and he braced himself for what came next. Instead, she craned her neck and then slanted her body until she was leaning over so much that he feared she was about to topple out of her chair. Then she squealed, jumped up and ran toward the entrance.

Crosby folded his napkin and placed it next to his plate. He searched and found Sami hugging a behemoth of a man. Crosby's mouth dropped. This wasn't just any man, either. Taller than Crosby, who topped six feet, this guy must be a model or an actor given his good looks. His jet-black hair was perfectly groomed and his blue eyes would have given Paul Newman a run for his money. The man swirled Sami around as if she was a toothpick before setting her down once more. Sami reached for the man's hand and dragged him toward Crosby.

For the second time that night, every eye in the restaurant gazed in their direction and Crosby thought he heard a couple of sighs from a group of women at the corner table.

"Crosby, you won't believe it." Sami was quivering with excitement as she hugged the stranger's arm. "I was just thinking of Jeremy today, and guess what?"

"This is Jeremy." Crosby's words came out garbled and high.

"Crosby, such a strong name, very memorable." Jeremy reached out his hand, and Crosby rose from his seat to shake it.

"It's my grandmother's maiden name, plus my mother's favorite movie was *White Christmas*." He kept his eyes from bulging out at Jeremy's strong grip.

"Any friend of Sami's is a friend of mine," Jeremy said warmly, grinning from ear to ear.

"Jeremy, I can't believe it's really you. Why are you here in Violet Ridge?" Sami motioned to the chair next to hers. "Care to join us?"

"Just for a bit. I'm meeting friends for dinner, and I'm early." Jeremy settled in the chair between Sami and Crosby. "My aunt lives here, and she offered me a place to stay, since I'm the new lounge singer at the Wilshire Ski Resort. Aunt Marilyn and I have always been close, and now I can help her while she's undergoing chemo."

"Oh, I'm sorry to hear that." Sami patted his hand. "I always remember you saying the nicest things about her."

"Her prognosis is good." Jeremy smiled wider, his teeth perfectly straight and pearly white. "You'll have to come hear me sing. I'll get the two of you ski passes, and we can make a day of it."

A shadow crossed Sami's face, but she pulled herself together. "It'll have to be sooner rather than later."

"Of course. You're right. It has been too long since we've seen each other." Jeremy released the utensils from the napkin. He turned toward Crosby, who felt like a third wheel. "She's such a whirlwind, isn't she?"

The server came over and took Jeremy's drink order, an imported lager. Jeremy delivered a dazzlingly white smile toward her. "Thanks, Marla. And could I have some fresh chips?"

Marla nodded. "I'll bring a new basket and more guacamole. The chef just finished making a batch."

Sami ordered churros, and then Marla departed without even glancing in Crosby's direction. Sami and Jeremy began chatting, and Crosby debated whether to pay his share of the bill and go home. But that would be rude, so he sipped his water while wishing he could read his book.

Jeremy glanced his way and robustly patted Crosby on the back. Fortunately, Crosby kept from pitching forward.

"Here I am a guest at your table, and I'm monopolizing the conversation. Tell me about yourself, Crosby."

Before Crosby could answer, two women approached their table, whispering to each other and then staring at Jeremy.

"It can't be him," the first woman said.

"I tell you it is." The second woman faced Jeremy with stars in her eyes. "Are you the man who rescued those two teenagers in an avalanche last weekend?"

Jeremy blushed bright red and waved his hand as if it was nothing. "I was just in the right place at the right time. I visited them at the hospital yesterday. They're making a full recovery."

The first woman practically swooned before sending Sami a big smile and a sigh. "You're one lucky woman to be his date."

They left the table as Marla appeared, holding aloft a tray with the chips, salsa and guacamole while promising to return with Sami's churros and the beverages. Jeremy thanked her, and Crosby could practically see Marla floating away from the table.

Jeremy sampled the guacamole and expressed his approval. He looked at Sami, then Crosby. A sheepish expression overtook his features. "Here

I am, interrupting your date. Tell me about the man who's captured Sami's heart."

"We're not a couple." Sami laughed and reached for a chip, dunking it in the guacamole, before pushing the rest of the plate in Crosby's direction. "Crosby's my best friend, and the smartest person I've ever known."

Yet another affirmation of their status as just buddies. If anything, he owed Jeremy a debt of gratitude for this interruption. Otherwise, Crosby might have done something he regretted, like asking Sami out on a real date.

Or even worse, told her he loved her.

Crosby started to rise. "Time to get back to work."

Sami looked at him with a hurt expression. "At this hour of night?"

Jeremy's phone chimed with a text. He read it and shrugged. "My friends backed out, so it looks like it's the three of us. Can you stay a little longer, Crosby?"

Jeremy looked so hopeful that Crosby didn't have the heart to say no. Crosby nodded and sat back in his chair again. "The prologue I'm writing can wait until tomorrow."

Crosby caught sight of Sami trying to get his attention before mouthing "later" at him. Then she asked Jeremy another question about his singing, and Jeremy launched into a story. Crosby reached for a chip and chomped at it. Jeremy looked like a male model with his stylish hair and fashionable cashmere sweater.

Crosby winced. Was this Operation Crosby 2.0? Or had Jeremy been front and center in Sami's mind when she offered to give Crosby a makeover?

Was this actually a way for her to turn him into Jeremy 2.0?

CROSBY HELD THE door open for Sami. She stepped out of Mi Casa and buttoned her white wool coat. The wind had picked up, and snowflakes swirled around her. Although the chill was unlike anything she'd ever experienced, it was glorious. While she extracted her gloves, Jeremy joined them and blocked their path.

"What's next? My ride is arriving in an hour, so let's keep the party going." Jeremy's voice boomed in the night air. "Is there a bar nearby? A place with dancing or a pool table?"

Crosby frowned. "Tomorrow's a busy day at the train depot, so I'll leave you two to continue getting reacquainted."

Sami wasn't going to let Crosby leave without telling him about her thoughts for the makeover. It was crucial she talk with him tonight, especially since she had scheduled the first stage for tomorrow evening. If he left now, he'd find some excuse to cancel everything.

"I know you, Crosby Virtue, and you're not escaping that easily. You're coming with us." She glimpsed Jeremy's raised eyebrow but that didn't faze her. Seeing Crosby living up to his full potential before she left town was critical to his well-being as well as his relationship status. "Besides, you grew up here. Don't you want to show Jeremy the best of Violet Ridge?"

She linked her arm in Crosby's, too aware of the possibility she was turning into her mother, always demanding perfection in her appearance, but she wanted him to hear her out. If Crosby was still determined to back out of the speech after the haircut and clothes shopping and whatever else she could come up with, she'd personally talk to Ben Irwin and Zelda Baker until they relented. She just wasn't about to share that info with Crosby until he gave this a chance.

Conflict warred on Crosby's expressive face, and she smiled at him. His shoulders relaxed. "Violet Ridge is at its finest this time of year thanks to two women who head the decorating committee. They used to cause quite a commotion in town because they had a tremendous feud going. Now that they work together, everyone is the better for it."

Crosby motioned toward the town square, and they started walking in that direction. Sami felt the excitement pumping in her veins. Seeing towns and cities at their finest satisfied something deep inside her.

The sights and smells of the holiday season were as captivating as the town itself. For the past six months, the residents had embraced her. Well, at least, they embraced Amanda, who endeared herself to people wherever she went, and tolerated Sami.

Jeremy stopped in front of the Holly Theater, which she'd heard so much about from Daisy's triplets. He sniffed the air. "Something smells delicious."

"It's Oren Hoffman's chestnut stand," Crosby said.

Sami unhooked her arm from Crosby's, the aroma enticing and sweet. "Let's go."

It wasn't hard to find as there was a line queued in front of the stand. They waited their turn and chatted about the weather.

When they reached Oren, Crosby read the sign advertising popcorn and frowned. "What happened to the chestnuts?"

"I sell chestnuts the week before Christmas. This week it's popcorn." Oren waved his arm over the seasoning canisters. "Thirty different flavors. What'll it be?"

Jeremy held up his hand. "How about I order for you? I'm always right when it comes to guessing people's favorite flavors." He placed one arm around Crosby and his other around Sami. "Especially since I ended up eating most of the churros."

Crosby escaped Jeremy's reach and motioned toward the stand. "Can't wait to see if you're right."

Minutes later, the trio headed toward the town square and the decorated Christmas tree. Sami winced at the bag Jeremy had selected for her: candy cane popcorn with crushed peppermint sprinkles. Instead, she eyed Crosby's jalapeño cheese popcorn, which smelled divine. Jeremy threw a handful of plain buttery popcorn in his mouth. "Absolutely delicious."

They strolled the rest of the way to the town square. The main tree lit up at night didn't disappoint. Jeremy faced Sami and Crosby once more. "Thanks for letting me hang out with you two. We'll have to do this again." He stepped toward Sami and flashed a smile. "Want to have dinner with me next week? The ski lodge has a terrific restaurant."

She reached for her phone and handed it to Jeremy. "Just enter your number and I'll text you later." Together she and Crosby watched Jeremy leave, and she looked at her bag of popcorn, then his. "Want to trade?"

Crosby let out an exaggerated sigh of relief. "I thought you'd never ask."

They traded popcorn. She preferred savory flavors, and Crosby's sweet tooth was legendary. In fact, she had ordered the churros for him, knowing he loved them and wouldn't consume a full serving without her eating something.

Only the sounds of munching broke the comfortable silence between them. Around Amanda, Sami always felt like she had to prove something to her sister. But with Crosby? She could be herself.

"Now about the makeover—"

"How about we scrap it altogether?" He selected one kernel and popped it in his mouth while she grabbed a handful, savoring the crunch. "You're going to be busy with clients, maid of honor dress fittings and holiday festivities. Maybe those are all signs we should just enjoy the season before the ball drops on New Year's Eve."

Crosby could be so stubborn sometimes. She held her ground, determined to win this battle. "I brainstormed a sensational plan." She walked with care on the sidewalk, well treated with salt, and the slush was already shoveled to the other side. "This is my Christmas present to you, and it's going to be fun."

"A whole plan? I was thinking you'd call it quits after a haircut." He pointed toward Harold's Barbershop and then rubbed his jaw. "And suggesting a new type of aftershave. That would be more than sufficient."

"How will aftershave bring about real change?" Besides there was nothing wrong with the way Crosby smelled: fresh and crisp with a lingering note of spice. "By working on your outward appearance, you'll gain confidence and your keynote will flow out of you."

"Confidence isn't the problem. It's my fear of public speaking." Crosby grumbled and separated his arm from hers. "This seems a lot of effort for one evening."

She had to admit that he was putting up a gallant and stubborn fight. "There's nothing wrong with wanting to look your best." Perhaps she should thank her mother for that lesson. "Look at me. What do you see?"

Crosby set his gaze on her. "The white of your hat and coat brings out the pink in your cheeks."

"That's called blush." She laughed away his compliment and led him to the town square. "Look around you. Notice how the lampposts have red bows on them. Now above you. See how the strings of lights extend from side to side, bathing the shops and businesses in a soft glow."

Nestled in the Rockies, Violet Ridge was one of her favorite destinations any time of year, but during the holiday season? The town's charm was enchanting with one window display featuring Santa and his elves while another showcased painted wreaths and a family of snow people. Then there was the square itself with a glowing Christmas tree and a menorah. Sami had to admit it had risen to the challenge of looking its best.

Now it was time for Crosby to do the same.

Crosby pointed toward the closest lamppost. "Did you know that lamplighters had an important job in the eighteenth and nineteenth centuries? They'd start before dusk and go around lighting the lanterns, originally with fish oil, ensuring people would be able to travel in safety."

"Fish oil? How smelly. Thank goodness for electricity." Sami shivered and nestled into her coat. "I love how everyone puts a little more effort into spreading cheer and making the town look its best this time of year. Just like I'm going to help bring out the special quality in you so everyone will see you the same way I see you."

He jammed his hands in his coat pockets. "And how do you see me, Sami?"

She tapped her chin and contemplated his appearance. There was something different about him tonight. She couldn't pinpoint what, and that bothered her. "I see my best friend who has so much potential." She closed the distance between them and removed his glasses. "After I'm done with you, you'll be everyone's first choice."

It was rough settling for second place, not that Crosby was that in her eyes. No, he was her best friend, but she knew only too well what it was like to feel disappointment. She didn't want him to feel that way after his speech. Too often she'd stand on the stage with the other finalist, both of them waiting for the announcement about who would be crowned the winner. Every time she was the runner-up, she'd plaster on a smile and endure the long car ride home with her mother railing against the judges before hatching yet another scheme to catapult Sami into the spotlight. Sami had always burrowed in the back seat, only wanting to make her corner of the world brighter and happier.

She wanted more for her best friend. She wanted to see him happy and find the right woman for him. Someone unassuming and calm, someone who could keep him on his toes while sharing his interests.

Sami gave Crosby his glasses, and he untangled his fingers from hers. After his glasses were affixed to the bridge of his nose once more, he sighed. "Tell me about this makeover."

Unlike her smiles on the pageant stage, his was genuine.

"It has five stages. Haircut, contacts, poise lessons, new clothes and a mystery element. That's where I choose something outside of your comfort zone for you to try."

He whistled. "That's a lot considering New Year's Eve is in a month, and we both have jobs and commitments."

"It won't take as long as you think." She let out an exasperated breath. "Look, if the Miners' Cottage needed publicity, you'd go to Amanda, right?"

"Of course. She's good at marketing."

"And I'm a great cosmetologist."

"Never said you weren't. You're wonderful at your job."

"Then accept my help." She swallowed the rest of her popcorn and threw away the bag. Another one of Crosby's strengths was keeping her secrets, and she knew he wouldn't tell Amanda about her insecurity. "Sometimes it's hard being at the dude ranch and feeling like everyone's comparing me to Amanda."

Crosby halted, another kernel of popcorn halfway to his mouth. "My grandparents would never do that. They love you."

"I love them, too. They're special people." She smiled as the images of Bridget and Martin flashed in her mind. "Nevertheless, it's intimidating to be Amanda's sister. You wouldn't understand as you're brilliant, but I've been on stages where everyone is judging you. On the night of your speech, I don't want you to feel like that."

He threw away his bag, still half full, a look of inevitable surrender coming over him. "But five stages? Couldn't we eliminate one, or four, of them?"

She chuckled and then grew serious. "Since yesterday, I've considered each step. This morning I looked a fright and went to the dude ranch kitchen to ask our favorite cook for used tea bags. You should have seen the look Ingrid gave me before handing them over, but there's nothing like them to eliminate eye puffiness." She swiped at her eyes for maximum effect. "You'd have run away screaming."

"Never." His voice sounded funny, and a coughing fit came over him.

"Are you choking?" Alarm rang out in her voice. "Crosby?" She quickly went over, the Heimlich maneuver top of mind, and approached his back, ready to encircle his rib cage with her arms until he held up a hand.

"I'm fine. Tonight's been…" He paused as if trying to come up with the right word. She waited as it wasn't good to rush him. "Interesting."

Satisfied he was okay, she stepped back. "The mystery element is the most crucial." She halted at the window for the Rocky Mountain Chocolatier. Her friend Emma had crafted a beautiful display with chocolate truffles taking the shape of little mice all gathered around a Santa mouse reading from a gingerbread book. "That way you'll be prepared for any contingency on New Year's Eve."

He looked at her as if she was barking up the wrong tree, but he'd see. She was right about this. "When do we start?"

She grinned. "We don't have a minute to lose. Be at the Porcupine Suite tomorrow night at six sharp. You're getting the works."

He gulped, and terror crossed his face. "What's the works?"

She waggled her finger. "I'm not giving anything away. Otherwise, you might not show up." She pointed to his coat pocket. "Give me your phone, and I'll set an alarm and program a reminder for you."

He grumbled but pulled out his phone and let her do just that. "I'm getting better. I'm only late when something's not important."

"I'm important." She held her head up high. "I'm going to make a swan of you yet, Crosby Virtue. On New Year's Day, the women in this town will be lining up at the doorstep of the Miners' Cottage."

The cold must be getting to her. For the first time, the thought of Crosby hanging out with another woman sent a tiny ping of alarm through her, but she recovered quickly. She'd be long gone from here by then, walking along the beaches of San Diego while plotting her next destination.

CHAPTER THREE

ON THE TRAIL between the main lodge and the barn, Sami practiced her speech about moving to San Diego so she wouldn't lose her nerve about telling Amanda. Curtains and picket fences were fine for her sister, but Sami wanted suitcases and souvenirs. There was a whole world waiting for her.

Around her, the Rockies rose in splendor, and Sami's anticipation skyrocketed to see Denali, Mount Kilimanjaro and even Everest, although she had no intention of climbing the famed mountain.

Steeling her spine, Sami entered the barn that wasn't used for storage or for animals. Rather, it was the site for weekly dude ranch dances and special events, like Amanda and Seth's wedding next February. She found Amanda kissing Seth under the mistletoe. The two obviously didn't see her. After a while, Sami cleared her throat and the pair startled. Amanda looked in Sami's direction.

"Don't sneak up on people like that." Amanda rubbed her arms together, her fuzzy pink angora sweater perfect for her fair coloring.

"I've been standing here for two minutes," Sami said with a wry chuckle.

Seth pointed to a pile of boxes. "You arrived just in time to help us decorate the tree."

Sami scuffed at the dirt of the barn floor. Her secret was becoming a huge anvil on her shoulder that she wanted gone. "Can I borrow Amanda?"

"Can this wait until tonight at the bridal shop? It's the one night of the week they're open late." Amanda focused on the box cutter she was using to slice through the tape. "We have to decorate the entire barn this afternoon."

The fitting had slipped Sami's mind. She whipped out her phone and texted Crosby to be here at five sharp instead of six. Then again, Sami's news might change Amanda's mind about her role in the wedding. She had already disappointed her sister in the past. Would this second strike cause Amanda to ask someone else to take her place as maid of honor? Someone like Seth's sister, Daisy, who had so much in common with Amanda?

Sami dismissed the very thought. Her sister was sweet and kind, not vindictive.

"Not really," Sami replied.

Seth took the box cutter from Amanda. "I'll contact the staff and see if someone can step in, although it won't be as fun without you." He dropped a kiss on Amanda's cheek and she all but glowed. "You'll just miss the boring part. I'll see you later."

This was part of the reason Sami would miss Violet Ridge. For the first time, she was around happy couples, who made romance seem like the biggest adventure of all.

Amanda grabbed her puffy knee-length coat. "Come on, Sami. We can have lunch together."

Seth ripped into another box. "Don't rush. Take your time."

Sami and Amanda left the barn and walked alongside each other on the path to the main lodge. "Is this about the dress I picked out for you?" Amanda asked, facing Sami. "I know you prefer bright colors, but the dark pink will look great on you, and it is Valentine's Day."

"It's not that." Sami traced a line in the dirt with the stiletto of her boot. "How about I find some lunch for us in my suite?"

They stopped in the lobby. "I have a better idea," Amanda said. "Ingrid made her special chicken potpie, and lunch will be served in an hour. How about we grab some hot spiced cider and head to the library until then? I want to find a book to read."

Cider would warm Sami's cold toes. In no time, Sami found herself curled up in one of the extra-comfy armchairs in the library. Seth's retired Australian shepherd, Trixie, was at her feet, while the other retired working dog, Hap, was sniffing Amanda, who reached into her pocket and pulled out two dog treats, one for each of them.

"You're happy, aren't you, Amanda?" Sami wasn't sure why she asked that for Amanda was beaming with happiness.

Steam wisped out of Amanda's mug, dissipating in the air. Amanda blew across the top and then lowered the mug without taking a sip. "I've never been happier. For too long, I let others dictate my life. First, our parents and then my former boss. Standing up for myself has brought me a newfound sense of peace and purpose."

Sami searched her sister's face. It was satisfying to know that Amanda was content with her life. Grasping control of her destiny was a big step in claiming her own happiness. She took a deep breath and decided to blurt it out all at once. "I'm turning in my notice to the Virtues this week. I'm moving to San Diego after your wedding."

Shock bloomed over Amanda's pretty features, and her mouth dropped. "I'm sorry. I must have misheard you." She laughed and rubbed her ear. "I thought you just said you were leaving the best place in the world."

Trixie whined as if sensing Sami's distress. The sweet dog nudged Sami's hand until she rubbed the underneath of the Australian shepherd's jaw. "I did, and I am."

The look Amanda was giving her was why Sami hadn't said anything sooner. Even though Amanda didn't realize the impact of it, Sami did. She'd seen the same look in classrooms when teachers realized that she wasn't the same conscientious, straight-A student as her sister. She'd seen it in her mother's gaze whenever Sami asked if she could stop competing in beauty pageants.

Amanda blinked and placed her mug on the large table. "But home is best."

"For you, yes." Of this there was no doubt in Sami's mind. Amanda belonged here as much as Crosby and the rest of the Virtues. He was the one person who never seemed disappointed in her. They'd had so much fun in the past six months whether climbing Hartman Rocks or watching the sun set together over Lake San Cristobal. She'd miss having him follow her anywhere. "Not for me."

"Your body language is telling a different story." Amanda leaned forward, concern overtaking her pretty features. "Are you worried there won't be any clients in the snowy season when we're closed? I can help with your small business..."

"I've already informed my regulars that I won't be here next year." Sami sighed. "I was just thinking about Crosby's reaction to my announcement."

"You told Crosby before me?" Amanda threw

herself back in her chair, her face turning ashen. "Am I the last to know?"

Trixie whined again until Sami lavished more affection on the loving dog. "You're not the last. Besides, you know how much Crosby means to me." Friends and boyfriends would come and go in her life, but Crosby? Unlike Jeremy, who'd been absent from her life for the past few years, Crosby would always be there for her.

Amanda retrieved her cider, blowing across the top of the mug once more. After sipping it, she rested the mug on her thigh. "Sami, there's something you should know about Crosby."

"Before you say that he's going to be lost without me, I'm fixing everything so he won't even know I'm gone." She outlined the concept of Operation Crosby 2.0, growing quite excited about her plan. Crosby was funny and serious at the same time, cute and handsome, smart and lovable. Any woman would be fortunate to date him.

"So you see yourself as Henry Higgins?" Amanda downed the rest of her cider.

"Of course not." Crosby certainly wasn't Eliza Doolittle. He was simply a diamond in the rough, and she was enhancing his exterior, giving it polish that would let his substance shine. Deep down, he'd still be Crosby Virtue, the man captivated by a strong story and the past. He'd still be late for everything, too. "If all goes as expected, you won't recognize Crosby at the Midnight Express

New Year's Eve Celebration. He might even be in a committed relationship by Valentine's Day." Just as well she was leaving then. No way could she stick around while women lined up on the doorstep of the Miners' Cottage, hoping to date Crosby.

Amanda placed her empty cup on the table. "Why not wait until after Cassie and Jase's wedding to leave?"

"There will always be a reason to stay but my heart is telling me that going after yours is the perfect time to leave."

Being careful not to disturb Trixie, Sami rose and paced the room while outlining her friend Asia's request. Sami stopped in front of the mantel and studied the tallest nutcracker standing on pine garland. Turning it over, she found the initials *GF* on the bottom. "Did Grandpa Garrett make this?"

"Yes, for Grandma Lou. Bridget let me put Grandma Lou's nutcracker collection in here for everyone to enjoy." Amanda joined her and rubbed the base of another nutcracker. Her throat bobbed up and down, emotion welling in her expressive face. "I miss Grandma Lou. During those summers I spent with her, she made me feel special. They were wonderful."

Sami hadn't shared in those carefree experiences with her sister. Her mother had kept Sami with her in whichever town they were living, preparing for the next beauty pageant and keeping up with the steady regimen of dancing and singing lessons. "I don't have many memories of her or Grandpa Garrett." Trixie arrived at Sami's side. It was like the dog was herding her and trying to keep her close. Sami had no doubt her sister would do the same if she could. "Although I do remember the time she visited us in California."

Amanda smiled, her eyes misty as they stared off into the distance. "She loved the Pacific Ocean."

Sami let out a small sigh. "I was only eight, but one of our conversations has always stuck with me. She told me that Grandpa Garrett and I were kindred spirits with wanderlust in our veins."

Amanda picked up the smallest nutcracker. "And I'm more like her, a homebody."

"I don't want to look back and have regrets about what I didn't do." Sami heard the pleading in her voice. She wanted her sister to do more than just understand what she had to do.

She also wanted Amanda's approval.

Amanda gripped Sami's hands in hers. "What about relationships? I just got my sister back."

Friends and family were the only reason she was staying in Violet Ridge until Amanda's wedding. "We'll always be sisters, and I'll be back for holidays and to meet any future baby Virtues."

Amanda searched Sami's face and gave her a tiny smile. "Sisters forever."

Sami gave Amanda's hands a tiny squeeze. "You won't even notice I'm gone with Seth nearby."

Earlier in the barn, Amanda hadn't even noticed Sami's presence at first. That was all the proof Sami needed to know that was true.

"Not true." Amanda lifted the right side of her mouth up in a small smile. "If you go, who's going to leave me little handmade chocolate caramels on my desk every Monday morning?"

Busted. "I'll make sure Seth knows which ones I buy from Emma's shop."

Amanda hugged her, and Sami leaned into the embrace, letting all her emotions rise to the surface. She'd just reconnected with Amanda, but if she didn't follow through now, when would she escape Violet Ridge? In a way, she was doing this for Grandpa Garrett as much as she was doing this for herself.

Sami stepped back and wiped her cheek with the back of her hand, the mascara smear dark and evident. "I've got to fix this."

"I love you, my sister, my maid of honor." Amanda reached out and gently touched Sami's arm. "You always have a home here."

Sami affixed the grin that won her more than her fair share of beauty pageant titles. "Wild horses won't keep me away for long. See you tonight at the bridal salon."

Sami left the library, Trixie still by her side. Stopping abruptly, she patted Trixie's head and told her to stay. She needed to get the ball rolling on the project that would change Crosby's life for the better.

AT THE FRONT of the miners' cottage, Crosby finished guiding the six tour participants through the museum. Talking to a group this size wasn't a problem, especially since he was so comfortable in this space. His speech anxiety only reared to life with larger crowds or unfamiliar surroundings. An older woman from Idaho asked a question about life in the nineteenth century. Crosby took his time explaining his answer before presenting the children with special souvenir pins.

Waving goodbye to the family of four, plus the retired couple, Crosby headed to his office and checked on Sundance, who had accompanied him to work today. With the iguana munching contentedly on his kale, Crosby took off his boots and got settled at his desk. He picked up the train conductor's diary and started reading. Transfixed, he absorbed the conductor's anecdotes in the era marked as one of great change; even the railroad switched from wood rails to steel.

Coming to a new section, Crosby placed the bookmark between the pages and searched for his phone, but it wasn't at the corner of his desk where he usually left it. He frowned and then tapped his forehead with his fingers. Of course. He had set it on the entrance table when the tour arrived.

Leaving his office, he couldn't shake the feeling something was wrong. Why was it so dark at four in the afternoon. There should be sunlight streaming through the front window.

A persistent beep sounded from the entryway. *Oh no!* He grabbed his phone and let out a mild curse. Turned out he had not only worked through the first phase of Sami's makeover, but also fourteen texts from her. The first asked if he could arrive earlier as she'd forgotten about a dress fitting. They got progressively worse until he perused the last text and winced.

What did she mean she was canceling Operation Crosby 2.0 altogether?

As hard as it was to admit it, he needed her help if he was going to stand up in front of the town to give his speech and make his family proud.

Crosby called her, but she wasn't answering. A minute later, the fifteenth text came through.

You're not taking this seriously. I can't help you if you don't want my help.

He typed a return text but deleted it. No matter how many ways he asked her to reconsider, he couldn't get the words right, which didn't portend well for his speech.

Hold on. Sami was heading to Timeless Tailors for her bridal dress fitting. He ran out the door. The second his socks hit the pavement, he realized his mistake. He looked down, only to find he wasn't wearing shoes. Letting out an exasperated breath, he went back inside the cottage with wet cold feet that were in serious danger of becoming blocks of ice.

Too aware of every passing moment, Crosby quickly tugged on his boots. Thankfully, Timeless Tailors was a mere three blocks away. He didn't want Sami returning to the dude ranch without hearing his heartfelt apology.

Crosby hadn't gone far when he spotted Sami staring at the display in front of Reichert's Supply Company, one of Crosby's favorite destinations for it conjured notions of an old-fashioned general store. He especially enjoyed the retro candy sticks near the front, particularly the cherry ones that were a bargain at ten cents each.

Crosby was about to call out her name when someone else beat him to it. Jeremy appeared by her side, and they hugged each other. Crosby ducked inside the alcove leading into Corwin and Company Boot Shop. Despite the holiday rush, Crosby could see them just fine. They separated, and Sami pointed to something in the window. Jeremy let out a booming laugh that carried all the way to Crosby's hiding place. This was ridiculous. He should just show himself and march right up to them.

And do what? Explain he'd been watching them from afar? Then he'd sound like a jealous boyfriend, so he sighed and stayed where he was. Besides, he wanted to apologize to Sami when she was by herself and not with Jeremy.

He flattened his back against the store window, his breaths coming out in short spurts, the same way as when he was younger and yet another teacher had compared him to one of his siblings. Where was a book when he needed one?

Crosby changed his mind. He'd come clean and beg for Sami's forgiveness. He stepped toward the sidewalk but jumped back. Sami was already upset with him about missing the first stage of his makeover. If she found out he'd been lurking behind buildings, she might think he was spying on her. He counted to sixty and peeked around the corner again, only to find a large crowd gathering around a group of carolers. The distraction was just what he needed, and he used the opportunity to head in the opposite direction.

"Aunt Marilyn!" Jeremy's voice boomed over the crowd, which separated.

With Jeremy heading his way and without a second thought, Crosby ducked into a snowy hedge. Ouch! The prickly holly snagged on his sweater and scratched his arm, the cold starting to penetrate through him. Finally, it dawned on him that he'd forgotten something other than his boots, namely his coat. What started as a quick stroll to Timeless Tailors, where he'd have had a chance to get warm, was turning into anything but that.

If anything, he'd have an even harder time explaining why he was in a hedge than he would have had about skulking in building alcoves, so Crosby stayed hunkered down. The worst of it was he only had himself to blame.

Jeremy hailed his aunt and pulled the older woman toward Sami. The trio came to a halt right in front of him and the theater marquee that advertised *The Santa Who Forgot Christmas*.

"I've heard so many nice things about you. It's a pleasure to meet you." Sami greeted Jeremy's aunt with the same effusiveness she showed everyone.

"Jeremy has told me so much about you." Marilyn stepped toward Sami and hugged her before pulling away with a smile. "If anything, Jeremy didn't tell me how beautiful you are. You two make such a gorgeous couple."

"Aunt Marilyn!" Jeremy batted his aunt's arm, but Crosby noticed neither he nor Sami corrected Marilyn's observation.

Instead, the trio launched into a lengthy conversation, and Crosby pulled his sweater around him, trying to stay warm. He retreated deeper into the hedge when something like a gasp came his way, followed by a stretch of hacking coughs coming from Sami. Concern for his friend compelled him to peek through the hedge. Sami's face was beet red, and it took all of Crosby's restraint to stay hidden.

Sami straightened and cleared her throat. "I'm sorry to cut this short, but I have a pressing engagement that I must attend."

Marilyn expressed her dismay, as did Jeremy, until Jeremy mentioned the popcorn stand. The chummy pair headed in the opposite direction, and he watched Sami's boots travel away from the hedge.

Crosby's feet were frozen. He wiggled his toes until he was confident that he didn't have frostbite. Then he climbed out of the hedge and sighed with relief, yanking his sweater free.

Tomorrow he'd confess everything to Sami and beg for double forgiveness, but for now, he wanted to get back to the Miners' Cottage and enjoy the warmth.

He took two steps before Sami blocked his path. One look at her, and it was clear that he was so busted.

Sami folded her arms over her chest. "Are you in a hurry to go somewhere?" She arched one eyebrow as her gaze took in the sight of his favorite chunky beige belted sweater that had belonged to his father. "Or did you leave your coat in the bush?"

"You knew I was there?" Crosby jammed his hands in his pockets, having also forgotten his gloves.

"It's not every day you see the town historian hiding out in the hedges." Sami's voice held no hint of amusement.

"I was looking for you." He tried to smile but his face was growing numb. If only he had Jase's fast thinking or Daisy's ability to smooth over every situation with a kind remark.

"You found me." She let out an exasperated huff and motioned for him to follow her. "Come with me. You either look like a snowman come to life or a human about to become a snowman. I don't know which."

Minutes later, he luxuriated in the warmness of Blue Skies Coffeehouse with his hands wrapped around a mug of apple cider with a cinnamon stick stirrer. "Thanks for the drink."

Sami frowned at him. "No coat, no gloves, no wallet. What were you thinking?"

"About apologizing to you." He swirled the cinnamon stick through the amber liquid, the delicious scent barely registering over the disapproval in Sami's eyes. "For missing the first phase of the makeover."

"And you could do that in a bush?" She shook her head and picked up her purse from where it was hanging on her chair. "I'm sorry, Crosby, but I can't help you prepare for your speech."

The resignation in Sami's eyes went deeper than he cared to admit. It was almost as if she was walking out on their friendship as much as delivering the blow that Operation Crosby 2.0 was over. That same panic that had welled deep inside him that first day of kindergarten was taking root in his core.

"But I need you." He winced as that sounded like a lame way to justify his behavior over the past few hours.

Sami stood. "Everyone's waiting for me at Timeless Tailors." She was halfway out the door before she came back to him, and his heart went wonky at the possibility she might be giving him a second chance. "I know people think I'm too concerned about external appearances."

Crosby scoffed. "I don't."

Sami held up her hand, and Crosby stopped talking, stirring his apple cider instead. "My mother scheduled every minute of every day in hopes I would become famous. She lived vicariously through me without asking me if that was what I wanted." Crosby knew about Mrs. Fleming's attempts to profit off her daughter and didn't care for the woman's desire to control Sami, let alone pocket Amanda's hard-earned money. "At first, I circumvented her plans by taking it lightly and making it a game until I finally worked up the courage to live my own life. That's when I stopped going on auditions and attended cosmetology school. I will credit my mother for one positive thing, though. Everything in my childhood prepared me to help others feel happy with their outward appearance. Find the beauty in themselves and with life itself."

She did that, and more, every day.

"Please help me, Sami." The words came from his heart.

She looked troubled, and Crosby longed to do anything in his power to drive away that worry line in her forehead, and make her life easier.

Sami slowly took a step back. "I never listened to you and what you wanted. I forged ahead and developed the plan without your input. I was this close to turning into my mother and turning you into something you're not." She held up her fingers, a small space separating her index finger and thumb.

He refused to believe it. He knew the true Sami. "You did nothing of the sort."

She gave him a winsome smile, which caused the slight ache in his chest to bloom to full fruition. "Don't worry. The makeover idea is finished. Here's my advice about your speech. Deliver it with the same intensity as you dedicate to your books, and you'll knock it out of the park."

Sami hurried away before he could get a word in edgewise. Unsure of how to convince her to give him a second chance, he watched her leave.

CHAPTER FOUR

SAMI SNIFFED AND swept the same square foot of the Porcupine Suite that she'd been sweeping for the past ten minutes. By all accounts, she should be the happiest woman in Violet Ridge. Jeremy had just texted her and asked her to dinner at Miss Tilly's Steakhouse with him and his aunt Marilyn, who had finished her last chemotherapy treatment. Despite the sweet invite, Sami kept seeing Crosby's brown eyes brimming with uncertainty as she left Blue Skies Coffeehouse last night.

Throughout the fitting at Timeless Tailors, Sami had remained quiet. Amanda had picked up on Sami's somber mood, attributing it to her recent announcement about moving, and postponed the plans to discuss her wedding shower afterward. Sami hadn't had the heart to tell her about Crosby's hiding out in the hedge, not wanting Amanda to think any less of her future brother-in-law.

And even though she wanted to stay upset with him, she couldn't. Crosby didn't have a malicious bone in his body, and the thought of him spying for nefarious reasons was quite comical, almost as much as his actions, except for the fact that he had been shivering. Actually, he had looked quite sad.

Darn Crosby and his good-natured self.

Sami leaned her chin on the top of the broomstick, replacing the image of Crosby from last night with one where he was wearing a fitted suit and delivering a speech that ended in a standing ovation. Sighing, she shook her head. Taking over was her mother's way of doing things, not hers.

It was for the best she'd canceled the makeover. Now she and Crosby could go back to the way things used to be between them.

Shaking off any negative energy, she searched through her Christmas playlists. Nothing appealed to her. She shouldn't have walked out on Crosby, not when he had that empty look in his eyes. It was as if he thought she was turning her back on their friendship. She scoffed. As if that could happen. Not after all they'd shared in the past six months.

Like when he accompanied her on her first horse ride here at the dude ranch. Although Amanda had worked at a ranch one summer in Texas and was a proficient equestrienne, Sami had never ridden a horse before. She and Crosby had shared a first-rate adventure that day with the wind at her hair and the Rockies at their prettiest.

Or the time when she introduced Crosby to

karaoke. She laughed so hard at the memory of him belting out a version of Rick Astley's "Never Gonna Give You Up" that her shoulders started shaking. She wasn't surprised that Crosby had such good pipes, considering that everything he did, he did well.

"Sami? Are you okay?"

Bridget Virtue's voice came from behind, and Sami whirled around to find Crosby's grandmother, who was also her boss, standing there with both hands on her cane.

Sami hastened to reassure her that everything was fine. "I was just thinking about your grandson."

Bridget tapped her forehead. "Great minds think alike. Crosby has been on my mind quite a bit lately. He's so concerned about that speech he has to give on New Year's Eve. I'm so happy you're helping him get over his anxiety about public speaking."

So Crosby hadn't told his grandparents or siblings that she'd rescinded her offer. If only he hadn't been so exasperating yesterday. He should have been honest with her rather than hiding in bushes like some superspy or jealous boyfriend, neither of which applied to him. Crosby had his share of faults, but he was nothing like her exboyfriend Aaron.

"We actually agreed last night that my little experiment was a bad idea," Sami said, frowning.

She wasn't sure if it was a mutual decision, or unilateral on her part.

"That's a shame. Sometimes a little change can make such a difference. Like when you arrived at the ranch and cut my hair in such a flattering style." Bridget patted her silver bob that framed her face. "It was the first time since the stroke I'd really been pampered. It did me a lot of good and rejuvenated my spirits."

Sami waved away Bridget's praise. "I loved seeing Martin's face when he saw you. Thank you for letting me be a part of this for a little while."

Bridget rested in the salon chair and placed her cane next to the armrest. "Not just for a little while, but always. You're part of our family." She searched Sami's face and then smiled. "Amanda resembles your grandmother Lou more, but you have her presence. She always lit up the room, just like you do."

Sami let out a nervous laugh. "It's the training from my beauty pageant days."

"So humble, too. Just like Lou." Bridget reached out for Sami's hand. Sami connected with the older woman's gnarled fingers and received a light squeeze in return. "I wish I could remember what I did with that box of Christmas cards from her so I could give them to you."

"When you find them, give them to Amanda." Except for her pageant tiaras and gnome collection, Sami tried to keep clutter to a minimum.

Bridget patted the tote bag hoisted on her shoulder. "But I did find some mementos from my parents, along with photos taken at the train depot before my father was shipped overseas. Oh, how happy I was when he returned on New Year's Eve. I'd love for Crosby to see these as soon as possible. Can you take them to the depot for me?"

Only Bridget Virtue had the pull to make Sami budge from her desire to keep Crosby at arm's length. With reluctance, she accepted the bag and chatted with Bridget for a few more minutes before setting forth for town.

The depot was in plain sight, but Sami hesitated. Since the moment she met Crosby at the duck pond, she hadn't felt awkward around him. Their bond had been immediate. Why did their friendship work so well? After all, she concerned herself with people's exterior appearances while he sought out a person's internal story, the further in the past the better. He was the dreamer and she was the doer. Together they somehow created a meaningful friendship. All the more reason to go back to the way they were, two friends who had fun hanging out together and accepted each other, faults and all. Forgetting the makeover, which had done nothing but cause trouble, was for the best.

With that in mind, Sami climbed the stairs to the second story of the depot. What used to be the living quarters for the stationmaster and his family were now used as meeting rooms.

Beatrice, one of the historical society docents who often led tours at the cottage, greeted Sami and motioned toward the back. "Crosby's with the students. I forgot the juice boxes that are in my trunk. I won't be long."

Sami nodded and continued along the corridor.

She soon spied Crosby with his back to her. Twenty sets of eyes were glued to him. Once a week, students filed into the rooms where Crosby conducted after-school activities until it was time for their parents or guardians to collect them.

"Today we're making train ornaments," Crosby said.

As much as she wanted to watch from the sidelines, that wasn't her style.

"Is this offer reserved for your students, or can I make one for a friend?" Sami asked.

Crosby's back stiffened before he relaxed and turned around. A huge goofy smile graced his face until it disappeared. "I'm sure Jeremy will enjoy his."

"It's not for Jeremy." Sami rolled her eyes and spotted an empty chair, sliding into it. "My best friend is really into trains."

He pointed at himself. She nodded, and a trace of that smile returned. She never was able to stay upset with anyone for long. "But I thought we were not exchanging gifts, just getting each other…experiences."

She raised her eyebrow. "One more stunt like

last night and you'll be on Santa's permanent naughty list and you won't receive anything except coal."

Giggles from the elementary school kids reminded her that little pitchers had big ears. Crosby cleared his throat and brought order back to the group.

"Everyone gets to choose a red or a green train." He stopped in front of Sami's desk. "Can you help distribute the materials?"

Sami nodded. "But first where should I put this?" She raised the tote bag. "It's from your grandmother."

He scratched his long hair, her fingers still itching to style it, but she didn't say anything.

"Could you put it by the door, please?"

She did as directed and then returned for half of the kits. "You're stuck with me. Nothing can keep us apart for long, you know."

A tic in his jawline surprised her. Apparently Crosby hadn't known that she couldn't stay mad at him even after yesterday's stunt. He looked like he was about to say something, but he simply closed his mouth and started bustling around the room, assisting the students.

Crosby's eight-year-old nephew, Aspen, raised his hand and fidgeted in his seat. "Uncle Crosby! Uncle Crosby! I got an important question."

"The bathroom is right across the hall, Aspen. But come right back." Crosby kept helping Aspen's sister Rosie, who deliberated between red and green.

Aspen continued to hold his arm high. "That's not my question. Why trains? Why not something exciting like motorcycles? Oh, or planes?" He swooped his hand in a gliding motion, right into the face of his other sister, Lily.

"Ouch!" Lily wrinkled her nose and folded her arms together. "Aspen, don't hit me."

"Sorry, Lil." Aspen sounded contrite. Then he moved to look directly at her. "I didn't hit you hard enough for the freckles to go away."

Sami covered her laugh with a cough and approached Lily. "Your freckles are beautiful. Don't let anyone convince you otherwise."

Lily smiled and reached under her seat, pulling out the book she always carried with her.

Like uncle, like niece.

"Sorry, Lily." Crosby tapped the cover. "It's not time to read. It's time to make and decorate train ornaments."

With a big sigh, Lily placed her book back under her seat. "Do you have any purple ones?" Crosby shook his head, and she chose the last pack of green Popsicle sticks.

After all the kits were distributed, Crosby took his place at the front of the room while Sami stood to the side. "Kids, Aspen asked a great question. Why trains? It took five years to restore the Violet Ridge Thunderbolt, a narrow-gauge steam locomotive."

Crosby launched into an age-appropriate explanation of the importance of the Western Rocky Railroad System in this part of Colorado. After which he began demonstrating how to glue the sticks together to form a wooden train.

Beatrice returned with the juice boxes and pulled Sami aside. "Can you help Crosby while I make a quick phone call?"

"No problem."

Sami assisted the students at one end of the room, while Crosby aided those at the other. Eventually there was as much glue on fingers and sleeves as on the ornaments themselves. After everyone left their trains to dry, Sami helped Crosby distribute juice boxes and cheese sticks to the group.

Aspen made choo choo sounds before munching on a strand of cheese. "Uncle Crosby? I still like planes better, but trains are pretty epic."

"Glad you're giving them a chance." Crosby slurped the last of his juice box and smiled.

Aspen imitated Crosby, finishing his juice, and then stared at his uncle. "Can we go on the train next?"

Everyone murmured their approval until Crosby tamped his hands for noise control. "I'm sorry, no. It's still undergoing renovations, but there are tickets still available for the Christmas Eve train ride."

Rosie rushed over to her uncle. With an angry look, she stomped her foot in front of him. "They'll have to change the date. There's a very important play going on that day."

"It's okay, Rosie." Crosby patted his niece's shoulder. "The organizers thought of everything. The play will occur earlier, and the train ride isn't until evening."

"What about Santa?" A kindergartner's eyes grew big as he gazed at the Santa hat on Crosby's head.

Crosby turned his head in either direction with a degree of stealth. "Shh! I'll let you in on a little secret. There's a rumor Santa will be making an appearance on the Violet Ridge Thunderbolt before he starts delivering toys and presents all over the world." Crosby pushed the tip of his Santa hat to the other side of his head. "I have something wonderful for you. If everyone is quiet and respectful, I'll get Sundance from the other room and you can say hello to him before you go home."

Cheers erupted. Penny O'Neal, the daughter of Jase's fiancée, Cassie, reminded everyone they had to be very quiet around Crosby's pet iguana. While Crosby retrieved Sundance, Sami guided everyone over to the carpeted area. Soon Crosby returned with Sundance on his shoulder while toting his portable carrier with a built-in heat lamp. Everyone exclaimed over Sundance's matching Santa hat until Penny glared at the group, and silence reigned once more.

One girl inched backward until her back came

into contact with Sami's ankle. The girl shivered. "I don't like lizards or snakes."

"Sydney, right?" Crosby smiled at the young girl, who nodded. "Sundance is an iguana, and I'll tell you what I know of his story. One morning, Penny and Easton's mom woke up and found him in his terrarium on her front doorstep."

"I remember that day." Easton nodded with extra enthusiasm. "Mommy screamed really loud that morning."

Penny confirmed her brother's memory, and Crosby finished his story. "Sundance and I hit it off. Iguanas can grow very attached to their caregivers."

Sundance remained calm for Crosby while Sydney moved closer to the front. "Isn't it gross to feed him his food?"

Crosby kept his movements calm and deliberate but let a giant smile grace his face. Sami's insides melted the slightest bit.

"Iguanas are herbivores. They eat vegetables like leafy greens, peppers and snap peas."

Sydney frowned but took another step toward Crosby and Sundance. "What if I gave him a chicken nugget?"

Crosby placed Sundance back inside the heated terrarium and then squirted hand sanitizer in his palms and rubbed it into his skin. "He'd get very sick. Chicken meat can damage his kidneys."

Sydney shook her head. "Don't do that. He seems like a nice iguana."

At that moment, Sydney's mom appeared in the doorway along with other parents and guardians. They oohed and aahed over the finished ornaments. Soon everyone had gone home, including Beatrice. Sami wanted to stay longer, but Jeremy would be expecting her at Miss Tilly's soon. Still, she couldn't go until she cleared the air.

Sami picked up her finished train ornament. "I have a feeling someone might like this in his stocking."

"Trains never go out of style." Crosby blushed the sweetest shade of pink.

He gazed in her direction. For a second, he looked at her the way Seth looked at Amanda. That was crazy. This was Crosby, her good friend. Her best friend.

"I was pretty upset yesterday," she said.

"I was wrong not to make my presence known sooner." His cheeks transformed from pink to bright red. "I'm sorry, Sami."

"I accept your apology." She clasped the train ornament to her chest. "I have somewhere I need to be."

Sami headed for the exit but then heard Crosby's voice. "I still need help with my speech."

She halted at the doorway. Part of her wanted to keep walking to Miss Tilly's and enjoy a pleasant evening with Jeremy and Marilyn, yet the rest of her wanted to erase this awkward tension forming between her and Crosby. She faced him once more. "You seemed fine talking to the students." She tapped her chin. "And you give tours at the cottage. Why do you need my help for the Midnight Express New Year's Eve celebration speech?"

"For one thing, there will be many more people at the celebration. They expect more. It's not hard talking to kids. They soak up everything." Crosby shrugged. "Besides I've known Rosie, Aspen and Lily since they were born."

"It's too bad Rosie isn't ten years older. She'd deliver a great speech."

"I love her sassy confidence, but that part of the New Year's Celebration is past her bedtime." Crosby met Sami halfway. "Any advice for me? I'll take anything since I want to do my best for the volunteers who worked tirelessly to make this happen. You know how strongly I feel about historical preservation."

She stayed where she was. "Just be yourself, Crosby. After all, you just made an impact on Sydney. I wouldn't be surprised if she asks her parents for an iguana for Christmas."

They both laughed, and he reached for her hands. "You might be onto something, using your past experience on the pageant circuit to help alleviate my concerns about my speech. Please, Sami, I need your help."

It occurred to her how well he'd communicated with his audience today.

"But the way I want to help you isn't conventional. Maybe your time would be better spent just practicing your speech until it's perfect."

He shook his head and squeezed her hands. She ignored the small tingle zooming along her fingertips.

"You've never steered me wrong, and something needs to give in my life. You're right. I should start thinking more about my appearance before I catch frostbite or something." He gave a wry laugh.

"I can't guarantee my approach will fix any of that, but it might alleviate your concerns about giving a speech to a crowd." She met his gaze, and it was as if something was changing between them right this minute. She pulled her hands away as if he was a hot curling iron. His eyes darkened, and he looked hurt at her jerky motion. She hastened to add, "But it might make you irresistible."

"Then let's go for it." He took off his glasses and grinned. "But be gentle with me."

"You're incorrigible." She chuckled and shook her head.

"Only in the nicest way. I'm also yours." He winked at her. "Mold me into the man of your dreams."

"It's not every day that someone gives me carte blanche. You're going to be the talk of the celebration." Sami rubbed her hands and narrowed her eyes as if she was plotting some diabolical scheme. "New Year's will be here before you know it, and then Valentine's Day."

The idea of her departure caught her off guard. She grabbed her purse, shouting an order to Crosby to be on time tomorrow night. Halfway to Miss Tilly's, Sami stopped rushing and took a deep breath. Suddenly, the prospect of Valentine's Day being the start of her new adventures seemed wrong.

Had they, in fact, already begun?

CHAPTER FIVE

TEN MINUTES EARLY! That was a first for Crosby. He stopped short of giving an exuberant shout of joy as he entered the Porcupine Suite. Sure, it took two alarms and a tied string around his finger, but he was here. Although, he was positive Uncle Billy's trick from the holiday movie *It's a Wonderful Life* wasn't really the cause of his newfound punctuality. Still, being on time allowed him the luxury of taking a minute to admire Sami. As always, she looked beautiful, and today her long crimson cashmere sweater, paired with jeans and high stiletto boots, matched the season. But how did she walk around in those boots all day long?

After he returned the hat that she'd forgotten at the train depot yesterday in what seemed like a rush to escape, he winced. Sami had whipped out a giant lavender cape and held it aloft for him. Crosby eyed the cape with skepticism, and his muscles tightened, especially around his shoulders. "Harold doesn't make me wear one of those."

"Harold also only knows two ways to cut hair—

short or very short." Sami arched her eyebrow and continued holding the cape out toward him. "I know what I'm doing. I've been licensed as a cosmetologist for over a year."

He approached and she snapped the cape in place. "And you're the official stylist of the entire Virtue family," he said.

"They know a good thing when they see it." She guided him to the salon chair and ran her fingers through his hair. "Your hair is thick and curly just like Seth and Jase."

Crosby tensed. This was the last place he expected to be compared to his siblings before he caught himself. She was talking about hair texture and nothing more.

"What about Daisy?" he asked.

"Hers has a different feel with less wave." Through the mirror, he could see her tilt her head to one side, then the other. "I originally just wanted to cut and contour, leaving a bit of length. Now that you're in the chair, what do you think of going shorter and accenting those great cheekbones?"

"I don't see how this will help me deliver my speech, but I trust your judgment." So far, he hadn't written a single word of his first draft, but there was plenty of time yet.

"Crosby, relax. You're too tense." Sami left her station and went to a nearby shelf. She brought back a candle, lit the wick and placed it on the counter in front of them. "This is rosemary and mint. If you like the scent, I'll send it home with you. Rosemary is designed to reduce stress, and mint helps clear the mind."

"This might be the first time anyone has described me as tense." He prided himself for being the most laid-back of the Virtue siblings. Yet, at this moment, he was on edge, most likely due to this environment, which was most unusual to him. Still, he liked seeing Sami showcase her skills and talent.

"Change is inevitable, Crosby." She returned and rubbed the strands of his hair between her fingertips. "I'm going to apply a deep conditioner. It will do wonders for the damage caused from years of sun on the ranch."

He flinched. "I always thought I spent more time inside with my books than outside." On second thought, when Grandpa Martin and Grandma Bridget had saddled horses for outings with the dude ranch guests and his siblings, Crosby had been right there in the middle of the pack.

With a book in his saddlebag and a story floating around in his mind.

She rested her hands on his shoulders. "There's a whole world out there beyond books. Haven't you ever wanted to see Paris in springtime? Or go to Australia when it's winter here and summer there? Or see an elephant in the wild in Africa?"

"I can see all of that in books or online." Crosby

pushed his black-rimmed glasses back to the bridge of his nose and turned to face her.

"There are some things that are better experienced in person." She pushed at his shoulders until he was staring at the mirror once more. "Now, we have to get something straight. When I have scissors in my hand, you can't swivel around whenever you feel like it. You might end up with a gaping bald spot or a mohawk."

"Point taken."

"Thank you." She lifted her hands off his shoulders and held out her hand. "I need your glasses."

He hesitated, suspicion lurking in those light brown eyes. "Hal never takes my glasses."

"I bet Hal spritzes your hair with water, right?"

Crosby smiled and nodded. "Yep."

"Hal does a fine job, but you're in my salon now." Sami rubbed her hands together and delivered a cackling laugh before she winked. "As my best friend, you're entitled to the works."

"The works?" That sounded more sinister than her fake laugh.

"Your glasses?" She kept her hand raised.

He removed them, folded the arms and placed them in her palm. "Why do I get the feeling I'm about to undergo more than a simple haircut?"

Sami escorted him to the professional sink and chair for the official washing of the hair. "I have the whole evening planned. First, a haircut and then a facial."

Crosby glanced at the door, wondering if it was too late to bolt. "What? A facial?" His voice cracked, and his mind flooded with excuses to leave. Sundance could be having an iguana emergency. He'd finally hit upon the thesis for the book about the history of Violet Ridge. He had a mad crush on her and that's all that it could ever be.

She wouldn't believe any of them, even the last one, which happened to be true.

"It was that or my new special feature—body wraps." She pushed him into the chair and indicated that he should lean backward. "But I thought that would scare you away."

She was right. "It sounds like something they did to mummies in ancient Egypt," Crosby said.

The sound of water hitting the sink reached him, and he braced himself for what would come next. "My body wraps are quite delightful. They soften your skin and improve circulation. They're relaxing, and that's what I'm trying to do for you before New Year's Eve."

A jolt of cold water was not relaxing in the least. He yelped and jumped in his seat. "That's not working."

"Oops." Genuine remorse sounded in her voice, and she diverted the stream of water back to the sink. A minute later, a warmer stream drizzled over his scalp. "Is that better? I checked it against my wrist this time."

Much better. He started relaxing. A few seconds later, a pleasant smell reached his nose, a woodsy scent mixed with ginger. "What's that?"

"My special shampoo." Her fingers massaged the top of his head. It felt wonderful, and he relaxed under her magic fingers. He might have to buy a bottle of that if she had any for sale.

She rinsed off the shampoo. When he began to say something, water dribbled into his mouth. Crosby coughed. He started to rise when she placed some gentle pressure on his shoulders. "I'm not done yet," she said. "Next up is the deep conditioner."

She massaged more wonderful-smelling gunk into his hair, and his scalp tingled in a good way. "I could get used to this."

Before he knew it, she tapped on his arm and motioned for him to sit up straight. "You don't know how long I've waited to run my hands through your hair." Even without his glasses, he could see her cheeks pinken. She wrapped a warm towel around his head. "You have a great head of hair, thick and curly. That's what I meant to say."

"Then why do you want to cut it if it's so great?"

"Everyone can use a change once in a while, even the king of keep everything the same." Sami escorted him back to the other chair and blotted the excess water with the towel.

"Can I have my glasses now?" Crosby asked,

squinting in her direction. "I can't see myself in the mirror."

"Nothing much to see. I'm just selecting the best shears for your haircut." She closed the drawer and made snipping sounds with the scissors. "I'll give you a choice. You can have them back or you can wait for the big reveal and leave everything to my nimble fingers."

He stretched his neck and considered her offer before shrugging. "You can keep them for now, but you have to find some new trust-building exercises for our friendship."

She chuckled. "It's a deal, and you made a wise choice. Tell me about your day."

He never talked to Harold. "Why? Don't you work best in silence?" He did. Weaving together a picture of historical facts and figures was best done in silence; at least, that's what he'd always found. "I wouldn't want to say something that might cause your fingers to slip so that I'd leave with a gaping bald spot or a mohawk."

"On the contrary. I find the rhythm of voices soothing, and people usually like talking to me." He could hear the smile in her voice. "I'm quite likable, you know."

Crosby knew that firsthand.

"Just remember that you asked." He launched into an account of his day. "I traveled to our nearby Ute community and met with folks to seek approval to record interviews. Once the recordings are done, I'll get them uploaded to the oral history station alongside the display of chronologies and local arrowheads and other artifacts they approve. Creating more interactive exhibits has sparked attendance again."

They conversed about his trip while she used the shears to snip his hair, an ever-growing pile of which was now on the floor. "Almost finished," she said in a joyful, singsong voice.

Crosby tried to stay calm. He closed his eyes while she waved the blow-dryer around his head, the warm spurt of air quite pleasant. She switched off the apparatus, whipped off his cape and handed him his glasses. "What do you think?" she asked.

He almost didn't recognize himself with his hair so short. The last time he'd had it shorter than Seth's was probably around the time their parents died in a tragic car accident. Crosby was four. It was as though a new man was staring back at him in the mirror. "Wow! You're good."

"Thank you, kind sir." Sami performed a mock bow and crossed over to the shelves of hair care products for sale. Muttering to herself about which ones would be best for his new style, she plucked a bottle of shampoo, another of conditioner and a small can of styling mousse off the top shelf. She deposited the products into a tote bag emblazoned with the Lazy River Dude Ranch logo and returned to him. With patience, she delivered detailed instructions about how to use each and presented him with the tote. "It's an early Christmas gift."

He accepted it with reluctance and stared inside. "Is all of this necessary?" He pulled out the mousse, raising the bottle in the air.

She reached over and ran a manicured finger through his locks. "Your hair'll be out of control if you leave it as is."

Right now, his heart was beating out of control. His mind worked overtime to convince himself that she was treating him just like any other client. You didn't call someone you liked the king of keep everything the same. There had never been strings attached to their friendship, and it was for the best that there never would be. Disappointment bloomed in him, but at least she was still a part of his life. He wouldn't do anything to change that, so he reached deep inside himself and kept everything light.

"You think I'll blow-dry my hair?" Crosby laughed until she stared at him. He was joking about her livelihood, and this was serious to her. He stopped and shrugged. "I don't even own a blow-dryer."

"Buy one and thank me later."

He accepted the tote bag, covering his hand over hers. A shock passed through him, and she moved her gaze to her high-heeled boots. "Static electricity."

So she had felt something pass between them as well. *Huh.* "When is the next stage?"

"Right now. I promise it'll be fun." She smiled and winked at him, more signs that the sizzle between them was just that, a flash of chemistry that disintegrated in a snap. "I downloaded the best action holiday movie of all time, which I know is one of your favorites. We can watch it in my suite while the mud mixture works its charm on us."

Her bright laugh followed her as she departed for the White Fox Suite with Crosby on her heels. He didn't need a facial for Sami to work her charm on him. Just spending time with her was all it took, but he wouldn't ruin however long they had left together by forcing the issue. It was best if he put his feelings for her on the back burner where they belonged.

"This is a clay mask made with all-natural ingredients, including oats and chamomile." Sami mixed two teaspoons of a beige powdery substance with two teaspoons of distilled water until the paste was the right consistency. "I chose this one because I love the soothing scent. And it softens your skin."

Crosby stared at the goo with disdain. "Sundance doesn't care whether I have rough skin or not."

He wrinkled his nose, and Sami tried not to stare at him. She had styled over a thousand heads of hair over the past few years, but his stood out from all the others. If anyone ever doubted the wonders of a good haircut, Crosby would make them a believer. The shorter style brought out the sun-toned streaks to their advantage and showed off his chiseled cheekbones.

Crosby looked ready to bolt, but she dismissed his concern and kept talking.

"Self-care and maintenance can boost your spirits. Positivity and self-esteem will go a long way to alleviate your anxiety about giving that speech." She snapped a hair cap on him and then one on herself. "The audience will pick up on nerves. If you're calm and confident, they'll be more likely to give you their full attention."

Not that she'd ever thought of Crosby as anything but calm and, yes, confident in his usual surroundings. The man was a rock with the ability to stay chill in most situations. There was little he couldn't face with a book in hand and facts about the past on his lips. Look at how fabulously he interacted with those students yesterday. None of them had rattled him.

Crosby sniffed the paste and then pushed his glasses back into place. "The smell reminds me of something, but I can't put my finger on what."

Sami inhaled the earthy scent, the aroma boosting her endorphins. "Chamomile is part of the daisy family. This might be a good signature scent for your sister. Maybe Daisy's aware of that and has already adopted it for herself. That could be where you've smelled it before."

"I don't think so." He shook his head and then stiffened his shoulders. "Let's get this part over with so we can watch the movie."

Sami batted his arm. "When you're so relaxed that you fall asleep and wake up in time to see the credits, I'll be the one saying, 'I told you so.'"

Crosby laughed. "You're always the one who falls asleep when we watch a movie. You make the cutest snoring snuffles."

"I do not."

"Do so."

"Do not." She wrinkled her nose at him. Did she snore? And why did it matter so much that he noticed a little detail like that?

She stirred the clay mixture once more and directed him to the couch. "After this hardens a bit, I'll put it on our faces. It'll be ready to come off at the elevator scene, which will be the perfect time to clean up, reload our popcorn bowls and settle in for the rest of the movie."

Crosby shuddered as he handed her his glasses. "You won't take my picture and send it to any of my siblings, right?"

Without his glasses, he resembled a superhero. For the second time in almost as many minutes, she had a glimpse of what he'd look like as he approached the podium on New Year's Eve. Surely single women in the audience would be as impressed as she was.

She shook off the image of future Crosby and focused on the here and now. "Hmm, a little light blackmail sounds too enticing to pass up. So many delicious possibilities of what I could ask for are going through my mind." She pulled out her phone and brought up the camera app. "How can I get you to do my bidding if I don't take the picture?"

Sami waggled her eyebrows and laughed, but Crosby looked as serious as ever. "Like you need photos of me covered in mud to do that?"

The air grew thick with something close to tension, something new and unfamiliar. If she didn't know better, she'd say it was romantic in nature. Something close to longing made her lick her lips and wonder what it would be like to kiss Crosby.

Kiss Crosby? What was she thinking? Nothing good ever came from dating your best friend. Didn't she learn anything from her cousin Isla? She had started dating the man who'd been her best friend in college before they called it quits, ending up as mortal enemies. When Isla and Henry had broken up, their friends claimed sides, and Sami had to comfort Isla because most of them sided with Henry and wouldn't talk to her any longer.

Crosby had far deeper roots in Violet Ridge than she did. Without a doubt, there were no surprises in his future, which was already as settled as Seth and Amanda's. He'd live quite happily with Sundance in his house with a white picket fence while maintaining the Miners' Cottage as a historic landmark where visitors could learn about the region's history.

Sami wanted adventure and surprise, romance and mystery. Crosby was her complete opposite, embracing the past and stability. That's what made them such good friends. Best friends.

She reached for the bowl of clay. "This will harden if we don't apply it now." She coated his face with the mud mixture and then did the same to hers.

After handing him a cooling under-eye mask, Sami put hers in place. She tried to relax and watch John McClane save the day, but Crosby's presence suddenly had her on edge. She took deep breaths of the aromatic blend of chamomile and other natural essential oils, letting the soothing mask work its wonders on her skin. Soon they'd both have dewy skin and she'd fetch the popcorn before Hans Gruber announced his demands. Then, once she was absorbed in the plot of the movie, she'd no longer be thinking about what it would be like to have Crosby wrap her in his arms…

"Sami?" Crosby's voice intruded into her thoughts and held a note of panic. He sounded anything but his usual calm self.

"Yes?" Was he sensing the same shift she was? She held her breath.

"Should my skin be tingling?" Urgency crept into his words, and she threw off her mask. Even with the dim lighting in her living area, she could tell something was wrong. He was flexing his fingers. "I feel like I want to start itching."

This wasn't good. Sami rushed him to her bathroom and flicked on the lights. Once her eyes adjusted to the brightness, she began washing the hard clay mask off Crosby until every trace of it was gone. Then she gasped. Angry red welts had popped up all over his face and neck.

She collected herself. "Crosby, are you allergic to anything?"

"Not that I know of."

He brought his hand to his face, but she grabbed it. "No matter how much you want to itch, you can't scratch. Wait here."

She ran to the living room and retrieved her phone. Her hands shook as she rushed back to the bathroom. "Should I call Seth or 9-1-1?"

"For now, Seth. He's the one who tends to the guests' injuries and my older brother might have some insight on whether I've ever had this type of reaction before. If it gets worse, we'll head to the hospital right away."

Within minutes, Seth and Amanda arrived at her suite with a first aid kit. Sami led them toward the bathroom, where they all squeezed into the tight space. She winced at the pitiful sight of Crosby, a scarlet rash covering his neck and face.

"Are you having any trouble breathing?" Seth asked while unlatching the kit.

"Not until you two showed up." Crosby raised his hand as if to scratch but Sami pressed it down again. No way would she let him permanently damage his skin. "I'm sort of mortified at looking this way in front of my older brother."

Seth rifled through the kit. "Why? That's what family's for."

"Dr. Yang is asking for the ingredients of the mask. She'll let us know whether Crosby needs to go to the hospital for an allergic reaction." Amanda redirected Sami's focus.

Sami fetched the small jar and read the ingredients to Dr. Yang, who was on speaker.

"Chamomile and ragweed are in the same family. Have you ever had a bad reaction to ragweed before, Crosby?" Dr. Yang asked.

Seth snapped his fingers. "Do you remember when you were little? Mom had to give you allergy medication for a week when you played in the ragweed patch. Dad cleared that area that very night so you wouldn't have the same reaction again."

Crosby shook his head. "I must have been really young at the time, maybe two or three? I had just turned four when they died."

Sami's heart went out to Crosby. The makeover

had been going well and they'd been having so much fun. Now he was not only in the midst of an allergic reaction to the mud mask but he was also reliving a painful incident when his parents had perished in an unfortunate car accident.

They listened to Dr. Yang's instructions. Seth found the allergy medication and gave Crosby the pills. Amanda brought Crosby a glass of water while Sami, a mere bystander, washed the cracked mud mask off her own face.

In no time, the four of them settled in to watch the holiday movie together so they could all keep an eye on Crosby. Scene after scene, Sami noted how Seth and Amanda had laced their fingers, holding hands. Sami tried to concentrate on the screen. Anything so she wouldn't look at Crosby with hydrocortisone cream dotting the rash on his face and neck.

While Sami had the best of intentions, this was an ominous start to helping Crosby overcome his anxiety about public speaking. There was no doubt, though, it had kept her from doing something she would have regretted: kissing Crosby.

CHAPTER SIX

THE SNOW HAD finally tapered off, and Crosby locked the Miners' Cottage behind him. He was due at the optometrist's office in fifteen minutes, and he'd best hurry. With a fast step, he might even be early for a change. For the first time in nearly a week, his rash had finally faded. Thank goodness for that. He had faced a barrage of questions about it, and answering each one was almost as bad as resisting the urge to scratch.

But those both took a back seat to what was really bothering him. Since that night, he had sensed a change in Sami, as if she was seeing him in a different light. It was only a haircut and Sami had never been superficial in that way. She cared about what lay beneath the surface while wanting to enhance the beauty surrounding her.

Crosby took care to avoid a slushy pile of ice on the sidewalk. Could it be that Sami held herself at fault for his reaction? She couldn't have known he was allergic to chamomile since he hadn't known, either. Was that why she had been avoiding him?

He hadn't liked the break from her company for a mere few days. How would he get used to her absence after Valentine's Day?

Still, this week wasn't a total loss. He had learned how to use the plethora of hair products she'd given to him. He had even broken down and purchased a hair dryer. His hair had never looked so good. If she was right about that, there stood a good chance she was right about the results of the makeover itself. For the sake of the Miners' Cottage roof, he hoped so.

As far as the other part of her promise—the one regarding the impact of the makeover? The one about finding a girlfriend? While he craved what his siblings had found in terms of love and support, he wasn't sure that could happen for him. Between his family and his job, he was so distracted, he couldn't devote himself to a relationship, at least, not the kind that Sami deserved. Besides, relationships led to commitments, and he didn't want a permanent one. Too many things in life, especially people, could be gone in a moment's notice. The pain of losing his parents rose once more. Maybe that was why he'd fallen for her. She brought joy and light to everything.

Admittedly, he hadn't revealed his feelings to her, and he couldn't. Not with her so happy to be leaving.

Crosby spied his optometrist's building at the same time that he saw one of the oldest residents of Violet Ridge, Mr. Hawk, using his walker to navigate the salted sidewalk. The elderly gentleman seemed to be in need of assistance. Crosby hurried to his side.

Mr. Hawk squinted. "Crosby Virtue. I've been meaning to find you. I must talk to you about the Violet Ridge Thunderbolt. You're making a terrible mistake that must be remedied before its first run on Christmas Eve."

"I have an upcoming optometrist appointment, but what's on your mind?" Crosby used his boot to clear the ice in front of Mr. Hawk's path.

"What's this nonsense about scarlet cushions?" Mr. Hawk raised the metal walker and tamped it on the cement for emphasis. "I distinctly remember being a young whippersnapper, riding on the Thunderbolt to go to meet my cousin who had been serving in Korea and was coming home on leave. The cushions were robin's-egg blue."

Crosby bobbed his head as Mr. Hawk elaborated on the meals served in the dining car. The elderly man's eyes lit up when he described the dishes and silverware and the delicious food served on them.

When Mr. Hawk stopped for breath, Crosby interjected, "I'd like to interview and record you soon, but I stand by my research. When the Violet Ridge Thunderbolt started running in the nineteenth century, the cushions were a deep red."

Mr. Hawk wrinkled his nose. "They were blue

when I rode on the train. I was so excited to sleep in the upper berth."

Crosby didn't want to interrupt him, but he was growing concerned about his appointment. At that moment, Sami approached them. She was a vision in her white coat and a bright red cashmere scarf, which looked new. "Merry Christmas, Mr. Hawk. How's life treating you?"

Mr. Hawk's expression turned from vinegar to honey. "Better now that you're here. Maybe you can talk some sense into Crosby and convince him he should order blue cushions for the train."

"I assure you the train will look its best on Christmas Eve, Mr. Hawk. The engine has been restored, and the plow on the front will ensure any snow won't block its progress." Crosby pulled out his phone. "I want you to be my guest at the grand unveiling and see for yourself how nice the scarlet cushions look."

Mr. Hawk sniffed. "I'll think about it and talk to my daughter. I'll have an answer when you interview me this week."

"I hope you don't find me incredibly rude, Mr. Hawk—" Sami waited while Mr. Hawk protested the contrary "—but Crosby has an appointment with the optometrist shortly. Can we see you to your car?"

"My daughter's meeting me for dinner at Miss Tilly's Steakhouse. It's her birthday." Mr. Hawk glanced at his watch. "Oops, I was supposed to be there five minutes ago."

There was no way Mr. Hawk could walk there by himself. Crosby looked over Mr. Hawk's head and relayed a silent message to Sami, who had already started moving alongside the older gentleman, chatting with him as if he were her long-lost grandfather. That was Sami for you. She made you feel as if you were a cherished part of her family within minutes of meeting her.

Inside the restaurant, Sami made sure Mr. Hawk found his daughter, then wished her a happy birthday. Crosby echoed Sami's sentiments and watched Sami interact with the Hawk family. She was vibrant and kind and totally captivating. Sami waved goodbye, and they were back on the sidewalk when Crosby snapped his fingers. "I should tell his daughter about the interview and set up a time to record Mr. Hawk."

Sami moved them in the direction of the optometrist's building once more, keeping as brisk a pace as possible considering the current conditions. "You know perfectly well she'll bring him to the Miners' Cottage at her earliest convenience once you ask her. Besides, it's a family celebration, and you're due at the optometrist's office in one minute. You're stalling."

The fact that she understood him so well might be the hardest part of letting her go.

They walked alongside each other. "I've done

fine with glasses, so it seems rather pointless to switch to contacts."

Sami hooked her arm through his and cuddled close to his side. "Confidence isn't pointless. Neither is trying something new and getting out of a rut. You'll thank me on New Year's Eve after your speech is a success."

The speech that he still needed to write. Winging it would lead to complete disaster.

Before he could work on his speech, though, he needed help decorating the train and she was the perfect person for such a task. "Any chance you could help me get the Violet Ridge Thunderbolt into shape next week?"

"As if you even need to ask."

Once again, the optometrist's building came into view, and Crosby held the door open for Sami. A burst of warmth from inside greeted him. "Thanks for coming with me. I'd have never done this on my own."

"That's why you have me. To make your life better." Sami sent him a dazzling smile before she squealed. "Jeremy? What are you doing here?"

Jeremy placed the magazine on the table and rushed over to Sami, giving her a hug, his bigger frame enveloping her. Then they separated and he grinned. "My aunt has an appointment today. She's getting her eyes dilated so I drove her."

Crosby excused himself and signed in with the

receptionist. Returning, he found they were still chatting and he felt like a third wheel.

"Do you remember that time in California…" Sami began.

"When I took you to the optometrist after you had to walk out of the audition?" Jeremy laughed and nodded.

Sami started giggling and touched Crosby's arm. "You should have seen me…" She was laughing too hard to continue talking.

"She had one bright green eye and one deep brown eye." Jeremy finished her sentence again.

One more giggle escaped before Sami squeezed Crosby's arm. "I had auditioned for a role, but the director wanted someone with green eyes so I ordered contacts. The tech, though, had been called away in the middle of placing my order. When she returned, she entered the wrong code for the right eye."

Crosby delivered a wobbly smile as Jeremy's aunt came into view. Jeremy brought Marilyn over to Sami. "Aunt Marilyn, look who I found."

Marilyn squinted and then hugged Sami. "How delightful. I hope Jeremy invited you over for eggnog. You won't believe all the work he's done around my house. The sink no longer leaks, and he fixed my refrigerator light." Marilyn motioned for them to follow her to the reception desk. "I'm so happy you and Jeremy reconnected. The two of you make such a handsome couple."

The receptionist gasped. "Sami, you didn't tell me you were dating." She grinned at Jeremy. "I hope you can talk her into staying in Violet Ridge. Other people can come and go, but I need Sami here. She's the best hairstylist I've ever had."

"Aw, Vickie. You're so sweet, but I'm still leaving after the holidays." Sami bumped Jeremy's arm. "I'll miss all of you when I'm gone."

Vickie winked at Sami. "Maybe you'll reconsider that move since the two of you look so cute together."

Crosby noticed Sami didn't correct Vickie. Of course, if Sami were going to stay in Violet Ridge and change her life, it would be for someone who was handy around the house and bore a striking resemblance to a well-known actor.

"Crosby Virtue!" One of the technicians called his name, and he was relieved. He excused himself and followed the tech, who led him down a hallway. "Since you've already had your yearly exam, I'll just be teaching you how to put in the contacts."

Crosby listened to the technician demonstrate the recommended technique. As he was removing his glasses, he spotted Sami come around the corner.

"Jeremy took Marilyn home since her eyes were feeling strained." Sami pulled up a chair and sat beside Crosby, then looked at the technician. "I'm not too late, am I? If I'm allowed to help, that is."

"It's up to Crosby." The tech smiled at them and then grabbed her tablet. "I have a couple of patients who'd be grateful if I saw them now, if you could stay here and give him some pointers?"

Crosby agreed. Should he ask Sami why she was here with him instead of on her way to be with Jeremy at Marilyn's house? If he were matchmaking for Sami, he'd pair her with Jeremy in an instant. Instead, he kept silent, laid his glasses on the table and reached for the contact lens solution.

"We're finally alone, Crosby." Sami adjusted the mirror so he could see himself. "I can just be myself around you. That's why you're the perfect friend."

His stomach sloshed at how casually she said the word *friend*. If only she knew how he felt. Then again it was for the best she didn't. Like she said, they could be themselves around each other. That type of bond was something you didn't find every day. While he loved his siblings, he still couldn't help but feel like they had expectations regarding his future. That he'd be late, which he inevitably would be, or that he'd have the perfect anecdote for any occasion. That was why he always volunteered to spend time with his nephew and nieces. They only wanted to have fun with him and didn't care about such things. Even the town had high expectations for him since Mr.

Hinshaw, the previous historian, was professional and beloved. Every time someone compared him to Mr. Hinshaw and ended the conversation by calling him Dr. Virtue, he felt another brick weighing on his back.

He picked up a contact, the slippery quality rather surprising, and yet it was exactly like his friendship with this beautiful blonde. It was flimsy and could tear too easily unless he protected it. He'd do everything in his power to keep their friendship intact, even if it meant letting her leave without telling her he was beginning to fall for her.

SAMI EXITED THE optometrist's office, only to find dusk descending on the downtown district. It had taken Crosby longer than expected to master inserting contacts, but he had finally succeeded. Under the pretense of checking a text, she let her gaze linger on him, the glow of the antique lamppost surrounding him. She would barely have recognized him, so handsome and composed with his shorter hairstyle and those contacts.

Then she winced at how superficial she sounded. If Sami was this concerned about Crosby's exterior, that was a bad sign that she was turning into Wendy, who had ended up hurting both her daughters. After all, her mother had drilled how important appearances were into Sami morning, noon and night. Not only had she been a stage mother while Sami had been young, but recently, she and

Sami's father had emptied her bank account and fled to New York City, lured by the promise of a get-rich-quick pyramid scheme. Thankfully, Amanda had allowed Sami to stay with her. Eventually, they had ended up living in Colorado with Sami working for the Virtue family and Amanda engaged to the oldest Virtue sibling.

Ever since she arrived here, Crosby had been her one constant.

But now that the immutable Crosby was changing? It shook her more than she expected.

As soon as Crosby grew out his hair and spilled something on his sweater or arrived a day late, she'd be herself again and these butterflies in her stomach would go away.

"Thanks for your help," he said.

She had it worse than she realized. Even his voice sounded deeper and fuller.

This was only a harmless crush. It would fade away as soon as she left behind Violet Ridge's city limits in mid-February. If she went home and got some sleep, it might go away even sooner. On that note, she shivered and denied his claim. "You'd have figured out how to do it without me."

"You made it fun." Crosby dismissed her objection. "To tell the truth, I was getting frustrated toward the end of my contact lens lesson."

Sami pulled her coat around her and concentrated on buckling the belt, anything to keep from noticing those flecks in his irises that were now easier to see. They were amber, like liquid gold. "You hid it well."

"What can I do to thank you? There must be something. Can I buy you dinner?" Crosby asked.

Spending time with Crosby tonight would be a mistake of epic proportions. Once more, she remembered holding her sobbing cousin Isla in her arms after her breakup with Henry. Sami would never make that kind of mistake and mess up the best thing in her life.

She really needed to wake up tomorrow with a fresh perspective.

"Thanks, but I'm meeting Amanda and Cassie at the holiday market near the town square tonight. There'll be craft vendors and trumpeters. I'd invite you but I know how you feel about shopping."

They looked at each other and burst out laughing. Crosby disliked shopping with a passion she reserved for cheap nail polish, the color chartreuse and monotony.

"Then I'll say adieu." Crosby waved and took a few steps away.

"But we haven't discussed the next part of the makeover! Poise!" Throngs of people had suddenly descended from nowhere, and she almost didn't hear her phone, which chimed with a text. She read it and groaned.

Crosby halted and then returned to her side. "What's wrong?"

Sami frowned. "Poor Easton isn't feeling well, so Cassie canceled. Amanda's decided to stay home with Seth and watch a movie. I guess I'll head back to the ranch."

With only three weeks until Christmas, she was growing concerned about how few presents she had purchased for her sister and her closest friends and coworkers. She considered asking Crosby for his advice but quickly pushed that thought aside.

Crosby performed an exaggerated bow. "If the fair lady would allow me to escort her to the holiday market, I would be most appreciative for a chance to return some of the bounty she has bestowed upon me."

"Are you sure?" He nodded and she mimicked his bow. "I'd be honored, kind sir."

"And, once you've purchased some finely crafted items, I'll even hold your bags for you." He winked and winced, rubbing his eye. "It's taking me a while to get used to these contacts. I've been wearing glasses since I was seven. Don't pay any attention to me."

That was the problem. She was paying too much attention to him, so much so that everything about him seemed magnified and electrified.

If she was going to fall in love, it would be with someone like Jeremy, whom she had so much in common with.

She linked her arm through his. "If you can

help me find something for your grandparents, I'd be forever in your debt."

Keeping it light and superficial was her best defense to stemming these new feelings. There was no reason to panic yet. Tomorrow she'd wake up and realize she was having a knee-jerk reaction to all the change swirling around her.

Then it hit her. She was just responding to the magic of the season when everyone seemed to be part of a couple except her. There was Amanda and Seth, Jase and Cassie, Emma and Dominic, Ben and Daisy.

That was it. She felt better.

They walked to the edge of town where the market stalls had been constructed with overhangs. Yesterday's snow had been pushed to the side, and space heaters kept the area comfortable. Portable lights illuminated the different vendors, and Sami squealed at the rows of crafts and holiday treasures.

They explored a couple of booths before a four-person band wove its way through the thoroughfare, playing a lively Christmas medley. She and Crosby stepped aside. When she started to clap and dance in place, Crosby laughed. "You have a way of making everything fun, don't you?"

Sami's grin grew broader. "If you can't have fun here, where can you?"

She regretted the question as soon as it left her

lips for it sounded like she was questioning her own motives for leaving.

The band passed. Crosby's stomach grumbled so loudly the people next to them gave them a strange look before scurrying away.

"Can we check out the food trucks next? Then I'll help you find something for my grandparents." Crosby held up his hands and looked so earnest that Sami couldn't resist his plea.

After they filled up on brisket and yeast rolls, Crosby was somehow still hungry and bought a giant gingerbread cookie. With chagrin, she refused his offer to share it. They explored the rest of the market as he ate.

On the main stage, the high school band brought a lively twist to favorite holiday selections. Sami tapped her foot and sang along with the crowd. Then they kept walking until he pulled her over to look at a booth selling handcrafted wooden puzzles. Crosby pointed out the one he thought his grandfather would like best, which happened to be Sami's choice as well.

Sami paid for it. Then they visited several other booths where she purchased trinkets for Daisy's triplets and Cassie's children. She paid particular attention to whatever Crosby admired. Not that she had changed her mind about getting him an experience rather than a material possession. Sami would always treasure memories over something that could be bought, but Crosby was different from her. He liked items that could be passed down and cherished.

They arrived at a booth selling quilts in traditional Christmas colors, but Crosby steered her past that one. "My grandma Bridget gave us each a quilt when we graduated high school. Since the stroke impacted her sewing skills, she's enlisted Nelda, who's an excellent seamstress, to help her fashion a quilt each for Seth's wedding gift and Jase's."

Sami heard the yearning in Crosby's voice for that type of love and commitment. She doubled down on her determination to finish this makeover. Once she left town, Crosby's loyalty and constancy would appeal to someone. He was a genuinely good guy, and the woman who fell for him would be fortunate to have him by her side.

Sami gravitated to the next booth. Hand-blown glass ornaments of various shapes and sizes were attached to a tree in one corner, while shelves with houses and nestling dolls also beckoned to potential customers. Sami went over to a ceramic house that resembled the one where Amanda was currently living. She faced Crosby, who was holding her purchases and steering clear of the tree so he wouldn't break anything.

"What do you think about this?" she asked.

Crosby waited until a couple moved toward the register before he neared her and winced. "It reminds me too much of my parents' house." Then comprehension dawned on his face. "You mean for Amanda and Seth. It'll be perfect for them."

"I'm sorry." Sami placed it back on the shelf.

"Why?" Crosby asked.

"Because I forgot you used to live there." She reached for her purchases, and her hand brushed his. She savored his warmth, most welcome as she was getting cold surrounded by the crisp night air. "I've never considered whether it's rough on you that Seth and Amanda are moving into the house that belonged to your parents."

He shook his head. "I know my siblings don't like to hear this, but the truth is I don't have many memories of Mom and Dad. I was so young when the accident happened." He shrugged and then glanced at the house, his familiar calmness settling in his eyes once more. "I'm thankful my grandparents kept all of us together. Do you know that my mother's brother wanted to split us up? Grandma Bridget made sure we all stayed in one place."

"I can't imagine the four of you being strangers to each other." She had often envied their bond, especially given as how she and Amanda had struggled with their own relationship, due in part to their mother, who had always favored Sami. It was hard knowing that her mother had played favorites and treated Amanda the worse for it.

That made Amanda's efforts to salvage their relationship all the more meaningful. It would have been easy for her sister to blame Sami or think that she had done something to encourage their mother. Maybe for the first time, she and Amanda were true sisters.

As for their parents? It was best that, for now, they had as little contact with them as possible.

"You've witnessed firsthand that it's been a group effort. For a long time, Jase didn't feel like he deserved to be a part of the family because of his misplaced sense of guilt at having survived the car crash." Crosby's throat bobbed up and down before he turned toward the shelves once more. "I'm just glad he's home for Christmas."

"So am I." But that still left Sami with the quandary of whether to buy the house for Amanda and Seth. She looked at the variety, ranging from Tudor-style houses to Georgian mansions to cottages. "If you could choose one, which would you choose?"

Crosby scanned the offerings.

She started surveying the houses, seeing if she could find his perfect match before he did. Her gaze landed on a blue Victorian home with turrets trimmed with white and a long front porch decorated with green garland and red bows. It was the exact replica of a house one mile from the Miners' Cottage. What would it be like to live there with Crosby and grow old with him? She brushed away that very notion. She changed her nail polish color every week and never ordered the same ice cream flavor twice. Settling down was the furthest thing from her mind. Besides, if she did ever marry, she'd take a page from her sister's book and find someone similar to her.

Someone like Jeremy Haralson.

Crosby pointed to the Victorian. "This one." There was that look again. The one Seth gave Amanda when no one was watching. Then Crosby started rubbing his eye with a groan. "Are contacts supposed to itch this much?"

She was instantly concerned, since his right eye was tinged with red.

"You need to get that contact out." She was about to reach for the house to buy it for him but changed her mind. "Come on. I'll take you home."

"Stay and buy the present for Amanda and Seth." He waved away her objections and handed her the rest of her bags. "Please."

He hurried off as the owner of the booth asked, "Are you interested in buying that? I have a nice box if it's a Christmas present."

Sami searched over her shoulder, but Crosby had already disappeared. With a sigh, she returned her attention to the vendor and gave him her credit card. He started to head for his register when she called him back. Sami pointed at Crosby's dream house. "That one as well, please."

The owner totaled her purchases while Sami resisted the urge to laugh at herself. The yearning gaze she thought she'd seen Crosby give her was nothing more than his realization that he'd lost a contact.

With that, she thanked the owner. As she walked away with her treasures, though, she couldn't help but wonder how it would feel to be on the receiving end of a real gaze like that from Crosby.

CHAPTER SEVEN

AT THE TRAIN depot platform, Crosby lifted a container marked *garland* and carried it inside the Violet Ridge Thunderbolt with extra caution. In the forty-eight hours since he'd visited the optometrist for the second time in as many days, everything required extra care, thanks to the eyepatch he had to wear with his glasses.

He raised the tote high enough so he wouldn't bump it against the seats before finding a good place to set it down. Upon opening the container, he groaned. This wasn't garland; this was a box of tree ornaments. What had he been thinking last year when he stored everything?

That's right. He'd been in the thick of researching his doctoral dissertation. To say he'd been enthralled with the connection between silver smelting and the rise of the train system in this area was an understatement. He hadn't surfaced for months except for meetings and anything to do with the Thunderbolt.

If the ornaments were here, where was the garland that would hang along the top of the car? Sighing, he hefted the box back to the staging area and searched through the remaining containers. None of them were labeled correctly. He checked his watch and found the volunteers were set to arrive within the hour. He hoped he'd have enough time to correct the labels before the decorating party began in earnest.

"You've been the hardest person to track down." Sami's voice came from behind, the lilting sweetness of it melting his bad mood. "We still have to do the next step of the makeover, namely poise and grace. That's why I arrived early. I knew you wouldn't be able to get away from me so easily."

With a bit of trepidation, Crosby faced her. Her loud gasp was a reminder that he had decided to wait until he saw her in person to reveal his latest setback. "About that."

"You're wearing an eyepatch?" She rushed over and then squinted. "Is that a snowman on your patch?"

He shrugged and nodded. "The clinic had holiday patches, and I thought my after-school students would at least get a chuckle out of this one."

She folded her arms across her chest. "Are you okay? How long will you have to wear that?"

"Only for a few days." She started tapping her foot. So much for getting away without telling her the whole truth. "The allergic reaction from the facial mask caused my eye to swell. Wearing contacts for the first time aggravated the swelling to the point where my right eye was irritated."

More like infected, but he didn't want to alarm her.

"I caused this?" Her high-pitched voice proved he already had.

He reassured her that she wasn't the source of his problems. "This was an accident." If either of them was at fault, it was him for not telling the technician about his reaction to the chamomile.

"This is just temporary, right?" She tensed until he nodded. Then she relaxed and continued, "We'll deal with it and adjust accordingly."

Her resiliency was reassuring to the point where he could focus on the totes again. "Thanks for arriving early. I'm in a bind. Everyone else is due to turn up soon." He admitted how his preoccupation with his thesis had led to the current mix-up. "This decorating has to happen now so the open house can start on time tonight at the Miners' Cottage."

"That's one advantage of moving as often as I have. I'll have this sorted out in a jiffy," Sami said while taking off her coat and opening the nearest container. "I can't wait to see everyone at the open house, all happy and in a festive mood for the holidays."

Sami's willingness to pitch in and help was saving him yet again.

In no time, they sorted the boxes. Sami labeled

the last tote as the first volunteers began arriving. Zelda Baker made a beeline to him, her frown most unlike her usual serene expression. "Crosby Virtue! Is this eyepatch your latest attempt to get out of giving the speech on New Year's Eve?"

Zelda never would have asked Seth or Jase if they were trying to get out of something important. Crosby let out a deep breath. "No. It's just temporary to help some eye inflammation."

"That sounds painful." Zelda winced and patted his arm. "Sorry I thought so badly of you."

Her twin sister, Nelda, arrived at her side and scrunched her nose. "Crosby? Do you have pinkeye? Are you contagious?"

Crosby launched into an explanation when Sami swooped in. She gave an apologetic glance to Nelda and Zelda. "I'm so sorry, but I need Crosby."

If only that were the case and she did need him enough to stay in Violet Ridge. He winced at how selfish that sounded. Yes, he'd love it if she lived in town for keeps, but he could never ask her to stay here for him.

Sami escorted him inside the train. "What was that about? Were you rescuing me?"

"You don't need rescuing. You can hold your own with anyone." Sami pointed to the ceiling and handed him a length of silver garland. "Your longer arms can manage attaching this better than I can."

Crosby navigated his way between the seats and raised the garland above the windows. "Is this what you had in mind?"

She tilted her head. "A little to the left."

Crosby did as directed, and then she approved the placement. No sooner was the garland hung than she handed him red bows to spruce up the trimming. Crosby attached the bows and moved to another row of seats.

"I don't see why we need to decorate everything in sight," he grumbled. "It just causes more work when we have to take everything down again in January."

"Okay, Mr. Grinch." Sami's light laugh echoed in the train car as she handed him the next bow. "Decorating may add to your workload, but it's cheery and pretty and brings people together. No matter what's going on in your life, it spreads joy and peace. For a little while, everything is merry and bright."

Her holiday spirit was most uplifting. She squeezed in next to him. The tight quarters of the train left her no choice. She was so near, close enough for him to smell her signature floral scent and feel the softness of her cashmere sweater. She reached for his hand holding the bow, lifting both to the apex of the garland. "I was thinking right about here."

Bringing her arm down, she met his gaze. Something electric jolted his system. He tried to remember ever having felt this way but was at a loss. Did he dare hope that Sami thought the same? He searched her blue eyes for some sign that she wanted him to kiss her as much as he wanted to embrace her. "Sami?"

"Yes?"

Before he could ask if he could kiss her, she rose onto her tiptoes and gripped his cardigan sweater. She pulled him closer. "Crosby?"

How could something seem so inevitable and feel so right?

"Hell-ooo?" Jeremy's voice echoed in the confines of the train compartment. "Sami? Are you in here?"

Crosby jumped. He moved away from Sami to the aisle and motioned for her to go ahead of him. Sami glanced his way, and he couldn't tell whether disappointment or relief lurked in those beautiful features. Then she started toward Jeremy, who carried a box that blocked her line of sight. "I'm in the back with Crosby."

Jeremy moved the box and spotted them. "Hi, Crosby! Isn't this a great day? I'm so glad Sami told me about this decorating party. Where do you want the silver bells?"

"Space is tight but bring it over." Crosby took another step away from Sami.

No sooner had Jeremy entered the compartment than a host of volunteers followed. Sami set up a speaker and seconds later, holiday music filled the air. Zelda produced a tin of frosted sugar cookies and distributed them. Crosby accepted his with a smile and resigned nod. While his head knew it was for the best that he and Sami stopped before they crossed a line of no return, he had a hard time convincing his heart of that.

Crosby kept busy hanging bows and bells, finding ways to stay at the opposite end of the train from Sami. After a while, he got a phone call about the correct antique fixtures for the main railcar and headed outside, away from the music and the happy sounds of the decorating crew.

When Crosby returned to the main compartment to take an inventory of what decorations remained, he realized, with everyone being so busy, there was practically nothing left. He heard Sami's boots before he saw her approach. He rose from the empty totes and found her standing there with a gingerbread man, which she held out to him. "I saved this for you."

Crosby crunched the head off the cookie and swallowed. "Thanks." Little gestures like this were why he'd have to settle for her friendship. "I couldn't have done all this without you. The boxes are empty so you can go ahead and leave."

Then he looked up and spotted mistletoe. Where did that come from?

"Crosby..." How did she turn his name into a sigh?

"We should talk about what almost happened."

"What's there to talk about?" He munched an arm next and hoped she'd go, but she stayed rooted in the spot. Her no-nonsense look left him little doubt they would address their almost-kiss now.

The mistletoe practically winked again, and Crosby considered seeing what would happen if he kissed her for real, instead of talking about the earlier miss.

Zelda and Nelda entered the compartment and nodded at him and Sami. He could almost kiss them for interrupting.

Nelda gestured at the transformed train. "It cleaned up so well. Christmas Eve…"

"Won't arrive soon enough." Her identical twin, Zelda, finished her sentence for her.

Too soon for Crosby's liking since that would bring them closer to Valentine's Day, when Sami would leave Violet Ridge.

He bit off the other arm and nodded. "Thank you for your help."

The twins departed and Crosby stacked boxes on top of each other. Perhaps Sami would get the hint and they could table this discussion for another time. Like never. He picked up four boxes and started for the exit. He hadn't gone far when he felt his grip on them loosening. One, two, the whole pile collapsed and fell onto the carpeted aisle.

Sami knelt beside him and reached for two of

them at the same time he did. "You're being stubborn."

Maybe he was, but the holidays were hard enough without the added pressure of the speech and her looming departure.

"I've got this under control."

She laid her hand on his until he had no choice but to look at her, even if the eyepatch impacted his line of sight. "*We've* got this. Crosby, you're my best friend."

Her heartfelt tone wasn't lost on him. He left the boxes where they were and sat in one of the window seats, the new cushions comfortable and historically accurate.

Sami settled next to him as he knew she would. He glanced out the window, encouraged to see the merry decorating crew headed for the diner.

"Friendship. That's exactly why I won't try anything like that again." It was too tempting to cup her soft face, so he laced his fingers together. "It was for the best that Jeremy interrupted. I was carried away by the holiday magic and having you so close. Now that the moment has passed, I realize I was reacting to all the changes. We're friends, and that's all."

"Do you really believe that?" He heard the incredulity in her voice, and he longed to act on impulse and actually kiss her this time.

But it wasn't in his nature to do anything without deliberate contemplation. He was Crosby, the steady sibling who had earned his place through studying and careful preparation. Otherwise, he'd just be Seth and Daisy and Jase's younger brother.

Besides, losing Sami's friendship would not only hurt him, but it could place a strain on his and Seth's relationship. It would be his fault if things grew awkward and affected the whole family.

"That's all we can ever be. And I won't do anything to jeopardize our friendship."

"Stop putting the weight of the world on your shoulders, Crosby. I wanted you to kiss me, but you're right. We have to put our friendship first," Sami conceded before laying her hand over his. "Don't discount holiday magic, though. That quality brings out something special in everyone. It makes the season sparkle."

Crosby removed his hand and decided to address the reindeer in the room. "It's going to be hard not seeing you every day, but I won't ever hold you back."

Sami nodded, then rose and left the train. His resolve would have melted in a second if she had looked back. He would have jumped out of his seat and kissed her and never let her go.

But that seemed to be an impossibility now.

Entering the Rocky Mountain Chocolatier, Sami picked up a basket and savored the aroma of sweetness in the air. She wandered around the store and paused to trace the top of a box of caramels with her index finger. Perhaps she should mix things up and leave Amanda her treat on a Thursday instead of a Monday. Sami added the caramels to her basket and spotted chocolate cream truffles. Crosby's favorites. Perhaps she should buy him a surprise gift. It would give her an excuse to talk to him. Like she needed an excuse. He was Crosby. Kind, deliberative Crosby, who was always there when she needed him. Someday they'd have a good laugh over what would have been a massive mistake if they had kissed.

Would it have been a mistake, though? Honestly, she really wished she had kissed him.

Sami gulped and walked over to the display of truffles. She picked up a box and then put it down quickly.

"Sami? Is everything okay?" Emma startled Sami, although she should have expected the shop owner to ask her if she needed assistance.

"Of course." Sami faced Emma with a smile. "Why wouldn't it be?"

Emma raised an eyebrow and shrugged. "Maybe it's because you've entered and exited my shop three times in the past fifteen minutes."

Heat flooded Sami's cheeks. Had she been that out of sorts that she hadn't even noticed that she had been walking in and out of the same establishment? Come to think of it, she may also have entered Lavender and Lace and Saucy Sal's a few times as well.

"Sorry about that."

Emma reached out and patted Sami's arm. "Don't be. I'm always here if you need to talk. That's what friends are for."

Sami blinked at the unexpected comfort from one of Amanda's bridesmaids. "I appreciate you saying that. I just didn't think…" She stopped talking before she put her foot in her mouth for the second time that day.

"Didn't think what?" The bell over the door jingled. "Hold that thought," Emma said.

The shop owner greeted a couple and let them know she'd be right with them. Then she turned back to Sami, repeating her earlier question.

Sami bit her lip and examined the nearest package of handmade candy, until Emma's gentle look made her blurt out the truth. "I thought you were Amanda's friend."

"I'm yours as well." Emma didn't seem fazed by the comment. Rather, she hugged Sami. "My assistant is sick today, so I have to help those customers, but we'll talk more when we plan Amanda's shower, okay? Cassie O'Neal has offered to host it at her farm. The three of us will have fun coming up with games and a menu."

Emma went over to the fudge display where the couple was debating which flavor to buy. Sami let Emma's words sink in. She had moved so often that she had gotten used to seeing people slip out of her life. It was easier to find new friends than stay in contact with those she'd never spend time with again, although she had been in contact with Asia on and off over the years.

Yet Violet Ridge felt different. From the camaraderie to the seasons to the town itself. Plus, Sami truly cared about Emma and Daisy and Cassie.

All of them had entered her life courtesy of Amanda, but they included her without hesitation. Sami headed for the exit when Emma called out her name. Sami came back and waited until Emma sent the customers off with a smile.

"Could you do me a favor?" Emma reached under the counter and pulled out two large cardboard boxes with the shop's logo. "Like I said, my assistant is out sick, and Crosby ordered two of my large variety trays for the Miners' Cottage open house. Can you deliver them for me?"

Still rattled by that almost-kiss, the open house had slipped Sami's mind. Tonight was important to Crosby, though, which meant it was important to her.

"No problem," Sami said with a bluster she didn't feel in her heart.

Sami accepted the boxes, and Emma opened the front door for her and thanked her for her trouble.

Except this was just the opposite. He loved that

cottage and all the history residing there. Tonight he'd recount stories in his inimitable style, and she'd see him for his true self: an absent-minded professor who'd spend his life content in one place. Then everything would return to normal. Her heart intact.

Crosby was right when he said they should stay friends. How would her sister feel if Sami and Crosby started dating only to realize they had made a big mistake? Their breakup would create tension in the Virtue family, particularly between Seth and Amanda, if either of them felt like they had to take sides.

Whew! She had averted potential disaster when Jeremy arrived in the train car just as she was about to kiss Crosby. She repeated that sentiment until she believed it herself.

By that time, she was approaching the Miners' Cottage. The holiday transformation was spectacular with the exterior outlined in big white bulb lights. Even the picket fence was decorated with pretty green garland dotted with red bows. A huge pine wreath hung front and center on the gate. Black lanterns with tea lights were set along both sides of the sidewalk leading into the house. Inside the former home was even more festive. A fresh pine tree with candleholders and tiny glass ornaments stood resolute in the entryway, and pictures of reindeer were posted behind the ticket booth.

Sami spotted and nodded to one of Crosby's favorite volunteers. "Hi, Beatrice!" She held up the boxes. "These are from Emma's."

"Thanks. Just put those in the classroom on the table with the other desserts and drinks. Your suggestion to add refreshments to our monthly gathering has helped increase attendance as you can plainly see." Beatrice turned and struck up a conversation with some early guests, and Sami moved along.

She noticed Crosby, also occupied with visitors. Normally, the group gathered to discuss a book about Colorado or its history. But this month, however, Crosby had chosen to throw a holiday party and invited the town. He gestured about as he relayed a story, a content expression on his face. She smiled, reassured that their previous encounter hadn't left a scar.

A crowd was gathered in the room with the refreshments. Sami made her way to the dessert table.

"Sami!" Jeremy hailed her and reached for the boxes. His aunt Marilyn scooted platters of petit fours and cookies aside to make room for the new treats. "You didn't return my text."

She groaned. *Is he actually pouting?* She searched her purse before finally finding her phone and read his brief message that said to call him as soon as possible. "Sorry about that."

"Aunt Marilyn, will you excuse Sami and me

for a minute?" Jeremy waited for his aunt's nod before he resumed speaking. "Remember our conversation at dinner last week?"

Sami mulled over the nice memory, but one without any of the attraction she was starting to feel for Crosby. *Argh*. Why did she keep thinking about Crosby? Finally, she gave up and shrugged. "Which part?"

"I told you about my friend Mario, the HR rep for the cruise line that departs from San Diego."

Now she remembered. "What about him?"

"He's waiting for your call. They have a variety of openings, and you have your choice of destinations like Hawaii or Costa Rica or Fiji!"

Sami squealed and threw her arms around Jeremy's shoulders, pulling him into an embrace. "Amazing! Jeremy, you're the best. All those cruise ships were one reason I chose San Diego as my next destination."

Over Jeremy's shoulder, she saw Crosby enter the room before someone called out his name and he left again. She released Jeremy and took a step back.

A pretty woman that Sami didn't recognize came over and asked Jeremy about the avalanche from which he'd rescued two teenagers single-handedly. Jeremy blushed before updating her about the teens' progress. "They're out of the hospital and doing fine. I'm just happy I was in the right place at the right time."

Another woman in a long suede coat and leather boots joined them and raved about seeing Jeremy's set last week. "You're a great singer. What's the funniest thing that's ever happened to you during one of your gigs?"

Jeremy began regaling the pair with stories about his lounge singing, including how he had spent last Christmas in Switzerland. Soon, others brought their plates and drinks over to listen to Jeremy, who kept everyone entertained.

He smiled wide and all but dazzled the growing crowd. "I'd call myself a crooner, more than a singer."

Sami noticed yet another trio of women hanging on Jeremy's every word. A woman in a leopard-print dress came forward and asked him which was his favorite holiday song. Jeremy motioned for everyone to gather close.

"Does everyone know the words to 'Deck the Halls'?" He hummed the first few bars before launching into the song itself with everyone joining in on the fun.

Within minutes, Jeremy transitioned to yet another old standard with everyone singing the refrain. From there, he introduced the next carol with his aunt providing the harmony.

One of the women from earlier nudged Sami's side. "You're so lucky that you're dating the life of the party."

Sami hastened to reassure her she wasn't when

Crosby once again entered the room accompanied by a gaggle of new guests. Even with his eyepatch, Sami could tell he was surprised at the impromptu sing-along but he joined in on the last refrain.

The gang insisted Jeremy continue and that led to more good old memories and more singing.

Jeremy might be the liveliest member of the room, but Crosby belonged here. The hours seemed to fly by.

Eventually, at the end of one very rousing medley, followed by much applause, Crosby stepped forward and thanked the crowd for coming, while urging them to watch for next month's book selection in a future email, along with a plea to take home a dessert or two.

Jeremy came over and hugged Sami. "Aunt Marilyn is getting tired, and I have a full day tomorrow. We'll talk soon, Sami. Goodnight."

Marilyn and Jeremy took their leave. Meanwhile, Crosby was engaged in a fierce debate about local wildlife and new measures the town council passed to protect certain species. Sami watched Crosby lose himself in the discussion. He was so determined. So compassionate.

The rest of the crowd dispersed until there was only Crosby, Beatrice and herself. Crosby asked Beatrice for the trash bag and urged her to go home. Beatrice didn't put up much of a fight and was out the door before Crosby could repeat himself.

Crosby met Sami's gaze and pointed to the door. "I've got this."

Sami would have none of it. "And you've got me to help you." She looked around and shrugged. "Where's Sundance?"

Crosby pointed across the hall. "Last time I looked he was sleeping. I locked my office so no one would disturb him."

A clatter erupted at the entrance to the cottage and they went to investigate.

A mail carrier started apologizing for his late appearance. "I've been socked with deliveries since early this morning." Crosby waved away the man's protests as he signed for the large package. The mail carrier said good-night and left in a hurry.

Crosby approached the big box and whooped for joy. "I've been waiting for this. These are the historical costumes for the volunteers on Christmas Eve. There are special outfits for the conductor, the engineer and the crew." He slipped behind the ticket booth and produced a box cutter. With care, he cut a clean line across the top of the box. "Timeless Tailors requested a week to do any alterations."

"Why don't you just take the box to the tailor and text everyone to head there at their earliest convenience?" Sami suggested as the anticipation at seeing the costumes welled within her.

"You're a genius!" Crosby smiled at her.

Only the thought of running along a San Diego beach stopped her from kissing him.

"But I want to see them first," he said.

His eyes sparkled like a little kid's on Christmas morning. She smiled back. "Me, too."

Crosby pulled out the first costume, a dark brown buckskin coat with layers of fringe on the front. "I didn't order this." Then he reached for the second, shaking his head, before shoving it back into the box. "There has to be a packing slip somewhere."

Curiosity prickled at Sami, and she snatched another outfit and held it up. Instead of a modest dress from the early twentieth century, this hot-pink-and-black number was better suited for a Wild West show. It had a plunging neckline and a ruffled bottom, ending well above her knee. One giggle turned into two, then Sami started rollicking with laughter, until she saw Crosby's crestfallen face.

"Oh, Crosby." He hid his face in his palms. His chest heaved, and Sami's eyes grew wide with alarm. "Crosby?"

He moved his hands and his chest shook. Relief poured through her. He was laughing, not crying. Just as he did with everything else, he was putting his whole body into this moment. They glanced at each other and laughed even harder.

He held up a black shirt with white fringe forming a V down his chest. They looked at each outfit before he sat on the floor with his back to the wall. She found the packing slip at the bottom. "Do you want to read it?"

He tapped his eyepatch. "I'm having trouble with fine print, so will you do the honors? Please tell me I didn't order these."

"Why else would they have arrived here, though?" Sami scanned the paper and grimaced. "You ordered ten cowboy outfits and ten showgirl dresses." She retrieved the hot pink number and held it up for inspection. "We can make this work. It's just different from what you expected. Different isn't always bad."

Crosby shook his head. "I won't be able to show my face in town for months, let alone go to the dude ranch on Christmas Day. I'm letting my family down."

Sami went over to Crosby, where he was sitting with his back to the wall, and plopped down beside him. "No matter what you do, you could never let Bridget or Martin down."

Crosby grimaced. "Thanks for the pep talk, but you don't know what it's like growing up in your siblings' shadows."

Sami scoffed. "Don't I? Amanda was the smart sibling, whereas our mother believed I would rake in the big bucks because of my looks." She rose and headed for the remaining dessert selections in the other room, selecting the last chocolate cream for Crosby and a pecan tart for herself. She also grabbed a fistful of napkins. Returning to his side, she held out the chocolate, which he accepted. "Why would you feel like you're in their shadows? As if you could be anything other than your intelligent, lovable self, but they care about you, and they'll be there for you on Christmas Eve. No matter what."

"Thanks, Sami. You always know the right thing to say." Crosby bit into the chocolate and grinned. She handed him a napkin, and he wiped at the corners of his mouth. "And you're right. I know how much they do care. They'll say this mistake doesn't matter, but…"

"It matters to you. Sometimes, though, you just have to make lemonade out of lemons. I promise, we'll turn this fiasco into a positive. The Wild West Violet Ridge Christmas Eve Thunderbolt! It'll still be fun for the whole family. We'll figure out a way." Sami nibbled the pecan tart as something about the packing slip nibbled at her mind. "Come with me."

She stood and, with Crosby looking over her shoulder, compared the packing slip with the box label, which had the Miners' Cottage address on it. The packing slip, however, had a different address and phone number.

"The buyer!" they exclaimed in unison.

He slipped the paper out of her fingers and waved it high. "I didn't mess this up. They put the wrong slip and costumes in this box, which must mean the other buyer has my order!"

Swept away by the excitement, Sami hugged Crosby. The scent of pine and musk and Crosby hit her with the force of an avalanche. Her eyes widened and she separated from him before she ruined the joyful moment.

"Call the vendor," Sami said.

Sami held her breath and concentrated on listening to his end of the conversation. Anything so she wouldn't look at how his shoulders filled out that old sweater of his father's that he always favored. Or how his grin was widening every second. Crosby sent Sami a thumbs-up, indicating he'd reached an actual person and it was going well.

"You need the costumes tomorrow? Can you drive here?" Crosby frowned. "You can't, and you're a couple of hours away. That's a problem because I can't drive long distances for the next few days."

Crosby patted his eyepatch, and Sami pulled at his sleeve until she had his attention. "I'll drive. We'll make a road trip out of it." Sami mouthed the words and pointed to herself before reaching for the phone.

Talking to the woman on the other end, she volunteered herself as the driver and arranged for a time to switch costumes. Luckily, Crosby's order had ended up in the box delivered to this woman. She pressed End and handed the phone back to Crosby. "What I tell ya? Lemonade."

"Pueblo's about three hours from here. Are you sure you can spare the time?"

"Like you even have to ask." She resisted the urge to hug him again and instead mimicked his earlier action of a thumbs-up. "I'll be here at eight a.m. sharp, and be prepared. Tomorrow will be double special. We'll start working on the poise aspect of your makeover."

With that startling tidbit leaving Crosby's face in a state of shock, she quickly waved, threw on her coat and skedaddled. As friends, she and Crosby could bare their souls to each other. As friends, they could find solutions to tricky problems. As friends, they could always have each other's back.

She wouldn't take the chance of ruining that, especially with the real possibility of losing Amanda if a romance between her and Crosby went south in a hurry and her sister sided with her fiancé over Sami.

CHAPTER EIGHT

In the small space of Sami's compact car, Crosby awakened to the sight of red rocks and mounds of snow passing quickly outside the passenger window. He blinked as he adjusted to yet another day with the eyepatch. Crosby was already counting down the hours until he could get rid of it. He tried stretching his long legs, but the cramped quarters prevented that.

"Good morning. I was concerned you were going to sleep all the way there. You were snoring quite loudly."

"I snore?" His voice came out as much hoarse as horrified.

She laughed. "Not a single bit. I was a little dismayed as I had hoped you would. It would give me something to tease you about since you do everything so well." Sami handed him a cup of coffee from the console while keeping her concentration on the road. "You missed the drive-through, and I went ahead and ordered your favorite—coffee with one packet of sugar and a pump of vanilla creamer."

"How did you know that? I always drink it black at the ranch." His siblings preferred their coffee without any added sweeteners or flavored creamer, so he always followed suit.

"That you really prefer your coffee to match your sweet tooth?" Sami kept her concentration on the road. "I know."

If he wasn't more careful, little details like these promised to add up to major heartbreak down the road. For now, though, he just focused on being grateful for his morning pick-me-up. "Thank you for noticing."

"I notice a lot about you, Crosby Virtue." She pulled over to a vista and parked the car. "I like you just the way you are."

Then why the haircut and the contacts? Sometimes Sami was a mass of contradictions.

Before he could ask her to elaborate, she opened her door and exited the car with her coffee cup. He did the same, and a stiff wind blew around them. The temperature was brisk but not so cold as to be uncomfortable. Besides, he'd lived in Colorado all his life and could adapt to blizzard conditions as easily as summer sunshine. Sami handed him her coffee to hold while she pulled her wool cap and gloves out of her coat pocket and donned them.

"If you like me as is, then why all this fuss

about a makeover?" Crosby handed hers back and then sipped his coffee, the sweetness already providing a burst of energy. "Why not just focus on elocution lessons?"

After she took a long sip of her coffee, he could see her smile. That sent yet another burst of morning happiness running through his veins.

"Because that's boring?" She wrinkled her nose and shook her head. "Fun and games aside, if you had your way, you'd have locked yourself in your office with Sundance until he could have recited your speech for you. You'd have rehearsed and refined it so much that it would be dry with nothing of you in it. On top of that, if one person seemed disappointed or fell asleep during your keynote, you'd blame yourself all through next year."

He felt the urge to defend himself after she made him sound as dull as a baker's unsharpened knife. "There's something to be said for memorization and deliberative analysis. It earned me my PhD."

"In that regard, those qualities are great, but life is about more than careful thinking and careful word choices. It's about adventure and trying new experiences." She flashed another smile at him. "Think about all that in terms of when you last went on a date."

He raised his cup to his lips and shrugged. "Don't suppose this counts? After all, you bought me coffee and we're alone in the middle of nowhere."

"If we were on a date, you'd know." Sami arched an eyebrow until it disappeared under her woolen cap. "I'm not letting you off easily, either. You have too much to offer someone to stay hidden in your office the rest of your life."

With his family? There was always something going on with one of his siblings. "As much as I'd like to hang out at the library and museum full-time, my family keeps me on my toes. I like being Uncle Crosby." Sometime in the upcoming year, his family would expand as he'd gain a niece and nephew in Penny and Easton O'Neal. Jase was already making plans to adopt them, a move supported by their absentee father.

She tsked. "But when was the last time Uncle Crosby went out on a date?"

Crosby racked his mind. All his free time over the past six months had been spent with this vivacious blonde, and he wouldn't have traded this time with her for anything. "Last Christmas." He mumbled the words and then sipped his coffee again.

"And with me helping you it won't be Christmas again before your next date." She motioned to the wide expanse of mountains before them, the white-capped peaks majestic and thrilling. "New Year's Eve will be as exciting for you as this scenery. You'll deliver an outstanding speech while revealing your new self to Violet Ridge. My fabulous makeover can help you connect with that special someone. Who knows? You might even kiss the love of your life at midnight."

Somehow he didn't see that happening. Not when he was halfway in love with Sami. Until she departed for San Diego, he wouldn't be interested in anyone else. The chill of the air was finally seeping through his thick jacket, and he sped things along. "Then please share with me why you pulled over here when we should be on the highway toward Pueblo."

She laughed. "Oops, I forgot to explain about the next phase of the makeover." She motioned at the idyllic view, almost as beautiful as Sami. "Part of public speaking involves the ability to handle whatever unexpected event happens while you're talking. Babies crying, people coughing, servers breaking a trayful of glasses. Pretty much anything."

"Sounds like you speak from personal experience?" He sipped his drink, the warmth filling him. "What did you encounter on those pageant stages?"

"The usual interruptions. There was that one time, though, when a judge sadly collapsed in the middle of my answer about world peace. One of my fellow contestants, who was interning in medical school, performed CPR until the medics arrived and resuscitated him. We finished the next night, and the intern won." She took a long sip before shrugging. "I don't expect anything like that to happen on New Year's Eve."

"I hope not." He shivered at how scary that would be. Then he searched the area around them once more. "But we're in the middle of nowhere. There won't be any interruptions."

A tractor trailer passed by them suddenly and hooted its horn. Sami nudged his side. "You were saying." She giggled and sat on a nearby boulder. "Impress me. If you can recite your speech to the mountains, you can give it anywhere. I'll watch you and deliver pointers about elocution and poise."

He joined her on the boulder and heaved a big sigh before tracing the lid of his coffee cup. "There's one little problem."

Sami waved away his objection. "If I could listen to myself rehearse the same answers over and over, I can hear your speech more than once."

If only it were that simple. He sipped the last of the coffee and threw the cup in the trash can before walking toward the guardrail, tripping over some rocks on the path. Righting himself, he turned toward her and let out a deep breath. "Good evening, ladies and gentlemen. Thank you for coming tonight to support the efforts to preserve a part of Violet Ridge's history."

He looked her way only to find her sitting calmly. "I'm listening," Sami said.

"That's as far as I've gotten."

Sami met him at the guardrail. He searched her features for some signs of disappointment but only found acceptance and a smile. "I almost forgot your legendary ability to pull things off at the last minute." She clicked her tongue and winked at him. "Seems we both have more work to do before New Year's Eve. You have to finish that speech, and I'll make sure you won't stumble on your way to the podium. Deal?"

She held out her gloved hand, and he shook it. Together, they hurried back to the warmth of her car.

A BIG SIGN above a wide set of wooden double doors of a vintage building announced the imminent grand opening of the Wild West Dinner Theater. Sami held the door open for Crosby, who was carrying the box of costumes that were no doubt destined for this production.

"Hello?" Crosby called out while Sami whipped off her sunglasses and placed them in her coat pocket.

He set the box on the red carpet as a woman's voice registered from the rear. "Be with you in a minute. If you're here to buy tickets, please visit our website."

While they waited for her, Sami took in the theater's refurbished interior. Western details set it apart from other venues. A string of holiday lights graced the neck of a bronze horse statue while an archway of intertwined ornaments separated the foyer from the door leading to the theater. Maybe she'd bring Amanda here for a girls' night out before leaving for San Diego.

Five minutes passed and no one emerged from any direction. Sami shrugged in Crosby's direction.

Just then, a young woman with short brown hair and a warm demeanor materialized, and Sami stepped beside Crosby.

"Sorry about that. How can I help you?" Her gaze went to the big box in front of Crosby, and she clapped and cheered. "Please tell me these are my much-awaited outfits."

"Happy to oblige." Crosby nodded at the woman and tipped his cowboy hat in her direction. "We spoke on the phone. I'm Crosby Virtue, and this is my friend, Sami Fleming."

Sami noticed the slight stress on *friend*, and her stomach flipped. What did she expect? They weren't dating. They'd never professed any feelings other than friendship. She had already determined keeping Crosby as a true pal and discarding this foolish crush was what was best, considering her future departure and Amanda's impending nuptials. But his proclamation still left a bitter taste in her mouth.

Besides, she couldn't let down Asia. Not after promising her she'd help with the rent for the upcoming year, not to mention in return for all her family had done for Sami. Asia was counting on her.

"I'm Jasmine Patel." The woman held out her hand, first to Crosby, then to Sami. "Thank you so much for driving here this morning. With the grand opening so soon, I couldn't spare the time to visit Violet Ridge, although I've heard wonderful things about your community."

Sami arched her eyebrow. Like Crosby was under less of a time crunch?

"No problem," Crosby said, looking around the foyer. "If you have our box of uniforms, we'll be good to go so you can get back to work."

"Follow me." Jasmine led them through the archway and stopped outside an office. Her name was on the door. "Crosby, I have to tell you I opened your box and love the retro style of the costumes. What's the event?"

Crosby launched into the story of the Violet Ridge Thunderbolt and how it had sat there until renovations made it viable once more.

"On Christmas Eve it will ride the rails and then on New Year's Eve we're celebrating everyone's efforts and contribution."

Jasmine seemed to hang on every word. A prickle of annoyance gnawed at Sami's stomach as Crosby and Jasmine were hitting it off. From there, they started discussing Colorado's transportation system and its impact on the Wild West.

Sami tuned out their conversation, instead reliving the moment when Crosby woke up in her car. He'd been downright adorable with his hair slightly mussed. The eyepatch had added a hint of mystery she hadn't expected, giving him a sort of rugged, dashing appeal like he was a pirate, ready to set sail, intent on adventure, possibly even danger.

Then she blinked. Haircuts and eyepatches only captured his exterior presence. She could see some changes in Crosby that went deeper and were more profound in nature. This morning, he had arrived on time for the road trip, and she couldn't remember the last time he'd been late. There was a newfound aura of confidence about him, even when he'd tripped over the rocks at the vista this morning. Sami gave him another look, his face animated as he never tired of talking about history. She transferred her gaze to Jasmine. Shock entered Sami's system. The woman, who looked very close to Sami's own age of twenty-seven, was obviously smitten with Crosby, enjoying his every word. Several minutes passed before Sami cleared her throat to no avail. The two continued chatting away about history. Jasmine mentioned her degree was in that very subject.

Someone emerged from another office and asked Jasmine about the staff meeting. Jasmine turned toward Crosby. "I have to attend, but listen, I'll be sure to make a visit to Violet Ridge in the near future…"

Sami picked up on Jasmine's hint that Crosby could escort her around town, but he was either oblivious to the young woman's flirting or didn't sense the same spark between them. With a big smile, Jasmine opened her office door and pointed to two boxes.

"I can carry one, Crosby," Sami offered.

"I'd give you a hand if it weren't for the staff meeting. Wait a minute." Jasmine opened one of the boxes and found the packing slip. Grabbing a pen from the cupholder, she scribbled something on the paper. "I'm pretty sure I put all the costumes back into the boxes, but in case anything is missing, that's my personal cell number."

Jasmine's smile was targeted at Crosby and Crosby alone. Sami's stomach reared up once more.

It couldn't be jealousy, could it? Despite her years on the beauty pageant circuit, Sami had never experienced this feeling before. She'd had no need to be envious of someone else earning the tiara when her heart hadn't been in the endeavor. She had always been genuinely happy for whoever had been crowned the winner.

Besides, she couldn't be falling for Crosby with everyone in town telling her how well she and Jeremy complemented each other. So many residents expected them to become a couple, but she still didn't feel any sparks with Jeremy. And when she fell in love, she'd want it to be with someone less broody and deliberative than Crosby, someone who could take off for a destination at the spur of the moment.

But hadn't Crosby done just that this morning by coming with her to Pueblo after ensuring that Beatrice could cover his tours and feed Sundance?

Crosby hefted one of the boxes and smiled at Jasmine. "Thanks for all your help, and the Violet Ridge Thunderbolt is only one of our town's attractions. There's also a first-class rodeo and the historic Holly Theater."

She beamed at him. "I'll have to make plans to visit soon."

Sami picked up the second box and sailed past them. She didn't stop until she reached her car, placing the box beside her compact while she found her key fob. After raising the trunk, she hoisted the box inside the small space and then bumped her head on the tailgate. "Ouch!"

"Sami!" Concern laced Crosby's voice, and she faced him. "Let me see."

He reached her and placed his box in the trunk before feeling the back of her head. Her scalp tingled from his touch, and she moved away. "I was just careless. I'll be fine."

"I can't feel any blood or a bump. That's a relief. I'd hate it if you were hurt because of me." He closed the trunk and then pointed toward the downtown district. "Shall we eat lunch before heading back?"

She couldn't find the right words and just stood there. Why was she upset about Jasmine when she was the one who kept insisting that Operation Crosby 2.0 centered on finding him a girlfriend? Maybe it was because Jasmine and Crosby were two peas in a pod. She could see him happy with Jasmine by his side, the two discussing history and sharing dessert at the Wild West revue.

Crosby was waiting for her decision, and her heart felt like it was being tugged in two directions. She needed to get home and pull the covers over her head until she was thinking rationally again. Rubbing her head, she countered the offer with a suggestion of fast food so they could head back to Violet Ridge faster. He seemed taken aback that she'd vetoed shopping or sightseeing, but one of them had to buckle down and get to work. She resolved to get back on track and keep him from suffering any anxiety on that stage on New Year's Eve. He deserved the best on that night, and she'd make sure it was an evening to remember.

CHAPTER NINE

THE NEXT DAY, Crosby tapped his pencil on his desk. Should he start his speech with a joke or a poignant story from one of the train engineer's diaries?

Deliberating between the two options, he felt something cold and wet ping his shoulder. If he were asleep at the Lazy River Dude Ranch, he'd awaken to the sight of Hap or Trixie snuggled up against him and delivering a wet doggie kiss to his face. As it was, he was neither at the dude ranch, nor asleep, which could only mean one thing. The Miners' Cottage roof was officially leaking. He looked up, only to have a drop of water plop on the lens without the eyepatch.

The roof he'd been hoping would hold out until spring was not cooperating. With a sigh, he called Gunther and Sons Roofers, which was the only one in town approved by the historical society. He was promptly put on hold.

Another drip landed on him, and he traveled to the kitchenette for a pot or something to collect the water. There were too many important documents and old books in his office for him not to do something. Perhaps he'd climb atop the roof and inspect the damage for himself once the bad weather had passed. Before he could act on that idea, the dispatcher spoke. Crosby explained the situation, and the dispatcher asked for a 50 percent retainer. He gulped as he didn't have that kind of money for this. Ben had said the funds wouldn't be available until June based on the estimate Mr. Gunther had already provided. Could Ben advance the money if it was needed early?

"Can I pay that deposit in January?"

The dispatcher requested that Crosby call back once he had the funds available. The line went silent. Crosby stared at the screen and was about to contact Ben before remembering that Ben and Daisy and the triplets were celebrating the holidays with Ben's father, stepmother and their extended families on this Saturday before Christmas. Gordon and Evie would be traveling to London tomorrow, where Evie, a famous singer, would perform a holiday concert.

Glancing at the window, he noted the rain and snow was slowing. There was nothing left to do except climb onto the roof and check the damage. If it wasn't too bad, he'd hold off until things were dry and he could use the tube of rubber sealant, which would hopefully work its magic one more time. Crosby searched his office for his toolbox and came up empty. Where was it? Oh, right. Sami had borrowed it when she was decorating the Porcupine Suite.

Crosby picked up his phone to call her when he received an incoming text from her, saying she was outside the cottage. He hurried to the front door and then excused himself and turned back without even looking at her.

"As soon as I feed Sundance and get my coat, can you drive me to the ranch?" He raised his voice while rummaging through the refrigerator for the plastic container with Sundance's collard greens and kale.

"But it's time for the next stage of the makeover," Sami said.

He rushed past her, but in his haste, he missed the counter and the green leafy vegetables spilled all over the carefully restored oak floorboards. Sami knelt and placed the vegetables into the container.

"Thanks." He picked the pieces of chopped-up kale off his favorite chunky sweater, the one that had belonged to his father. "I don't have any time to lose."

He headed toward Sundance's terrarium, and Sami followed him. "What's so important that you need to go to the ranch right away?" she asked.

Crosby opened the heated terrarium and fed Sundance, while explaining about the roof, the newest leak and Ben's family commitments. He ended with stating the exact location of his tools. Her bedroom closet.

"Would it be easier for you to bring them here?" he asked.

Sami whipped out her phone and held up her finger. "First, let me make a couple of calls."

"In the meantime, I'll get my coat." He looked at his socked feet. "And boots."

Crosby was pulling on his right boot when Sami appeared at the doorway. Maybe he should find some boxes and transport the most fragile of the documents and books to his small house until the roof could be repaired.

"Emma's husband, Dominic, is coming over to check on the roof." Crosby started to protest but she spoke first. "He's a qualified contractor, and Emma has raved at how well he remodeled the kitchen at Rocky Mountain Chocolatier and their home. I've visited their house. The part he's already renovated is gorgeous. At least talk to him first."

Sami was making a lot of sense, and he thanked her. A few minutes later, Dominic and his brother arrived at the cottage, and Dominic introduced himself and Joey to Crosby.

"I know you from around town, but I don't think we've ever been formally introduced," Dominic said. "I'm still waiting on my historic preservation certification from city hall, but I can verify the extent of the damage and give you an estimate."

Crosby appreciated Dominic's straightforward manner. The Martinelli brothers promised they'd have more to tell him within an hour. Crosby went back inside where Sami offered him a cup of coffee. The deep aroma of sugar and vanilla creamer calmed him almost as much as Sami's mere presence.

"Thanks for the coffee."

She tapped her long fingernails against her chin. For the first time since she'd arrived today, he found a moment to appreciate how beautiful she looked in a rich green cashmere sweater dress and black boots. Then again, she was always gorgeous no matter what she wore because her beauty was more than skin deep.

"You need a distraction." She checked her phone. "While Operation Crosby 2.0 isn't set to start for another couple of hours, I have a fantastic idea. Wait here!"

Before he could respond, Sami was already out the door. Crosby blew on his steaming coffee. It wasn't long until Sami was back, struggling with one of the boxes of costumes. Crosby rushed over and took the box from her. "We need to get these to Timeless Tailors today."

Sami nodded. "I thought we'd do that together, before my surprise. Although, I know nothing is getting you to leave this cottage until Dominic and Joey give you their estimate." She rifled through the box and pulled out the conductor's uniform. "This is yours, isn't it?"

Crosby accepted the folded uniform and pointed toward the box. "What about you? Care to try one on?"

Sami began sorting through the remaining outfits. "I don't mind if I do." She pulled out a costume in protective cellophane. "I'll change in the bathroom. Just open your office door once you've finished changing."

In no time, Crosby buttoned the gold buttons of the conductor's suit jacket over the matching vest before tying the bow tie around his neck. Since there wasn't a mirror in his office, he didn't know what he looked like, but he felt transported to another era wearing these clothes. That feeling became more pronounced when he donned the conductor's hat and adjusted his eyeglasses.

He opened his door to find Sami standing there in a long A-line skirt paired with a white dress shirt and matching navy jacket, also adorned with gold buttons. She had tilted her attendant's cap at an angle, giving her a jaunty air. She twirled around for him. His eyes grew wide with admiration.

"It's as if it were made for you," Crosby said.

"These are going to be such a huge hit on Christmas Eve and the relaunching of the Thunderbolt." Her gaze wandered along the length of him and she smiled. "Holidays and history—our two favorite things."

Scurrying sounds from the roof caused a flutter in his chest. They both looked upward.

Crosby shuddered. "I wonder how much longer they'll be up there."

"Dominic knows what he's doing. Emma says he's thorough and professional." Sami pulled the cap over his glasses before adjusting it again. "Same as you. How's your speech for the New Year's Eve celebration coming along?"

Crosby walked to his desk and picked up his notepad. "I was working on it this morning, but I'm not sure where to start."

Sami moved a pile of papers off a chair and placed them on the floor. "I'm a captive audience."

Sorting through the mess on his desk until he found the tome he sought, Crosby turned to a bookmarked page and picked up a pencil, tapping it on his chin. "Should I start off with a story from one of the conductor's diaries? Or a joke to make everyone laugh?"

She reached over and placed the book on the desk, spine upward. "Tell me the conductor's story in your own words."

Crosby lost himself in telling her about the conductor's diary with its emphasis on punctuality and who sat where. To her credit, her eyes only started glazing over after he started in on the improvements the conductor had wanted to make to the storage compartment, and he stopped talking.

"That bad?" Crosby saw the whole audience falling asleep, only waking once the band started playing as the clock struck midnight. "Back to the drawing board."

Sami blew out a deep breath. "It wasn't all bad, but there's definitely room for improvement. Any details about who was traveling on the train might be interesting." She gave him a wistful smile. "It's clear that you love your subject. Is that why you never worked at the ranch?"

More shuffling from the roof stopped him from answering right away. He glanced upward. "I should go outside and see if they need anything."

"They know where to find you." Sami shrugged. "If you don't feel like answering my question, I understand."

Ever since their first meeting, he felt at ease talking to her about anything. So he made himself comfortable in his office chair. "It was always understood that Seth would continue the family legacy. That ranch means everything to us."

Sami sat again and removed her cap, placing it at the edge of his desk. "I've worked there long enough to see that Seth would have made a place for you."

His brother would have done just that if Crosby had asked him to do so. "But then I could never have proved myself. In my chosen field."

"I get that. Part of me wonders if I'm moving on because Amanda is a force of nature and I'm only Amanda-lite." Sami's gaze never left him. "But why not agricultural science or still something related to the ranch?"

"You're not Amanda-lite. People love you because you're you."

Sami blushed but kept her chin high as she repeated her question about history. Crosby fingered the gold buttons on the conductor's suit coat. Growing up, he had sensed a big hole at the ranch from his parents' absence. Whenever he felt that emptiness, he'd cuddle up on his grandmother's lap and ask Bridget to tell him a story about his father. She'd always brush the hair off his forehead, give him a peck and then launch into his father's exploits when he was Crosby's age. As Crosby had grown older, Grandma Bridget had intertwined stories of his mother, Rosemary, into those talks. He searched his memory for any glimpse of his parents. Same as always, he only remembered what his grandparents and siblings told him about Peter and Rosemary. His father's inability to brew a decent cup of coffee. How much his mother loved big band music and would dance whenever she cleaned the house. The day his parents brought Crosby home from the hospital and introduced him to Seth, Daisy and Jase.

All these memories came to him secondhand, but they all kept his parents real to Crosby.

He relayed all of that to her and added, "Stories keep them alive."

Crosby rose and motioned for Sami to follow him, stopping first for his conductor's hat. He led her to the replica miner's room with cots and lanterns packed on one side with a sluice and tools on the other. "The miners worked sixteen-hour days. It was their labor that created revenue in this area, which drew ranchers and the whole community together. Their stories are part of the town, just like my parents were a part of the Lazy River Dude Ranch."

Sami set her hand on the rope partition that prevented the public from touching the period pieces. "The past is everything to you, isn't it? This town, this cottage."

A knock at the front door preceded Dominic's entrance and stopped Crosby from having to respond to her, although her question seemed more rhetorical than inquisitive. Crosby met him near the ticket booth with Sami on his heels.

Dominic didn't waste time. "The substantial weight of the slate roof has put a strain on the main frame of the cottage. There are serious structural issues that need to be rectified and soon…" Dominic pulled out his phone and showed Crosby pictures to support his claim. Then he presented Crosby with his estimate, which was significantly lower than what Gunther and Sons had implied, even with more substantive repairs. "I can't perform any of these repairs until city hall approves my request to become certified in Violet Ridge."

"The mayor is my brother-in-law, but I try not to take advantage of our family connection." Crosby winced. All this history and the Miners' Cottage, an important part of Violet Ridge, might be lost if the roof wasn't fixed properly. "If it's as serious as you claim, it has to be done as soon as possible."

Equally concerning to Crosby was the fact that Gunther and Sons hadn't been concerned about any of this.

"The sooner, the better." Dominic wiped his forehead with a bandanna. "It doesn't matter who does it. It just has to be done."

Crosby studied the estimate. "Your price is significantly lower than what another company told me to expect, even with more extensive work and labor." He tilted his head to the side. "Why?"

"My great-grandfather was a miner. This site means a great deal to my family." Dominic replaced the bandanna in his back pocket. "I'll talk to my mother, Kim. She might be able to convince the historical society to move up my accreditation date since she's been active on almost every committee for as long as I can remember. After the New Year, you can buy me a beer, and we'll review our options more."

Crosby thanked Dominic for his time and escorted him to his truck with Sami by his side.

After the Martinelli brothers drove away, he and Sami walked back to the front porch where she nudged his side. "Dominic delivered a lot of bad news. Are you okay?"

A headache was forming at his temples. He shivered as much from the bad news about the Miners' Cottage as the cold weather. His gaze traveled over the structure that had been the center of his professional life over the past ten years.

"The damage is more severe than I thought." His voice sounded distant, and he tried to process the news.

"Hey." Sami came over and tipped his conductor's hat askew. "Dominic is really good at his job."

Crosby tried to smile but couldn't. The cottage was crumbling around him, and he wondered what this said about him as a steward of such a place. "This is the oldest existing stand-alone structure in Violet Ridge. There was a fire on the other side of town in the middle of the twentieth century, and none of the ranch houses predate the Miners' Cottage. This is a piece of the town's history."

"You're doing everything you can, starting with taking action now." Sami walked along the pathway. "I hope Dominic gets that certification soon enough to help you."

So did Crosby. He didn't want to know what

the extra work would do to Gunther's revised estimate. "Dominic seems like a nice guy."

"He didn't bat an eye at how we changed into these uniforms." Sami stopped short of the porch steps and winked at Crosby. "I can only imagine what he must have thought about us appearing like this."

Until now, Crosby had forgotten they were still wearing these uniforms. He chuckled. "Just another day at the Miners' Cottage."

He wondered how many more there would be if things didn't improve around here.

"Aha! It's not often that you're wrong, but you are. This is a *special* day." Sami whipped her phone out of her purse and hustled over to the front door decorated with a giant wreath, a red bow and sprigs of holly and pinecones. "The holiday season is upon us, and you are quite dashing in your conductor's uniform. Yours won't even need alterations. Let's take a selfie in front of the cottage."

He positioned himself next to her, close enough for the floral scent of her perfume to flood his senses. "Is this good?"

"Yes, but I only wish I'd had time to style my hair like the forties and go home for my red lipstick. Still, we look pretty darn great, if I do say so myself." As if she could ever look less than stunning. She held out the phone and snapped several photos. The chill in the air brought a natural rosiness to her cheeks. "Now for some goofy faces."

Even with her tongue sticking out and nose wrinkled, she was beautiful. More so, she made a tough day better with her mere presence.

"Please send me the pictures." He wanted to remember this moment always.

She nodded and forwarded the images to him. "And the day isn't over yet. There's still the next phase of the makeover."

He groaned. "Go ahead and tell me about it now."

"All in good time."

Her optimism was already overtaking him. How would he handle the renovations without her?

The train attendant's uniform was a joy to wear. With some reluctance, Sami changed back into her sweater dress, thick socks and knee-high black stiletto boots. Arriving in Colorado in May, she'd been amazed the mountaintops still possessed a hint of snow. But nothing could have prepared her for that deep cold that came with the first snowfall in early October. Still, this was an adventure, and now she found she loved the cold. Come to think of it, she would miss frolicking in the sparkly white snow and how it felt to come inside afterward and chill by the fire. More reason to enjoy the layers of thick clothing and blankets and quilts while she could. The last time she had spoken to Asia, the daytime temperatures in San Diego hovered in the sixties, a far cry from Colorado's freezing climate.

Asia was excited that Sami would arrive in San Diego on the second of January, sooner than originally planned. Jeremy's human resources connection had come through and contacted her for an interview, which was now scheduled for the week after New Year's with the understanding she'd have to return to Violet Ridge for Amanda's wedding on Valentine's Day. While Sami had intended on telling Crosby all that, she'd decided to postpone her announcement given Dominic's devastating news about the cottage structure.

When should she tell Crosby that she had moved up her departure date by six weeks? Christmas Eve? Christmas Day? Was there ever a good way to break that type of news to your best friend? Not particularly, but she owed it to Amanda to tell her first this time. She'd tell him after she broke the news to her sister. Sami exited the bathroom with the folded uniform and found Crosby pacing the hallway.

"What's next?" he asked.

She was startled. One look at him and all certainty about going flew out the window. She wanted to hear more Crosby stories, to tease him about his beloved sweet tooth, to spend time with him. Then it dawned on her. He was referring to the makeover. Her efforts on his behalf were already having an impact. She wasn't the only woman to notice Crosby's new look. Jasmine in Pueblo had even given Crosby her personal phone number.

Calm and intelligent, Jasmine was the exact woman Sami envisioned for Crosby. The two obviously had a lot in common with their shared passion for history. They had also ordered authentic uniforms from the same vendor. And she was obviously interested in Crosby.

Knowing him so well, though, Sami realized he'd need a push to contact Jasmine. She couldn't bring herself to be that person, though. It was one thing to play matchmaker; it was another to see the results. He looked at her, waiting for her to say something.

"I barged in here without even asking if you're free this afternoon." In a way, she had taken him for granted, especially given how he was always available when she needed him. "Do you have plans?"

Crosby chuckled as if it was the silliest idea he'd ever heard. "Besides working on my speech?"

He didn't have plans with Jasmine. A nice person would give Crosby a push toward her. Since Sami would be departing Violet Ridge, she wanted to make sure he took the first step while she was still here. "Have you called Jasmine yet?"

Crosby scoffed. "Why would I? She lives in Pueblo."

That wasn't a rejection based on the woman's personality or character. "She's interested in you." As evidenced by the long-lingering appreciative look she'd given him while passing Crosby that number.

Crosby blushed before waving away Sami's observation. "Three hours is too far of a drive for a date. I can't do long distance."

Sami's insides twisted even more. San Diego was a three-hour-plus airplane excursion from here. "You can't ever have too many friends." She handed him the uniform, the desire for fresh air intense and pressing. "And you need time to work on that speech. I'll let you do just that."

This time she wasn't reacting to his hiding in a hedge or someone's surprising interruption. She wanted him to succeed, and he would because he was the best. As long as he conveyed his authenticity to the audience and showed them the real Crosby who loved stories, so much so that he sometimes got so engrossed in whatever he was working on that he lost track of time, he'd flourish.

"You said there were five steps," Crosby said. "I'm nothing if not thorough. Come on. What's the next phase?"

"Look at you. All dapper and handsome. I declare you have officially graduated from the Sami School of Makeovers."

"I don't deserve that diploma yet." Crosby placed her uniform on the ticket booth and grinned. "Whatever's next must be a doozy. Lay it on me. I'm yours to command."

Sami laughed at his puppy dog look and decided to let him decide about her next phase. "I thought we'd check out the dance studio that just opened in town after dropping off the costumes at Timeless Tailors. Renee Napier is giving a recital of her favorite scene from *The Nutcracker* along with a free ballet lesson."

He went pale and touched his eyepatch. "Ballet might not be a good idea until this comes off. Do you have a backup idea?"

She winced as she hadn't even considered that his limited range of vision might preclude this activity. After the facial and contacts had ended in disaster, she was more than willing to pivot, but to what? She tapped her long fingernails against her chin and came up with a new idea. "Do you happen to have a pair of sweatpants handy?"

CROSBY ENTERED ON THE RIDGE GYM with some hesitation. Sami's backup to ballet was yoga? For some reason, she was convinced his limited range of vision wouldn't be a problem with this activity. Between hiking with Sami and spending his spare time at the ranch, he considered himself to be in good shape, but this was something else. Still, he was game for most things.

Once.

Sami was already here, dressed in yoga pants and a sports top. They approached the desk together and Sami asked the receptionist if there were any openings in the heated yoga class that evidently Amanda had been raving about for the past six months.

Gabrielle gave a wistful smile and shook her head. "Bree's class is full." She looked at Crosby and his eyepatch. "Are you contagious?"

Crosby explained his situation. "I can take the eyepatch off if necessary."

Sami glared at him as if he should have made that concession earlier before turning her attention back to the receptionist. "Are there any other yoga classes today?"

Gabrielle clicked on some buttons and held up her finger. "Wait here while I check on something."

Gabrielle departed in a hurry, and Crosby felt a tinge of apprehension. He gave an awkward chuckle to relieve some of his tension and faced Sami, wanting to clarify what he'd said earlier. "I didn't think about removing my eyepatch until Gabrielle asked if I was contagious."

Sami arched her eyebrow and then relaxed. "I believe you."

Their gazes met, and something about her expression zapped his inner core. He was taken aback. Could Sami be feeling something for him? Something more than friendship? This was it. The moment he was going to address the elephant in the room. He opened his mouth, and Gabrielle reappeared.

"Bree can't take any more students, but Lori has two openings in her seniors' yoga class. It starts in five minutes, and she's willing to let you join in if you're up to the challenge."

Crosby bit back a chuckle. Yoga with seniors? This might be a chance for him to really shine in front of Sami. He had this in the bag. "Sign me up."

After filling out the waiver form, Crosby joined Sami in front of the classroom door.

"Are you sure about this?" Sami glanced toward the exercise room. "I've heard they're an experienced group."

That gave him pause, but only for a second. This was new and exciting. He could try this with no repercussions and no expectations.

Sami's makeover was working. After being doubtful about this for so long, he could barely wrap his head around this latest development. Yet there was one thing holding him back, so he asked, "How does yoga alleviate my public speaking issue?"

"I think yoga might make you more conscious of your surroundings but in a good way." Sami launched into an explanation of how the stretches have many positive effects, besides helping his flexibility. "Strengthening your inner core and reinforcing your sense of balance might create a better awareness of those around you. Put you in tune with your audience."

Zelda and Nelda arrived, dressed in workout clothes with added holiday flair: Zelda wore an antler headband and Nelda sported a necklace made of tiny ornaments.

Zelda hailed them. "Are you brave enough to join us?"

Crosby met Sami's gaze and then nodded. "Bridget and Martin raised me to face just about anything." And they had. What was more, they always did just that as a family.

"You won't regret it." Nelda grinned. "We'll keep you on your toes."

Crosby held the door open for the ladies. They thanked him and filed inside the big room, where he recognized several of the participants. Sami led him to the spare yoga mats, and he selected a blue roll. They settled near Marshall Bayne and his girlfriend, Constance Mulligan, who had purchased the Holly Theater and never passed up a chance to talk about the next production.

Constance greeted them first. "Hello, Crosby and Sami. Merry Christmas! It's delightful having the triplets live next door to me. They're such darlings." She grinned at Crosby. He still couldn't get over the change in her demeanor. Constance used to be known around this area as part Grinch and part Scrooge, until Ben had moved into the Victorian that he now shared with his new family. "I can't wait for this year's production of *The Santa Who Forgot Christmas*. Your niece Rosie is such a natural on the stage."

Sami stopped unrolling her mat and stared at Constance, her eyes flashing fire. "You're not pressuring Rosie into acting, are you? She's just a child. Let her enjoy this time to be a kid."

Constance seemed taken aback at Sami's tone for a second. "Of course not. Ben and Daisy are very conscientious parents, and Rosie loves being in the production."

Lori gave a two-minute warning, and Constance and Marshall started some light stretches. Crosby was about to do the same when he noticed that Sami was unusually subdued, so much so that Crosby could hear Nelda and Zelda's animated discussion about holiday shopping. Nelda was gloating that she was finished while Zelda expressed dismay about having quite a few errands left on her list. He expected to find Sami smiling about this, but she was examining her nails. He neared her so he could speak to her without anyone overhearing him.

"Don't worry," Crosby whispered. "Daisy will let Rosie be a kid."

Sami sent him a wistful smile. "Sorry I got

upset. I guess I need to apologize to Constance as well. Sometimes it's hard to remember not everyone has a stage mom like mine."

Crosby furrowed his eyebrows. "Was it that bad?"

"Not all the time. There were good moments, but my mother seldom took my feelings into account." She frowned. "I tend to get defensive of children and forget that some of them genuinely love to be on a stage."

Before he could say anything else, Lori, an attractive brunette in her twenties, started the class. Crosby marveled at how limber everyone was. If anything, Zelda and Nelda were encouraging him rather than the other way around. His muscles screamed at him, and he was convinced they must be near the finish line when Lori announced they were halfway done. Everyone else had barely broken a sweat and had contorted their bodies into different positions with seemingly little effort.

Finally, the torture, or class, was over. Lori approached Crosby and asked if he'd enjoyed it. Crosby wiped the sweat off his forehead. "This was a genuine workout."

Lori nodded. "It really is. I've enjoyed getting to know your grandparents. Bridget and Martin have been regulars ever since her physical therapist recommended yoga following her stroke. Is everything okay with them? They canceled today. That's why I had two spaces available."

"They're fine. Jase's future mother-in-law is visiting so they're over at Thistle Brook Farm," Crosby said, relieved that his facial muscles could still form a smile.

Lori reassured him he was welcome to join her class anytime, and Crosby thanked her. She handed him her business card and circled her personal phone number. He accepted it and then stretched his back, unsure of how his muscles would feel in the morning.

Sami, who had been over at the water cooler talking to Marshall's brother, grinned. "It gets easier if you start doing it more often."

Crosby was sure she was telling the truth, but he wasn't ready to commit to anything quite yet. He and Sami exited the room, and he was about to ask her what was next when there were shouts and exclamations from somewhere nearby. He looked at Sami, but she seemed to be in the dark as much as he was. They followed the noise, and found a crowd congregated in the weight room where Jeremy was lifting himself off a bench. An employee patted him on the back and congratulated him.

The admiring crowd flocked toward Jeremy.

Jeremy noticed him and Sami and waved them over as someone handed him a towel. "Crosby! Sami! Having my two new best friends here makes the moment even better."

"What happened?" Sami asked.

The excited crowd was still chatting. Jeremy smiled and waved and blotted his forehead. "Oh, nothing much."

Les Tomasino, chief teller at the bank, scoffed. "Jeremy just broke the gym's record for bench pressing, that's all. Two hundred and twenty-five pounds. That's impressive."

"Aw shucks, you did a great job spotting me. Thanks, man." Jeremy wiped down the equipment and faced Sami and Crosby. "This gym has an amazing juice bar. Care to join me for a smoothie?"

Despite Crosby's protests, he found himself sitting with them at the juice bar. Jeremy insisted on treating them, and Crosby kept silent while Jeremy and Sami debated the merits of adding various ingredients to their smoothies.

Crosby sat and watched their interaction and easy banter. Even he had to admit they made a handsome couple.

He kept from groaning. Watching Sami with Jeremy, he couldn't help but see her with someone who was exactly like the affable bodybuilder, for he was her equal in humility, kindness and all-around geniality.

Of course, Sami would end up with someone perfect like Jeremy: an effervescent crowd-pleaser who could do no wrong. Sami deserved the best, and Jeremy was exactly that.

Did Sami want to double-date with Crosby?

Was that why she was asking so much about Jasmine?

Crosby rolled his neck. Jasmine was attractive, and they had so much in common. And yet Crosby didn't feel the pull to call Jasmine and ask her on a date. Maybe he'd feel differently post-Valentine's.

"Crosby? What do you say to that one?" Jeremy broke into his thoughts.

Crosby looked at Sami, who seemed bemused. "I guess... Yes?"

Sami raised her hand to her lips and started quivering. She couldn't hide her laughter, and Crosby had a bad feeling about his choice. A few minutes later, those fears were confirmed when three beverages appeared, and Jeremy handed him a slimy green drink that matched his own. He clinked his cup to Crosby's as if in a toast. Then Jeremy took a long gulp. "Delicious!"

Sami accepted her dark purple drink and kept her gaze on Crosby. "What do you think about yours?"

Ooh, that was low, but it couldn't be as bad as it looked. Crosby sipped his and used every bit of his resolve not to spit it out. He tried one more taste. This smoothie was just like that one time he'd fallen off a horse and accidentally eaten earth and manure.

Jeremy stared at him, waiting for his verdict. "Isn't it something?"

Crosby decided to be diplomatic so as not to disappoint him. "It's something all right. What do you call that?" He'd file it away for reference so he never ordered this for himself.

Jeremy beamed. "Green Supreme. It's loaded with great stuff like ginger, spinach, kiwi, apple juice and a scoop of protein powder. It's perfect after weight training or yoga."

"Perfect," Crosby repeated while his stomach rebelled against another sip. Still, Jeremy looked happy at Crosby's pronouncement. Disappointing him seemed on par with failing Aspen or Lily or Rosie. He twirled the straw in the smoothie.

Jeremy's phone chimed, and he whistled. "Time to head for the ski lodge to get ready for my set." He faced Sami and smiled. "Just text me a day when you want to ski and see my show. I'll score you a ski pass and tickets for the both of you. Gotta run."

Guilt kicked in at how Jeremy had accepted Crosby into his life, and Crosby had only experienced jealousy and pettiness in return. It wasn't Jeremy's fault he was practically perfect in every way, including being Sami's ideal Christmas match.

Jeremy was halfway out the door when Crosby called to him, "Same for you and your aunt. I'll get you both tickets to the Midnight Express New Year's Eve Celebration, if you can make it?"

Jeremy gave him a thumbs-up before he exited.

Sami tapped Crosby on his arm and pointed to the drink. "That's an interesting color."

In return, Crosby lifted his eyebrows and poked the side of her cup. "Yours is radiating brightness."

They glanced at each other and burst out laughing. Her giggles were music, the sound a melody of its own. Sami motioned for Crosby to follow her and they left the drinks behind.

He hurried out of the gym, eager for their next adventure together.

IN THE BACK booth at the Creamistry Old-Fashioned Ice Cream Parlor, Violet Ridge's newest restaurant, Sami savored her salted caramel milkshake, which had enough of a bite to keep it from being too sugary. She sneaked a peek at Crosby, who leaned back with his eyes closed and a content smile. He'd already finished half of his mocha chocolate chip milkshake.

"Thanks for rescuing me from the Green Supreme. You have my complete devotion." His eyes flew open, and his mouth went slack for a second. The air between them sizzled until he said, "Unless you ask me to another seniors' yoga class. Then all bets are off, and I will transfer my affection to Nelda and Zelda, who are more agile than both of us."

Sami's stomach performed a funny flip as he qualified his statement. For a second, she thought he was going to do something impulsive and wonderful like telling her he wanted to throw caution to the wind and see where romance carried them.

Sami blinked and sipped more of her milkshake, the cold treat bringing her back to her senses. She was destined for different adventures, ones that took her around the globe. She couldn't wait to explore art museums and go scuba diving.

Yet seeing the Louvre or coral reefs without Crosby didn't seem to have the same luster as a month ago.

This Christmas season had been so full of promise. Why was she ruining it by falling for her best friend, who also happened to be her future brother-in-law?

Tightness filled her chest. Violet Ridge was only supposed to be a brief stop until she gained her bearings. She had done exactly that with the bonus of connecting with her sister and finding a lifelong friend in Crosby.

It would be foolish to want more, and yet she found herself doing just that. She held her breath as something wonderful came to her. What if a romance wouldn't ruin their friendship, though? What if reaching for more brought out something rare and lasting?

"Crosby..."

"Jase! Cassie!" Crosby slid out of his side of the booth and greeted his brother and his fiancée along with Cassie's kids, Penny and Easton.

He invited his family to join them. Penny slid in next to Sami while Jase and Cassie excused themselves to place their order. Easton hopped up to sit by Crosby.

"Ms. Sami, will you show me how to do that special braid again? Please? I want my hair to look pretty on Christmas Eve." Penny pleaded with her hands and eyes.

Sami looked over at Crosby, who was already discussing the model train Easton had produced from his pocket. She started braiding Penny's hair and had just finished when Jase returned with extra chairs while Cassie delivered ice cream.

A couple of spills and two delighted kids later, Jase and Cassie and the children took their leave. Sami was alone with Crosby once more. He blotted water on his ruined white T-shirt.

"My shirt ended up with more of Easton's chocolate peppermint cone than his stomach." His laugh proved that he had no hard feelings. "I have ten of these back home. I'm just glad Easton wasn't upset."

"You'll make a great father someday." The words slipped out of her mouth, but she didn't regret them. Suddenly, she saw a little boy with Crosby's cowlick and her blue eyes licking an ice cream cone with the Eiffel Tower in view on a gorgeous summer day.

Crosby reached for his coat. "I prefer being Uncle Crosby." He donned his coat and held out

Sami's for her. "You'll be Aunt Sami once Seth and Amanda have children."

She would be, and she looked forward to it if it happened. How involved did she want to be with them? For certain, she didn't want to be a mysterious enigma who only showed up once a decade.

Crosby opened the door for her. They exited the establishment and strolled along the town square. Contentment settled into her. This type of peace often eluded her as she was always looking for the next thing. In a way, it was a continuation of her childhood when her father would inevitably lose yet another job and they'd move once more. Sami had pumped herself up by thinking of the move as a new chance to explore different places and meet different people. And that always happened until uneasiness settled over her as she waited for the boom to drop once more.

But what if this peace didn't have to be just for one night? What if she broke her own cycle and committed to her job here for the long term?

Before she could ask Crosby if he wanted to be a part of her present in a new light, they arrived at her car. She settled in the driver's seat and went to close the door when she glimpsed Crosby moving toward her.

Was he about to kiss her?

He neared her, and she realized how much she wanted his lips to claim hers.

She held her breath, and his fingers entwined

themselves in her hair. She leaned into his touch when he unlaced his fingers and held out a piece of ice cream cone.

"Now you're perfect again. Can't wait for my next adventure with my best friend." He winked at her and closed the door before she could take it upon herself to express her growing feelings.

A kiss would have been an incredible end to a topsy-turvy day that was anything but stagnant or boring.

Was it time to start reconsidering her future?

CHAPTER TEN

IN HIS OFFICE at the Miners' Cottage, Crosby admitted he was in over his head. With nine days until his Midnight Express New Year's Eve Celebration speech, he was stalled. Proof of that came from twenty crumpled-up sheets of paper, half of which had landed in his office trash can while the rest were dispersed around the room. If he could just figure out how to start saying what was in his heart, he had a feeling everything else would fall into place.

But the situation was worse. He had the distinct feeling he'd forgotten something important. He glanced at the calendar and scratched his head. Baking cookies? No, it couldn't be that since he had a full jar of homemade deliciousness at home. Decorating the tree? He'd done that several weeks ago. What was he forgetting?

He munched on a bowl of chocolaty puffed cereal and turned to Sundance. "Were you supposed to remind me to be somewhere?"

His pet iguana raised his head and kept silent

before returning to snack on his pile of collard greens while Crosby crunched another chocolaty puff. His phone chimed. He glanced down and read the reminder that he was due at the ranch in an hour for taffy pulling and wrapping presents.

Technology was a wonderful thing.

After scraping ice off the windshield, Crosby drove to the ranch. He parked the car, and his excitement grew at the idea of his family gathering in the kitchen for his grandmother's favorite holiday event. But before heading there, he had just enough time to check on the surprise he had planned for Christmas Day. He detoured to the stable and found Seth and Amanda mucking out stalls. Confused, Crosby pulled off his gloves and reached for a rake to help. "Aren't you supposed to be getting ready for the taffy pull?" he asked.

Seth turned around, a look of surprise on his face that even his beard couldn't cover. Amanda joined them and tapped on her watch. "Crosby, we didn't expect you for two hours."

Crosby checked the time. "Grandma Bridget told me to arrive at five and I set my alarm early for four thirty. I didn't want to be late again. Yet I must have messed up anyway. Still, looks like you just started. Good thing you have me to help."

Seth and Amanda exchanged a guilty look, and then Seth approached Crosby with a frown. "Everyone's meeting at six for the taffy pulling."

Crosby glanced at Seth, and then Amanda before he realized what was going on. "Message received."

He let out his frustration by mucking out stalls at a fairly rapid pace. Was his reputation for being late that legendary that his family had started telling him to be here an hour early? Crosby let out a long sigh as he finished the third stall.

Amanda came over and tilted her head. "Something's different about you." Then she tilted her head the other way. "Your eyepatch is gone. I miss it. It gave you an air of danger and suspense."

Seth approached her, and she kissed Seth to show her heart would always belong to him. As if there was ever any doubt.

"Seth, can I see you for a minute in the stable office?" Crosby asked.

Amanda accepted Seth's rake while Seth accompanied Crosby into the office off the main aisle. They settled into chairs, and Crosby chose to avoid confronting his brother about his family's remedy for Crosby's penchant toward tardiness. It was enough that he was working at it, and he was already seeing a genuine difference thanks to Sami. Speaking of whom, he asked Seth for an update on his Christmas Day present for Sami—a genuine, authentic sleigh ride.

"Everything's on track. There's even snow in the forecast for Christmas Eve night so it will be perfect for a morning ride before the family gathers at the ranch."

"Thanks." Crosby rose and nodded. "I'll see you later in the kitchen."

Seeing as he had time to spare, he'd ask for Sami's help wrapping presents for his nieces and nephew before the taffy pull rather than afterward. Minutes later, he was knocking on Sami's door. No answer.

With some time on his hands, he left the lodge and opted for the duck pond. So often while he was writing his dissertation, a good long walk or a snooze would provide a clue about how best to proceed.

He picked up some pebbles, but there was already too much ice to skip stones across the pond. Instead, he sat on a nearby bench, scanning the landscape. Colorado already resembled a winter wonderland, but he enjoyed the other seasons, too. He noted the spot where Sami would meet him at sunrise in late summer to go kayaking around the pond. Then there were the horseback rides when they'd discussed everything and nothing. *The speech, think about the speech.* Yet everything was sparking memories of Sami, making it impossible to focus on anything related to getting up in front of a large crowd and talking about the Thunderbolt and its place in the town's lore.

Would he find it difficult to return to the dude ranch after she left? For there were memories of her everywhere, like the dining hall where they'd snapped the wishbone at Thanksgiving. What had Sami wished for when she'd won?

"Crosby?" Sami's voice came from behind, and he blinked away the memories.

He didn't trust himself to look at her, and he stared at the pond. She repeated his name and sat next to him. "Were you the person knocking at my door?" Her light laugh sent his heart skipping. "I can't believe I fell asleep."

He remained where he was, staring out at the pond, letting the frigid air settle into his bones. She must have sensed something was bothering him for she entwined her fingers in his and just sat there with him, letting the silence build between them.

That was something else he appreciated about her. She always gave him room to mull over his thoughts, knowing he'd talk when he was ready.

This was the first time he'd have to hold back from her since he couldn't tell her what was truly in his heart. It would be for naught since she loved him as a friend. Why else would she keep wanting to set him up with someone who was just like him?

Where was the fun in being with someone just like you?

Crosby wanted someone like Sami, who was his opposite, the sunlight to his foggy self. But it was time to accept the fact that just like he couldn't touch a ray of sunshine, neither could he hold her back. She wanted to leave the place he loved the most, where stories of the past filled his days with purpose.

It felt like he was destined to stay here. He loved this ranch, this town, the Miners' Cottage. How could he leave all of this? How could he abandon his family? He couldn't leave.

It was time for him to get past this infatuation and be happy for her. After all, he wanted her to find the same joy she brought to so many others.

With that, he tried to move on. He pasted a smile on his face and stood. "Then you'll be well rested to help me tackle the mound of presents that need wrapping."

She jumped up from the bench and nodded. "Lead the way."

At his car, he handed her a box of presents, while keeping the other one to carry. Then he threw blankets over both to hide the contents from peeping eyes. Sami went to her suite, where she'd set up a table for wrapping. In no time, two piles of gifts started forming. Hers were perfectly wrapped with ribbon and a special touch whereas his looked like a five-year-old had done the honors.

She glanced over at him cutting a length of gift wrap and scoffed. "That's way too much paper. Here, let me show you." She neared his side, and he caught the scent of her light floral perfume. She batted his arm. "You made some great choices for these presents, even if you can't wrap them."

Her teasing tone and nearness tested his new resolution, but he stayed on track. "You'll have to give me lessons so I can master this and continue my streak."

Sami held up the box containing the journal and scented markers he'd chosen for his niece Lily. "You shouldn't use a whole roll of gift wrap for something this small."

Sami bumped into him and stumbled. Crosby reached out and steadied her, only letting go when he was sure she was safe. Shock spread over her face, and she parted her red lips, her lipstick perfectly applied. Time stood still as Sami pulled him toward her. She gazed into his eyes before rising onto her tiptoes, her lips close to his and—

There was a knock on Sami's door.

"Sami? Are you in there?" Amanda's voice reached them, and Crosby moved backward. Sami answered the door and Amanda rushed inside. "There you are. Sami, Grandma Bridget says she needs to see us before the taffy pull. She says it's urgent."

Crosby flashed back to his grandmother's stroke. Chills passed through him. "I'm coming, too."

With that, he followed Sami and Amanda toward his grandparents' suite, dismissing the romantic notions lingering in his head. For Sami's sake, he'd do better from now on.

"I FOUND IT!" Bridget held a shoebox out toward Sami and Amanda.

In the living area of Bridget and Martin's suite, Sami turned to Amanda. Her sister held her palms face up toward Bridget.

"Found what?" Amanda asked.

Bridget ushered them over to the couch. The older woman settled in the middle and patted either side of her until her gaze fell on her grandson. "Crosby? What are you doing here?" Then her grin widened. "Of course. Wherever Sami is, you're never far behind. Have a seat across from us. You'll want to see this, too."

Bridget was wrong, wasn't she? She and Crosby weren't always together. Then it hit Sami. Except for work, they had been inseparable since she arrived.

Was she the reason Crosby didn't have a girlfriend? Was her presence preventing him from finding his own happiness?

Sami blinked and concentrated on what was so important that Bridget called for a meeting with both Fleming sisters before the taffy pull. Perhaps the interruption was for the best as she had come close to kissing Crosby, whose gaze didn't waver from the shoebox situated on the coffee table.

Although Sami would love to kiss Crosby, everywhere she turned another reason popped up to keep them apart. Not only did she want to be in control of her future, but she didn't want to prevent him from meeting the person who was meant to walk alongside him, right here in Violet Ridge, where he'd work and stay while she did the same in San Diego.

Bridget removed the lid and passed the top letter to Amanda and the one below to Sami. "Your grandmother's Christmas cards! I knew I'd saved them."

Curiosity quelled inside Sami, and she noticed Crosby reaching for one as well. His hand halted at the edge of the box. "May I?" Crosby asked, looking at Amanda, then his grandmother, but not Sami.

Bridget nodded. A silence descended on the room as Sami read the letter inside the card. Then she examined the photograph of Grandma Lou and Grandpa Garrett standing in front of the Colosseum. Amanda switched with her so that Sami then found herself gazing upon a photograph of her grandparents that must have been taken on their honeymoon. They looked so young in front of Niagara Falls. Sami laughed at her grandfather's platinum sideburns.

After a few minutes, Amanda folded another letter back into the envelope. "I always thought Grandma Lou was a homebody like me. These letters show a different side of her."

Bridget reached for another card. "Garrett was in the military before he married your grandmother. He loved to travel and would have been happy living out of a suitcase, but he loved your grandmother more. They compromised and had the best of both worlds. She found she liked traveling but they settled in Texas and then your father came along."

So Sami got her sense of adventure from her grandfather. Staring at the photo, she searched out any other resemblance between them but found none. The door opening made her look up. She'd been so engrossed in the letters that she hadn't noticed Crosby take his leave.

Sami turned toward Bridget and patted her arm to get her attention. "Where did Crosby go?"

Bridget arched her eyebrow, then shrugged. "If anyone knew that answer, I thought it would be you."

Sami considered whether to go after him but decided against it. For once she wouldn't give in on her urge to act on impulse. Rather she'd stay here and be deliberative, taking a page from Crosby's book.

The last thing she wanted to do was hurt three of the people she cared about most in the world, namely Amanda, Bridget and Crosby. With Bridget and Amanda looking on, she picked up another envelope and read its contents.

CROSBY WAS SURE Sami had intended to kiss him while they were wrapping presents, but now she was face-to-face with proof that her grandparents had lived their best lives and followed their dreams by being world travelers. Who wouldn't want to follow in those footsteps? Besides himself, Seth and Amanda, of course.

But if that wasn't hard enough, here he was at the back entrance of the lodge, staring at his phone, trying to digest more bad news. Deena Meinster, the head volunteer for the inaugural Violet Ridge Christmas Eve Thunderbolt, had just called from her home where she was down with the flu. With a high fever and the event a mere forty-eight hours from now, she had no choice but to back out of her commitment.

Where was he going to find someone to replace Deena on short notice? Not to mention someone who would fit into her uniform.

Crosby pocketed his phone and began to wander, eventually ending up in the lodge's industrial kitchen. Tonight Ingrid had the evening off, and all the Virtue siblings and their offspring were gathered together in the massive space for the taffy pull.

Crosby slipped into the room just as his grandmother was directing everyone how to separate the warm batch of taffy into several portions before adding food coloring for maximum effect.

Standing between her brother and sister, Rosie

craned her neck for a better view. "Ooh, I hope I get to pull the pink taffy. That's my favorite."

Penny motioned to Jase until he bent down. She whispered in his ear, and Jase nodded. "You can twist two colors together."

"Jase was always my best helper. Stick by him and he'll show you what to do." Grandma Bridget smiled at her future great-granddaughter before clapping her hands. "Everyone, team up! We're ready to start pulling."

Easton immediately clung to Jase's side while Penny joined her mother, Cassie. Crosby searched the room until his gaze fell on Sami huddled with Amanda. He approached Aspen and claimed him and Lily. Rosie looked quite happy to have Ben and Daisy all to herself.

While the taffy cooled, Crosby helped Lily and Aspen wash their hands. Then the fun began as each group greased their hands with butter. Everyone worked together to stretch and pull the taffy until it formed one thin rope.

The fun kept going as Crosby twisted ropes of purple, blue and green together, making striped candy. They began cutting the ropes into bite-size pieces when Lily and Aspen started yawning. Over Rosie's protests, Ben and Daisy said their goodbyes and collected the triplets and their taffy. Crosby stayed on task, twisting the rest of the candy into ropes. He didn't see Sami approach until she stood in front of him.

"Nice color combo." Sami pointed at his efforts. "Sorry you lost your helpers."

"Seems this tuckered them out, especially combined with today's play rehearsal."

"Looks like they're not the only ones saying good-night." Sami tilted her chin toward Jase and Cassie, who were helping Penny and Easton into their coats, hats and gloves.

Crosby reached for the kitchen scissors and snipped off bite-size pieces. "If you and Amanda want to read more of the Christmas cards, I can finish up by myself."

His grandfather motioned for Crosby and Sami, and they walked his way. Grandpa Martin looked around as if to make sure no one could overhear him and then stood close enough for him to whisper. "Your grandmother has had a long day. There are a lot of festivities coming up and I don't want her overdoing it. Can you two offer to clean up so she'll get some rest?"

Crosby never tired of seeing his grandparents' love story in action. Even now, his grandfather's concern for his wife was on full display.

Maybe this type of love requires taking chances. Maybe loving someone doesn't mean losing them.

Crosby nodded. "I'll even make sure she doesn't catch on that you asked me to help."

Grandpa Martin winked at Crosby. "Good son." He returned to his wife's side. A few minutes later, to call the room to order, Crosby clapped his hands—a good deal more difficult than he'd anticipated, considering how much butter was still on them—and shooed everyone away.

"I'm about to rehearse my speech," Crosby declared.

That did the trick. Everyone scattered at once. His grandfather gave him a second wink while ushering everyone out of the kitchen until only Crosby and Sami remained. Moving to the sink, Crosby started running the hot water while Sami brought over dirty cookie sheets and bowls of butter.

"Where do you want me to put these?" Sami asked.

"Next to the sink." He squirted dishwashing liquid into the streaming-hot water. Bubbles started flying everywhere. "You don't have to stay."

"Didn't you say you were practicing your speech?" Sami found a dishtowel and whipped it over her green cashmere sweater, which had nary a stain, unlike his chunky beige sweater that had a smudge of butter and a bit of taffy stuck to his sleeve. "I can listen and give you feedback. Then we can finish wrapping the gifts together."

He brought his hand up to his forehead, leaving a trail of bubbles. "I forgot about the presents."

Sami nudged his side. "What will you do without me?"

A pall fell over the room, and he turned off the water.

"Wrap presents quite badly," he quipped before reaching for the dirty dishes.

In no time, the kitchen sparkled once more, ready for Ingrid to prepare breakfast for the guests in the morning.

Sami dropped her dishtowel on the counter. "You didn't practice your speech. I'll listen to you while we finish wrapping those presents. I'll meet you in my suite in ten minutes."

Sami departed and Crosby puttered around the kitchen until he felt composed enough to be in her presence. He grabbed his tin of taffy and then returned to her suite where Sami was playing music and singing along with Mariah Carey.

She directed him to the table. "It's time to finish what we started." Her gaze met his, and alarm bells clanged in his mind. He saw the same alarm in Sami's pretty eyes, and she hastened to add, "The gift wrapping. That's all."

He nodded, and they set to wrapping the last of the toys. "Would you mind if I leave these under your tree?"

"It would be senseless to take them back to your house just to have to return them to the lodge," Sami agreed while using the edge of the scissors to curl the ribbon on the final present.

He stood back and inhaled the fresh scent of the fir tree in her living area.

"Thanks for your help." He pointed to the stack

he had obviously wrapped. "Otherwise, they'd all look like that."

"Don't discount them." A mellow sweetness came over Sami. "They have a certain charm."

Her lips parted, and he backed toward the door. "Sundance will be wondering where I am."

His poor iguana probably thought Crosby was neglecting him with all the hours he was spending away from him. Crosby resolved to bring Sundance to the ranch in his portable terrarium on Christmas Day. Crosby's back bumped into the door with a loud thud, and he rubbed at the spot.

Concern bloomed on Sami's face as she neared him, his cheeks heating with embarrassment. "Are you hurt?"

"I'm fine." Crosby opened the door at the same time she reached for the knob.

"Crosby."

His chest tightened as much from the sound of his name on her lips as her proximity to him. Her light floral scent was most enticing, and he clenched his jaw at not being able to reach out and feel the softness of her skin.

"We can't keep up like this," she said, her words a whisper near his ear.

The moment he'd been expecting to happen for so long finally landed on his heart.

"I see," he said, his response more of a croak than anything.

Sami's hand reached out and caressed his cheek.

The contact startled him. "You're my best friend and always will be." She entwined her fingers in his, bringing him over to her couch. "Why don't you build a fire while I pour the eggnog?"

The pull of another evening with her was both agony and a source of deep contentment, which won out. "Just nutmeg for me. No alcohol." He'd be driving home to take care of Sundance. "I can't stay long."

"Long enough, though, for us to clear the air." Sami headed toward her small kitchenette.

Crosby stacked two logs in her fireplace, added some kindling and then used a long match to start the blaze. The flames were crackling and the atmosphere cozy when she returned with two holiday mugs, one bright red and the other green. She handed him the red one. "Eggnog-lite."

He thanked her and then sipped the creamy liquid. The warmth of the fire, along with the scene, made him long for more nights like this one with Sami by his side.

Sami approached her turquoise sofa where a blanket with five gnomes and the slogan "Gnome for the Holidays" scrolled in red rested on the arm. She moved the multitude of gnome throw pillows onto the floor and sat in the middle. Finding nowhere else to sit, Crosby settled on the couch as far away from her as possible, taking care not to spill any of the eggnog.

He raised his mug toward the fir and nodded. "Beautiful tree."

"Crosby." His name practically came out as a growl. "What's happening between us?"

Absolutely nothing, but that wasn't her fault. He stared at the mug of eggnog as though it was the most fascinating thing on earth when, in actuality, that was the person sitting next to him.

Maybe the best way to settle everything was to be honest with her. Tell her about how he'd fallen for her and let the chips fall wherever they landed.

And yet? The thought of making Christmas awkward for her, Amanda and Seth and all the Virtues stopped him. He set the mug on the coffee table and faced her. "We almost kissed earlier, and that scared me."

Sami placed her mug next to his and reached for his hands, holding them in hers. "Then we should do something about that."

She leaned toward him until there was less than an inch of space between them. Her gaze met his, and she nodded. He closed the distance and inhaled her light floral scent before their lips met in a kiss that seemed inevitable. It was everything he'd wanted, and more. It was like the best stories, the ones that captured real life and all the emotions of home and everything good in the world. The kiss deepened, and he unlocked his hands from hers, entwining them in her hair. The strands were as silky as they looked. Everything faded away except Sami and home and forever.

Except she wasn't staying.

With reluctance, he broke the contact and moved away from her. Her lips were red and plump, and her hair was mussed. She was always beautiful, but now? She was exquisite.

"Sami..." The word escaped his mouth, and he despised the plaintive plea that it seemed to contain.

She placed her finger on his lips. "I won't have you ruining this moment." She snuggled against his side and let out a murmur of contentment. "You're my best friend, and that kiss won't change that."

Best friend. Were there any two words that sent arrows through a man's heart more than those? Still, if he had to choose between her not being in his life and having her as a friend, he'd choose friendship every time.

At this moment, Crosby was in the present. Not the past or the future. He watched the flames in the fireplace, happy to be here with her pressed to his side. They fit together perfectly, and he'd been right to be scared about kissing her, for that kiss was everything he'd ever wanted. He was no longer scared of committing to someone out of fear of leaving them too soon.

And having her here in his arms? It was the best feeling and, oddly, the worst combined into one.

What if he offered to go with her on her travels? He immediately dismissed the idea. The Miners' Cottage roof was in a state of disrepair. The upcoming year would keep him busy with supervising those renovations and writing his book. There was no way he could go gallivanting around the world.

He'd always wanted to measure up to his siblings, but once again that wasn't going to be the case. They'd found love at the end of their stories, but his story wasn't going to follow suit.

Sami kept talking, her eyelids drooping, her words faint. Crosby waited until her breaths were regular and even, indicating she'd fallen asleep. With care, he extricated himself from the sofa, covered her with the blanket and headed home.

CHAPTER ELEVEN

CROSBY PERFORMED A final walk-through of the Violet Ridge Thunderbolt on the morning of Christmas Eve. The windows sparkled and the red seat cushions were plump and inviting. He crossed his fingers that everything would be a huge success and the train, once more, became an important community connection. However, Crosby still hadn't found a replacement for Deena.

His head throbbed when he thought about spreading his volunteer staff so thin. Worse yet, Deena had assigned herself multiple tasks, all of which now landed on his plate. At least this gave him a reason to turn down Sami's offer of lunch today. The Thunderbolt and writing his speech and the next chapter of his book were more than enough to keep him busy until New Year's Eve.

He was rather relieved at having an excuse to avoid her. They had shared the most amazing kiss he'd ever experienced and then she declared they were destined to remain best friends. For his heart's sake, he would have to find reasons to stay away from her until Amanda and Seth's wedding.

The sleigh ride! He groaned as that experience was to be his Christmas present to her. The thought of being alone with her on the most romantic experience of all could be a disaster of epic proportions. Then again, with five young children at the ranch on Christmas Day, he could simply fall into his favorite role of being fun Uncle Crosby. They'd love to join him and Sami, and having children with them would ensure there was no repeat kissing encounter.

Problem solved. He pulled out his phone but heard footsteps. He smelled Sami's light floral scent and knew it was her before he even turned around.

"After I saw the 'closed for the holidays' sign at the cottage, I had a feeling you were here." He turned and found Sami standing in the middle of the aisle. "You didn't return my text."

He held up his phone. "I was just about to do that."

She quirked one side of her lips upward. "Are you avoiding me?"

Darn it. She knew him too well. His chest clenched. There was no way around seeing her while she remained in Violet Ridge. "I have work to do."

A shadow crossed her eyes, a flicker of hurt that was gone so fast he must have imagined it.

"You are avoiding me. We won't kiss again so you don't have to worry about it in the future. Since we've settled that, you can take me to lunch."

He opened a window so the slight mustiness would escape. "Deena's sick, and I haven't found someone to take on her role, let alone someone who can fit into her uniform."

Sami furrowed her brow. "I just had a meeting with Daisy, Cassie, Emma and Amanda where we planned Amanda's wedding shower. No one mentioned that you reached out."

Crosby shuffled his feet. "Daisy will be busy with the triplets, and it's Amanda's first Christmas Eve with Seth. I couldn't ruin Seth's evening like that."

Let alone admit to his siblings that he didn't have everything under control. It was bad enough they now adjusted their schedules to accommodate his tendency for tardiness.

"Shouldn't you let them make those decisions for themselves?" Sami folded her arms and stared at him. "You haven't asked me, either."

That kiss was a perfect reason to refrain from asking, but for the sake of the guests, he had to ask her this one question.

"Samantha Willow Fleming," Crosby stated and took a deep bow. "Will you do me the honor of rescuing me once again and fill in for Deena?"

"Certainly, kind sir. The honor would be mine." She curtsied but then grew serious. "We can go to

Timeless Tailors now and see if Deena's uniform fits me. Maybe they'll be able to check on the alterations for my maid of honor dress at the same time, since I'm leaving the day after New Year's."

Crosby's heart thudded. "What do you mean leaving the day after New Year's? I thought you weren't moving to San Diego until after the wedding. That's in February."

Sami stooped down and picked up a few pine needles that had fallen off the garland they'd hung at the decorating party. Then she straightened, a fine mist covering her eyes. "Jeremy put me in contact with a friend of his." She explained about the cruise ship opportunity and her friend Asia's condominium. His insides hollowed. "So, you see, by the time I return you'll be in the thick of the roof renovation. That Miners' Cottage is going to be your whole focus."

He'd had the same thought, yet shock traveled through him. He wobbled and fell into the closest seat, gripping it until his knuckles hurt. Her gaze searched his, almost as though she wanted him to speak up and give her a reason to stay, but that was fanciful thinking on his part. Her actions and words were everything. She was leaving Violet Ridge sooner than he'd thought.

"But you'll come back and visit?" Crosby almost didn't recognize his own voice, all high and garbled. He cleared his throat and took a deep breath. "For Amanda."

"Of course, she's my sister, and she and Seth want a big family. Three children, if possible. Someday, I'll be Aunt Sami, just like you're Uncle Crosby." She grinned. "And I'll be back for Jase and Cassie's wedding, not to mention taking in Jeremy's show whenever I'm in town."

Of course, she'd be coming back for nearly everyone else from Amanda to Jeremy to the entire Virtue family. But then he reconsidered. She'd be coming back to visit him as well.

It took all his resolve but he managed a smile. "I'll have so many stories to tell you about the renovation when you come back. Eventually I'll show you a new-and-improved Miners' Cottage."

She gave him a sly smile. "And maybe introduce me to a special someone."

There it was again. Another reference to finding his Christmas match when there was only one woman who had a claim on his heart.

His heart, though, still sought out a molecule of hope that she might seek out a balance between traveling and him. That love might be a good reason to stay, a reason for him to make a lasting commitment.

Commitment? His heart accelerated at the thought of a lasting relationship. Surely what he felt for her was infatuation, a crush. That's all it could be.

But one look at her, and the truth ripped through him with the force of a blizzard wind. What had started out as infatuation had deepened. He loved Sami, and that wouldn't ever change.

"Don't you think?" she asked, staring straight at him.

Crosby blinked as he returned to the present from the fog he'd found himself in. "Can you repeat that? I was woolgathering."

She laughed. "That's what I love about you, Crosby. You're always thinking about Violet Ridge's past and its stories." Then she pointed to the exit. "We'd best be on our way to the tailor, so you'll have time to take me to lunch."

As he disembarked the train, following her, he clenched his jaw. If only she loved him as more than a friend.

CROSBY HELD THE door of the tailor's shop open for Sami, and she sailed inside. The establishment's warmth enveloped her in a hug, and she glanced at Crosby. In the middle of the night, she'd awakened to find herself still on the couch with the gnome blanket wrapped around her. He'd obviously taken the time to tuck her in before he departed. The moment she realized he had left, something inside her felt empty, like she was missing something.

And that kiss? Who knew staid, old-fashioned Crosby could kiss like that?

Yet that made her more determined than ever to leave right after his speech. She was holding him back, and he deserved love in his life. The romantic kind, not the kind you felt for your best friend. When he'd removed that piece of ice cream cone from her hair the other night, he'd confirmed that was exactly the role she played in his life.

Sami took off her gloves and scarf, jamming them into her coat pockets, and then hung her coat on the rack near the door. A booming laugh came from the next room. It sounded familiar. She investigated and recognized Jeremy standing in front of a full-length mirror.

Jeremy must have seen her and Crosby's reflection in the mirror. He waved enthusiastically at them and then turned around. "Sami and Crosby, come in. You've saved me the trouble of tracking you down."

The tailor warned him to stay in place. Jeremy looked their way in the mirror and shrugged. "Tuxedo fitting for my New Year's Eve concert at the lodge."

Sami was sorry to hear that. "You won't get to hear Crosby's speech."

"You could come to the lodge, Sami." Jeremy moved, and the tailor yanked on his sleeve once more. "It's going to be so much fun."

Sami lamented that she couldn't be in two places at once, but there was no way she'd miss Crosby's speech. "Thanks, but I promised Crosby."

"If you want to be with Jeremy, I understand."

Crosby had joined them but now hung back. "I won't hold you to your promise."

Why did Crosby never want to fight for her? Sometimes his passivity was quite aggravating. Sami kept from sighing and reached for Crosby's arm. "I'm celebrating New Year's Eve with you, Crosby."

Something in the depths of his eyes sizzled. Suddenly, solid, dependable Crosby seemed anything but passive. Her heart skipped a beat, and she ignored the pesky romantic feelings welling within her.

"I have your measurements, Jeremy." The tailor's pronouncement brought Sami out of her trance. "Crosby, you're next."

Jeremy stepped off the stand and asked them to wait there. A minute later, he returned with an envelope. "Here are the ski passes I promised you, and I checked the showtime. I might be able to come on New Year's Eve after all."

"That's great! And thank you." She faced Crosby and thumped the envelope against his chest. For some reason, the sheer solidness surprised her even though she always felt its firmness whenever they hugged. It was like she was seeing him in a new light this holiday season. "I haven't forgotten the makeover. Specifically, that special something designed to prepare you for anything that might catch you off guard when you're giving your speech. Skiing fits the bill."

"Since you just told me what the mystery factor is, it's not spontaneous, is it?" Crosby asked, that wry tone, which she loved so much, back for the first time in ages.

"Maybe, maybe not." She shrugged. "I stand by the gist of it. Sometimes life throws unexpected curveballs, and we need to be ready for them."

Crosby slipped the envelope in his pocket and thanked Jeremy. "I've never skied at this resort before. Are you working on Christmas as well?"

Jeremy shook his head. "It's just Aunt Marilyn and me. I'm glad I'm here so Aunt Marilyn won't be alone, especially as we're about to find out after the holidays whether she's in remission."

Sami swept Jeremy into her arms and gave him a hug before releasing him. "You're such a good nephew." She gasped. "I have a marvelous idea. Why don't you and your aunt join Amanda and me at the Lazy River on Christmas morning? Two more will only add to the fun." Sami raised her fingernail to her lips. Once again she had let her impulsiveness overrun her manners. "Would that be okay with your family?"

Before Crosby could answer, the tailor approached him and tapped his watch. Crosby nodded, whether at her or the tailor, Sami wasn't quite sure, but she'd take that as a yes to all of her ideas. Sami shifted to the hallway with Jeremy and conveyed more details.

With Jeremy around, Sami would have a reason to concentrate on something other than these pesky romantic feelings for Crosby that were growing stronger every time she saw him. Jeremy was exactly what she needed on Christmas Day.

CHAPTER TWELVE

IN THE AUDITORIUM of the Holly Theater, the actors took their bows following the best version of *The Santa Who Forgot Christmas* yet. Pride for his nieces and nephew almost exploded out of Crosby's chest, and his hands tingled from clapping so hard. He raised his fingers to his lips and let out a wolf whistle to Rosie's delight. She winked right at him, her grin charming. The curtain closed, and the audience began milling in the aisles.

This year's Christmas Eve production was just what Crosby had needed for his holiday spirit to blossom. It had withered after Sami's surprise announcement about her earlier-than-planned departure. But for the next while, he intended on concentrating on his family and living in the present, especially for tonight's train ride. He banished away thoughts of roof repairs or historical preservation society red tape.

Crosby glanced at Ben and Daisy, who were still beaming. His sister retrieved her purse from under her chair before turning her attention to other members of the Virtue family who had taken up two entire rows of seats.

"You're invited back to our house for cookies and eggnog," Daisy said. "Our house is big enough for everyone, which is yet another advantage of marrying this handsome man."

His sister joined hands with her husband.

Over the roar of acceptances, Crosby declined. As much as he would love to join in the celebration, he still had too much work for the Violet Ridge Thunderbolt train kickoff later this evening.

"You'll have to excuse me. I need to go backstage and talk to Teddy Krengle." Crosby produced a small tote bag with flowers peeking out the top. He handed the bag to Daisy. "Please give these bouquets to the triplets. They're small tokens for doing such a great job in the pageant."

Daisy hugged Crosby, and he relished the contact. Separating from him, Daisy briefly touched his shoulder. "They'll miss their uncle at the party, but they're looking forward to tonight," Daisy said.

Ben and Daisy scooted out of the aisle and headed backstage. Grandma Bridget stopped in front of Crosby and patted his cheek. "Don't work too hard. Everything will come together."

When Grandma Bridget turned to go, Grandpa Martin handed her cane to her. He kissed her cheek before they took their leave. Seth helped Amanda with her coat and whispered something in her ear while Jase did the same for Cassie. Penny and Easton were practically jumping up and down with excitement for Daisy's party.

Sami looked at her phone and scampered out of the aisle. "Look at the time. I have to go."

Jealousy skittered through Crosby. While he'd been occupied with the tailor, Sami had talked to Jeremy for quite some time in the hallway before she had returned. No doubt she was meeting the handsome crooner and spending time with him before she left town. He watched her leave.

To Crosby's surprise, both his brothers remained behind. Soon they were the only people in the auditorium.

Seth tapped Crosby's shoulder. "We have to talk."

"Can't it wait until tomorrow? I'll be at the ranch all day," Crosby said.

Seth shook his head and folded his coat over his arm. "Look. I understand. I've been in your shoes."

Crosby groaned. If Seth saw how lovesick he was, had everyone? Crosby might as well take out an advertisement on the front page of the *Violet Ridge Gazette*. As much as Crosby wished his story would have had a similar outcome to those of his siblings, all of whom had found love, it wasn't meant to be for him.

For too long, he thought he had to compete against them in almost every way. Now, he not only saw the futility in that, but he wanted what they had: love. Seth had found someone who grounded him and reminded him of how the ranch was a family. Daisy had found love, not once but twice, with Ben coming into her life after her beloved first husband's death. And Jase? Cassie was truly his better half as she had brought him back to his family.

Thank goodness they were all his friends. Having their support come January would be a good thing. But for now, Crosby wanted to get to work. "Your situation is nothing like mine."

Seth patted Crosby on the back. "Take it from me. It's exactly the same."

Except no one would be playing matchmaker for him the way he and Sami had done for Seth and Amanda. After seeing that Seth and Amanda were each other's perfect match, he and Sami hadn't been about to let them go on with their lives, miserable without the other. Last spring's road trip to Phoenix and back to help the couple get back together had been such fun.

Crosby delivered a wry smile. "I'm fine. I just have to get through today."

Seth laid his hand on Crosby's shoulders until Crosby met his gaze. "I know I haven't always protected you. I was concerned about Jase after Mom and Dad died and didn't look out for you like I should have." Some of Crosby's earliest memories revolved around Jase's leg surgeries after the accident. "But here's some brotherly advice. Working around the clock isn't healthy in the long run."

Crosby let out a deep breath, relieved that Seth was only worried that Crosby was on his way to becoming preoccupied with his writing and the Miners' Cottage. He hadn't guessed his secret after all.

"I couldn't ask for a better oldest brother." He looked over Seth's shoulder at Jase. "Or older brother. Neither of you has to trouble yourself about me. I love my work, but it's only one part of me."

Seth nodded and took his leave. Jase moved until he was parallel to Crosby. "Now that I'm back in the family fold, I consider it my duty to be there for you, Seth and Daisy."

Crosby's throat clenched as he remembered how Jase had distanced himself from his siblings, believing he'd been at fault for their parents' fatal crash, which had truly been a tragic accident and nothing more. "And now you have Cassie, Penny and Easton to add to that list. They're probably waiting for you."

Jase raised an eyebrow, and Crosby had the sudden feeling he was the one being interrogated. He stopped from squirming and instead changed direction to exit the row on the other side.

"Seth knows about your feelings for Sami. So do I." Jase's words halted Crosby in his tracks.

Crosby returned to Jase's side and searched his gaze. Jase was a qualified and decorated detective. As such, his eyes gave no hint of the meaning behind his statement. "Sure, I have feelings for her. She's my best friend."

"It goes deeper than that. You're in love with Sami." The tic in Jase's jaw emerged. "And you're going to let her go without telling her how you feel."

Crosby should have known nothing would get by his brothers. "You're right on both accounts, but her mother controlled her future for so long that I won't do the same by holding her back from reaching for her dreams."

Jase frowned. "If you don't talk to her, you won't know if she feels the same."

Crosby stood his ground. "From everything she's done and said, I know my feelings are one-sided. If she's told me once, she's told me a hundred times. I'm her *best friend*. Nothing more."

Jase shifted to face Crosby and looked him in the eye. "One of the most important tenets we learn early at the academy is to search beneath the surface. The reason we ask multiple witnesses for each of their observations is that no two people see things in the same way. Talk to her."

It wasn't lost on Crosby how his family had

come together this year. It was nice to know Jase had his back.

"I'll take your advice under advisement." Crosby started walking.

"One more thing," Jase said, causing Crosby to stop. "What if Sami *is* in love with you? There's been something different about her recently, and it might be that she's noticed what we already love about you—that behind the tardiness and clumsiness, there's a smart, compassionate man with a heart of gold, devoted to his family and town."

Crosby would like nothing more than to believe Jase, one of the most astute men he'd ever known.

But Sami was leaving the day after his speech.

In this case, actions spoke louder than words.

WITH A MERE three hours until everyone had to leave for the train depot, Sami gathered the five female volunteers in the Porcupine Suite. "Thank you for giving up your afternoon on Christmas Eve so we can surprise Crosby and make tonight even more memorable."

Nelda clapped her hands and held up a tin. "We're not giving up anything—"

"Because this is going to be a party." Zelda completed her twin's sentence and brought out another tin, opening it to reveal jam thumbprint cookies whereas Nelda's contained slices of thick gingerbread. Delicious smells combined with the fresh pine scent of Sami's tree to give off serious holiday vibes.

Christmas music played in the background as Sami got to work, styling the volunteers' hair so it would match their uniforms. Zelda would be covering her green pixie cut with a wig, which Sami had set last night.

The volunteers changed into their costumes, and then Sami applied satiny foundation, natural blush and red lipstick to complete the vintage look.

She finished her slice of tasty gingerbread before contouring her own eyebrows and used liquid eyeliner on her upper lashes for her own unique look. Moments later, she gazed at her reflection in the mirror and found the present merging with the past. No wonder Crosby loved history with such a fervor.

Sami noticed how well the '40s-style waves complemented everyone's makeup and outfits. Zelda and Nelda oohed and aahed at each other. If it weren't for Zelda's uniform being bright blue and Nelda's a cherry red, Sami wouldn't have been able to tell them apart with their matching hairstyles. The other women gathered and expressed their delight at the transformations.

"You simply have to do this more often, Sami," Nelda exclaimed, checking herself out in a handheld mirror.

"In the spring," Zelda said, nodding her approval. "We're hosting a theme party at the seniors' living facility to raise money for Cassie's garden."

The party was for such a good cause that Sami didn't have the heart to tell Zelda she'd have to find someone else as Sami would be long gone by spring. Her stomach clenched at the thought of missing out on the blooms where Cassie had started a gardening project for seniors. Speaking of Cassie, her children were growing up so fast. She wouldn't see them or Daisy's triplets very often. They might even forget her. She'd miss that and so much more if she left town.

Did she have to leave Violet Ridge to follow her dreams of seeing the world? Could this town be her port?

Before long, they piled into their respective cars and traveled to the train depot. On the short trip, Sami blared her favorite Christmas songs and couldn't wait to see Crosby's reaction to her surprise. A glimpse of the train depot was most invigorating. Sami emerged from her car. Light fluffy snowflakes landed on her eyelashes. She took a moment and let the beauty sweep over her. This would be the first time she'd ever celebrated a white Christmas. Thankfully, the train had a snowplow so it would still be able to operate tonight.

She waited for the other volunteers before heading toward the platform where Crosby was pacing. Worry creased his brow, and then he caught sight of the group.

His jaw dropped, and Sami stayed back, glowing with pride at his look of amazement.

Sami couldn't hold back any longer and hurried toward him. "Like it?" she asked, swinging around in a circle for him.

"More than you could ever imagine." His smile broadened and Sami's heart skipped a beat. Maybe more. "I didn't think anything could make this night more special, but I was wrong. You organized this for the ladies and did everything? Thank you."

His gaze locked on her, and Sami wished for a second that she could kiss him, the bond that strong between them just then. But the volunteers crowded Crosby, and the moment passed before everyone went to their stations.

Soon after, passengers started arriving and began a queue. Sami punched tickets, watching as they boarded with grins and gasps of appreciation for what awaited them.

Amanda presented her ticket and fawned over Sami's hairstyle before noticing the others. "So this was where you were all afternoon. You did a fabulous job."

Sami downplayed her role. "The real credit goes to Crosby. Do you know he was the driving force into making this happen?"

Sami launched into an explanation of how the

train had been rusting away until Crosby worked diligently, convincing engineers to visit Violet Ridge, and applying for grants before approaching the prominent Irwin family for funding. Gordon had become the key sponsor, but income from the ticket sales would help the train support itself. Over the past five years, so many people had come together to return the Violet Ridge Thunderbolt to its glory days. Now it sparkled and shined. Sami felt like she belonged truly here, and not just as Amanda's sister or Crosby's best friend.

Amanda placed her hand on Sami's arm. "I've heard that story about ten times from Seth."

Sami blushed. "Why didn't you stop me?"

"I wanted to hear you tell it to me. It says all I needed to know."

The next person waved their ticket, and Amanda moved on before Sami could ask her to explain her ambiguous comment. Sami punched the ticket while guests settled into their seats. The train's whistle blew a merry toot-toot that promised fun and adventure waiting around the next turn. She bustled down the aisle as Crosby closed the doors. The wheels began turning, and the train set off down the track.

A cheer erupted in the carriage. Sami snuck a peek at Crosby, who was observing the crowd enjoying themselves. His gaze met hers, and she was struck at how his eyes were glistening. Suddenly, electricity filled the air, but someone called Crosby's name. He sent her a smile and attended to that passenger before announcing the arrival of a special visitor from the North Pole.

Santa appeared with a mighty "Ho ho ho!" and began distributing bells and candy canes to all onboard.

After Santa made his rounds, Crosby led the passengers in a round of Christmas carols. No sooner than the last chord of "Jingle Bells" echoed in the rail car than they arrived at their stop in Gunnison. Sami followed everyone else getting off the train for some shopping and sightseeing. She passed Crosby, who was talking to the engineer.

The next hour flew by as Sami relished spending time with Amanda and the Virtue family. When they returned to the depot, Sami hurried to the other car and found the refreshments ready to serve on the return trip.

Once the train was underway again, Sami started helping Nelda and Zelda serve hot chocolate and apple cider.

Rolling her cart along the aisle, Sami had to stop at one row that was halfway to the front of the train car. Her heart melted at the sight of a little boy snuggled up against his father, asleep and most likely dreaming of Santa's impending visit. The boy's mother accepted a glass of cider for herself and one for her husband, thanking Sami with a whisper.

Sami moved on to the next row but glanced back at that sweet sight once more. She could see Crosby being that type of dad who'd welcome cuddles with his little ones, most unlike her father, who was always complaining about his circumstances and refusing any comfort from his daughters.

She pushed away the memory and focused on this happy time. At this next row, an older married couple had their hands interlocked while staring out the window at the swirling snowflakes. Their joy at a white Christmas and with each other was evident. While she didn't know how long they'd been together, their commitment touched something within her. She wanted that for her and Crosby.

Sami interrupted them and served them hot chocolate, and they thanked her for the treat.

Sami rolled the cart to the next row and saw Crosby talking with Daisy and Lily while Ben sat on the opposite side with Aspen and Rosie. Crosby stood, and she noticed how dashing he looked in his conductor's uniform. Everyone on the train was wearing their holiday finest, but Crosby stood out from all of them. "Crosby Virtue!" Mr. Hawk's reedy voice came from the next row. "I've been trying to talk to you since I got here. I have a bone to pick with you."

Crosby slipped around Sami's cart and deposited himself beside the older man and his daughter. "Merry Christmas Eve, Mr. Hawk." Crosby waved his arm about the cabin. "Maybe this could wait until after the holidays."

"Nonsense. If something needs to be said, it should be said in the moment." Mr. Hawk punctuated his words with an emphatic nod.

"Dad..."

"Let me speak, Enola." Mr. Hawk faced Crosby.

Sami thrust a cup of hot chocolate toward Mr. Hawk. "Here's a hot beverage for you, Mr. Hawk."

She brandished a can of whipped topping, hoping Mr. Hawk would get the hint and not ruin Crosby's special night.

"In a minute." Mr. Hawk dismissed Sami and focused on Crosby once more. "Seventy years ago on Christmas Eve, I rode this same train, and the cushions were, in fact, blue, but no matter. I thought nothing would ever live up to the memory of that experience, but I was wrong. This train needed a little TLC and you've brought her to life again. You did good."

"Thank you, Mr. Hawk." Crosby's voice was thick with emotion. "Coming from you, that means a great deal."

Crosby started to rise, but Mr. Hawk was having none of that. "Tell me about the engine specifications and have some hot cocoa that Sami seems so excited about."

Sami echoed Mr. Hawk's sentiment. Except for taking time for the play and for her makeover, Crosby had been working hard this season. Five minutes in one spot wouldn't hurt him. She handed Crosby a cup of hot chocolate and added an extra squirt of whipped cream, not bothering to wait for a yes or no to the extra topping.

Soon, everyone was laughing, talking and swapping stories, and Sami accompanied Nelda and Zelda to the kitchen car where they stowed the carts. Not long thereafter, the train pulled into the Violet Ridge depot. Crosby assumed his place at the front, wishing the crowd a Merry Christmas. Everyone filed past him and accepted a flyer for an Easter extravaganza. Mr. Hawk thumped Crosby on the back, and Sami saw the bashful smile Enola gave Crosby. Sami resisted the urge to claim Crosby on the spot. Instead, she focused on Mr. Grosvenor carrying away his sleeping preschooler. As the pair passed, the little girl mumbled that at home they had to leave cookies for Santa and carrots for the reindeer.

Minutes later, she and Crosby were the only ones left on the train.

"Who's on the cleanup crew?" Sami asked.

"Deena. Since she's sick, I'm now in charge." Crosby rubbed the back of his neck and groaned. His gaze traveled over her and landed on her face. "Somehow, you still look as fresh and beautiful as the minute you stepped onto the depot platform."

Her heart thumped, and she flipped her hair to her back. "Thank you, kind sir." Then she grew serious. "Why didn't you ask anyone to help with the cleanup?"

"It's Christmas Eve. Ben and Daisy have the triplets. Jase and Cassie have Penny and Easton, and Seth and Amanda are looking out for Grandma and Grandpa." Crosby motioned toward the aisle, and she followed him to the other car where he donned latex gloves and retrieved a trash bag.

Sami blocked his path back to the main car at the connecting door. "Why didn't you ask me?"

A shadow flitted across his face. "I assumed you would be busy with Jeremy."

"You assumed wrong." Sami went over and plucked out two latex gloves from the box.

"Don't you get it? I can't depend on you bailing me out all the time." His words were controlled yet it might have been the most emotion she'd ever heard in his voice.

The tension was thick between them. Sami's eyes grew wide as his attitude made it clear how aware he was of her impending departure.

Her mouth grew dry, and the gloves were still in her hands. What did he want from her? For her to stay? He'd never vocalized his feelings, and Asia was depending on her as was Mario, the HR director.

Sami looked down at the gloves so she wouldn't

see the anguish in his eyes, the same that gripped her heart. "I'm not bailing you out. That would imply you're underwater so deep that you need rescuing, which is the furthest thing from the truth." Her fingers were trembling, and she donned the gloves to calm them. "That's what friends are for. To be there for one another."

His eyes blazed, and he opened his mouth. Shaking his head, he just sighed and departed for the main car.

Sami followed him and started stuffing bells, and used cups into the trash bag. Working in tandem, they finished in no time.

Crosby held up a pair of sunglasses and a scarf. "I'll put these in the lost-and-found box. Do you have anything to add?" She shook her head and he continued, "We can stop for the night. I'll finish the rest on the twenty-sixth."

She peeled off her gloves and stuffed them in the trash bag. "That's the next day of Operation Crosby 2.0. We're going shopping during the after-Christmas sales."

He groaned and fell into a seat, closing his eyes. That was her Crosby, so focused on tonight, wanting to make sure everyone had a Christmas Eve to remember, that he probably hadn't slept for the past few nights. Exhaustion poured out of him, and she'd stay all night if it would help him.

She settled beside him and nudged his side. "I'll cut you some slack." Especially since he'd just given her and Mr. Hawk an adventure they'd never forget. "We'll go later in the afternoon so you can sleep in that morning."

Crosby opened his eyes, the corner of his mouth crooking upward. "Nope. Can't. I have to work on my speech and the next chapter of my book."

She poked his chest. "You haven't finished your speech yet?"

"I work best on a deadline. I wrote most of my dissertation the week before it was due."

"I can't believe that. The way you describe Colorado in the late pioneer days was so eloquent." She stopped before she let anything else slip.

"Why, Ms. Fleming." This time he gave a slow smile, full of charm and mischief. "Have you read my dissertation?"

She fidgeted with the edge of the navy uniform jacket. "I couldn't sleep one night and started reading. Little did I know it would keep me awake." She'd been enthralled at how he took the dry events of the miners' everyday lives and made them come alive. "You didn't answer my question, though. Why did you write your dissertation in a week?"

He took his time removing his gloves and dumping them into his trash bag. "I had trouble balancing everything by myself. I was already in the thick of the train restoration and taking over at the Miners' Cottage when Mr. Hinshaw retired.

Everyone loved him, and it was hard to convince people to try a new way of doing something."

"So you felt pulled at all ends?" Sami's stomach clenched as she understood that feeling too well. This growing fissure within her between Violet Ridge and San Diego was tearing her apart.

He nodded. "Then I did a one-eighty and insulated myself to the point I didn't know that Seth needed so much help at the dude ranch or about its precarious financial state." He took off his conductor's cap and laid it on the other side of the seat. "Or how much help Daisy needed with the triplets."

Crosby sighed. "I'm glad she fell in love with Ben, and he adores her."

Yet Sami could see the regret in Crosby's face that he'd been so preoccupied with his life to the point where he'd lost touch with his siblings. Would Sami have that same regret if she started traveling? What if she became so preoccupied with her life and years had passed by before she visited again?

"But you seem closer to them now than when I arrived."

"We've worked at our relationships. I'll let you in on a secret. For a long time, I felt like I had to compete with them and prove myself. Now I'm beginning to find out they accept me for me." Crosby stretched against the seat. "Is there any cider or cocoa left?"

Sami rose and did some stretches of her own. "Only one way to find out."

They set forth for the kitchen car where they spotted a couple of steel pitchers still warm with apple cider or hot chocolate. Crosby held one in front of Sami. "Shall I pour?"

Sami nodded and found two unused cups.

"Hello? Is anyone still here?" a voice called out from the other car.

Crosby quit pouring, set the pitcher on the counter and together they went to investigate.

Did her eyes deceive her? It looked like Santa himself was searching for something. Santa straightened and Sami recognized Teddy Krengle.

"Did anyone find a wallet?" Teddy asked, alarm registering on his plump face.

Crosby crossed over to the lost-and-found box and listed its contents aloud. "No wallet."

Teddy remained crestfallen, and it seemed wrong to see Santa's shoulders slumped like that.

"Hold on. We haven't cleaned the bathroom in the refreshment car." Sami rushed to the other car and returned a minute later, triumphantly holding the wallet aloft. "I found it!"

She handed Teddy his wallet. Teddy clutched it to his chest before he relaxed. "Thank you, Sami! Ho ho ho! Merry Christmas."

It was as if all was right with the world. For the next couple of days, it wasn't important about where she landed or where she'd spend next spring. This time with Crosby by her side was where she needed to be. Wanted to be.

Until New Year's, there was no reason to make any decisions heavier than what color suited Crosby best. Although she already knew the answer to that: anything in a shade of oatmeal would offset his brownish blond hair and dark eyes best.

Santa, for it was hard to think of him as Teddy while he was in costume, started to leave and then returned to them, a pair of candy canes in hand. "For the both of you."

After Santa departed, Crosby stuffed the candy cane in his pocket. "The drinks are probably cold by now. I'd best collect the trash bags and finish up. That will take a couple of minutes, but I can walk you to your car afterward." He started moving toward the kitchen car and paused. "Unless you need to leave now."

"I love chocolate, hot, cold or otherwise. I'm good with it." Sami wouldn't let him deflate her holiday spirit that easily.

She followed him to the refreshment car where they sipped the cold cocoa. Sami decided hers needed a boost so she crushed the candy cane from Santa into her drink, urging Crosby to do the same. She giggled at the satisfied expression on his face.

They finished their treat, completed their last tasks and, together, they headed for the main car, where they stepped out onto the platform. Big fluffy snowflakes were falling from the sky. Sami closed her eyes to capture the magical memory forever. She opened them again. Carefully, she twirled in a big circle so she could feel the cold breeze on her cheeks and inhale the fresh mountain air.

"This is your first white Christmas, isn't it?" Crosby waited until she stood still. "You'll love my surprise. Be ready around eight tomorrow morning. In the meantime, text me tonight when you get back to the ranch, no matter how late."

If anyone else had muttered those words, she might have bristled, but not Crosby after a car accident had claimed his parents' lives. She realized he was staring at her.

With the same expression that Seth had whenever he looked at Amanda and thought no one was paying any attention to him.

She closed the distance to him, right there on the platform. Crosby was slightly rumpled and had a cocoa stain on his navy conductor's jacket, but that was only the surface of a man who cared so much for this community. Cared for his siblings.

Cared for her.

"Kiss me, Crosby."

He was about to peck her cheek when she placed her gloved hands on the sides of his face and pulled him in for a real kiss. Snowflakes fluttered around them, but she only felt the warmth of his breath on her cheeks. Everything for the past six and a half months had led to this minute.

The kiss captured the spirit of the season but so much more, and she was captivated by the stubble on his cheek, the peppermint taste of him, the firmness of his arms. He felt like forever.

Forever.

That was such a long time and had such a heavy weight. They separated. Crosby pulled out his pocket watch and glanced at it while the nearby antique lamppost bathed him in a soft glow. "It's past midnight. Merry Christmas, Sami."

Anticipation welled in her at the prospect of finding out what experience Crosby had planned for them later today.

"Merry Christmas, Crosby."

CHAPTER THIRTEEN

CROSBY HAD ALREADY had quite a morning, wishing Sundance a Merry Christmas while giving him his favorite dandelions with his breakfast and sprucing up his terrarium before driving to the ranch. Arriving at the ranch, he headed to the main lodge and wished his grandparents a Merry Christmas. Everyone else was arriving later, so Crosby moved on to the stable. He was thankful for Grandma Bridget's many lessons on how to tack horses. Seemed as though she'd taught him so much that he was only now understanding.

With gratitude, Crosby began to prepare the pair of Percherons for Sami's special sleigh ride. As for the sleigh itself, it was made especially for today. Crosby had done his research and had been pleased with the result, which sat not far from here in another barn underneath a tarp. He'd informed Seth and the family that he intended to leave it at the ranch for them and their guests to use.

Crosby greeted Branwen and Cairn and straightened his cowboy hat. Both lived up to their names as Branwen had a rich dark coat and a striking presence while Cairn was as sturdy as the stones along the path that he and Sami would be taking for their ride. Crosby took a moment to appreciate the stillness of the crisp white morning. Then he brought the pair of horses to attach to the sleigh and added jingle bells to the handsome pair and drove along toward the main lodge.

As he neared the building, Crosby started having second thoughts about taking Sami on a sleigh ride. Last night's kiss was breathtaking, and he'd give anything to repeat the experience, but he couldn't. He didn't want her to think he was open to possibly risking their friendship for something more. He just wanted to give her an unforgettable present, something to make the holiday merry and bright.

Just like her.

With his resolve to keep today light and happy, he arrived at the entrance. Could he leave the horses long enough to personally get Sami and escort her outside? Perhaps a text would be better. To his dismay, she had silenced all notifications. He glanced at Cairn and Branwen and realized he could tether them to a post not far away. The horses couldn't, and wouldn't, go anywhere in the five minutes it would take him to find Sami and return downstairs. After all, it was ten minutes past eight, and she should be in the lobby by now.

He searched the lobby, but Sami wasn't there. With a last glance at the horses, he took the stairs two at a time. Standing outside her door, he noted he was breathless and excited. He'd been waiting for this for months. He knocked and stepped back, expecting her to answer right away, but she didn't.

He rapped again, louder this time. He was about to go check the rest of the lodge when she opened her door, adorably rumpled with sleep. Her blond hair was mussed, her cheeks still rosy red.

"I thought you said around eight." Sami yawned and rubbed her eyes. "You're too early."

Even her voice still held the last slumbers of dreamland.

"I'm on time." He checked his watch. "Oh, right. I forgot I set it ahead by half an hour. Sorry about that. But, Merry Christmas, Sami! Your chariot awaits. Make sure you wear something warm."

Crosby reached the ground floor when his grandparents pulled him into the dining hall over his objections. His grandmother insisted it wouldn't take long, calming his fear about the horses. "The worst that could happen is that they head back to the stable. Besides, you'll need something warm to drink on the ride."

He relaxed and entered the dining hall where a number of guests recognized him as the conductor who had organized last night's train ride. He grew uncomfortable as a couple thanked him for such a lovely holiday getaway. To his dismay, he found himself unable to extricate himself politely from the conversation. The older gentleman asked him about the train's history, and Crosby found his comfort zone offering an answer.

Minutes passed and Crosby looked up to find Sami standing in the doorway, wearing her pristine white coat, matched with a red-and-green-plaid holiday scarf. Her blond hair, tucked under a fashionable red woolen beanie, was curlier than usual and cascaded past her shoulders. Her makeup was expertly applied, and her blue gaze searched the room until she found him. Her beautiful smile lit up the space and took the wind out of him.

She made her way over to him and linked her arm in his. "Excuse me, but Crosby has promised me a morning to cherish."

His grandmother gasped and his grandfather patted him on the back. "We'll be waiting for the good news."

His grandfather sounded funny, but Crosby let it go. He and Sami exited the dining room before he realized he hadn't brought her anything to drink. "I meant to get you something warm for the adventure."

Sami brushed away his concern. "There will be coffee here after whatever you have planned for us. What is it?"

He couldn't hold back any longer. "A sleigh

ride. Cairn and Branwen will be escorting the most lovely lady around the ranch on this most glorious Christmas morning."

He meant every word. She was beautiful, inside and out. She'd given up hours and hours to make the train ride that much more memorable and special not just for him, but for all the passengers.

Crosby tugged her through the lodge entrance and waited for her gasp. Instead, he was the one who gasped as the horses were gone!

Where were they? Crosby scanned the area until his gaze landed on a runaway sleigh in the distance. He sprinted toward it, but a man in a slick black parka dropped his packages on the ground and ran after Cairn and Branwen. That man reached the horses first and hopped on the sleigh as if it were nothing to board a moving vehicle. He grabbed the reins as Crosby neared.

The other man was Jeremy Haralson! Of course it was. Out of breath, Crosby reached the sleigh, gasping for air, and thanked Jeremy for his quick action. He bit back a groan. Not a single hair was out of place, and no sweat beaded on Jeremy's forehead, unlike Crosby, whose skin was glistening. Jeremy clicked his tongue and pulled on the reins. Branwen and Cairn came to a complete stop, looking as innocent as a couple of newborn babes.

Jeremy looked down on Crosby from his vantage point in the sleigh. "I presume these are yours?"

Jeremy laughed as if he had delivered a funny joke before executing a perfect dismount from the sleigh as his aunt Marilyn and Sami arrived at the same time.

"Care to join us?" Crosby offered as he boarded the sleigh. Jeremy and his aunt would ensure there was not a single romantic vibe on the sleigh ride.

Sami clapped and cheered. "Oh, Crosby, I love my Christmas present." Then a look of something like alarm crossed over her expressive face, and she turned toward Marilyn. "Please come with us on the sleigh ride?"

The more the merrier on Christmas. To his surprise, Crosby found he really meant it. As much as Crosby wanted to feel some sort of jealousy toward Jeremy, who almost seemed too perfect, he couldn't muster any hard feelings for him. Besides, the Lazy River Dude Ranch was particularly beautiful this time of year with six inches of snow coating the meadows and trails. It would be a shame not to share this beautiful sight with all of them.

"Thank you, dear." Marilyn clutched a present in her hands. "But this Colorado wind is biting right through me. I'd love to see the inside of the lodge and have something warm to drink instead."

Jeremy placed a protective arm around his aunt.

"Let's get you inside." He faced Crosby. "Thanks for the offer, but I need to see to Aunt Marilyn. Besides, I've already serenaded quite a few couples during their proposals. You're on your own today."

Flabbergasted, Crosby watched Jeremy usher his aunt inside the main lodge. Then he tightened his hold on the reins. *Proposal?* His eyes widened as he also remembered the look in his grandmother's eyes along with his grandfather's words. People weren't expecting him to propose to Sami today, were they?

They'd never even gone out on a real date. And there was still the small matter of her moving to another state and—

Sami cleared her throat. He looked over and found her extending her hand toward him. "You said my chariot awaits."

Her eyes gleamed more brightly than all the Christmas lights in Violet Ridge. "Of course, milady."

He reached over and helped her climb the stairs until she cuddled by his side and covered their legs with the blanket he'd stowed for the occasion.

"I'm ready for my Christmas adventure," Sami said.

Any day with her was an adventure. She had changed him from a man who had only looked for experiences in the past to someone who was planning them in the present. Even if this was the only one he'd get to spend with her, this would be the best Christmas yet.

Just when she thought her first white Christmas couldn't get any better, Crosby had planned something this special. The wind on her cheeks was brisk as the horses pulled the sleigh along the snowy landscape. She could barely keep in her seat at how captivating everything was. The clip-clop of the horses' hooves. The plumes of air coming from the horses' mouths. But most of all the man sitting next to her.

Sami wanted, needed to give him something close to this magical experience. "Tomorrow, we'll go downtown and buy you a whole new wardrobe. We'll make sure everything is perfect on you and for you."

Beside her, his body stiffened. He pulled on the reins, bringing the sleigh ride to a stop slowly.

"Sami." He faced her and then pushed his cowboy hat back on his head. "Can we not talk about that today? Especially after..."

His voice trailed off, and he clicked on the reins, calling out praise to the horses. Once again, the sleigh glided over the snow. The sun reflected off the drifts, the sparkles brighter than any diamonds.

"No wonder you love the ranch so much." She changed the subject, pulling her coat belt tighter around her waist. "It's beautiful."

Crosby paid close attention to the horses and their needs. "Even though I live and work in town, this ranch is a part of me."

Something was on his mind, and she didn't think it was his speech or his book. Sami shifted in her seat. In all their time together, Crosby had never left anything unsaid.

Until recently.

That was yet another sign that their kiss had been an abject failure in his mind, although it had been the most wonderful, delectable moment for her. Crosby flicked the reins, but the horses maintained a steady pace, not speeding up at all.

"What were you about to say?" Sami asked, prodding for Crosby to confide in her. The way he used to before she brought up this makeover nonsense. He didn't need her to be authentically himself; he was successful doing that on his own. He was Crosby, and she loved him.

What? Her breath escaped her, and she studied his profile that she knew better than her own. His glasses gave him a slightly nerdy air, but that was what had drawn her to him in the first place. As a friend. She loved him as a friend.

Her inner reassurance brought her heart rate back to its normal rhythm. Something was still wrong, but she couldn't put her finger on what it was. Was it that she was lying to herself? Somewhere during this holiday season her feelings had crossed a line. She wanted something deeper, something real, and yet she also wanted to move to San Diego, meet new people, take on new challenges and have new experiences.

What should she do? The one person who could help her was the one person she couldn't ask.

She didn't have an answer.

Or she didn't want to face the truth. That settling in one place wasn't settling period.

She continued studying Crosby. He let out a puff of breath, a wispy cloud that evaporated in the wind. "I should have stayed with Cairn and Branwen and not been distracted. It's easier to focus without distractions."

Was she a distraction?

Instead of leading him on any more detours, she was determined to get him back on track. Eliminating his anxiety about that speech was her main purpose for boosting his confidence. Helping him find the love of his life was supposed to be a nice side benefit.

But what if she could be the love of his life?

That wasn't to be. Crosby despised change, and he said he would never do anything to jeopardize their friendship. Telling him that she was starting to feel something more between them would be too much change for him. She tamped down her feelings and reached for something less personal.

"How's your speech coming along?" she asked.

"It's stalled. There's so much I want to say about the town and the impact the train had on the area and the ranching community. Did you know its expansion can be traced back to the silver mines?"

She listened, caught up in his story, while the horses continued their steady pace around the ranch and he recalled more details about Violet Ridge, interspersed with anecdotes about the Virtue family.

Soon the stable was in sight. Crosby pulled on the reins until the horses halted. He faced her, his lips forming a thin line. "This was supposed to be about you. Instead, you let me ramble on about history."

"Christmas is about joy and being with the people who mean something to you." Her eyes widened. She had almost let the word *love* slip from her mouth. Thankfully, she had caught herself just in time. "I have good news for you. You just practiced your speech, Crosby. Just say that again and be yourself up there. If so, you'll be a huge hit."

Her gaze lingered on the reins, secure in his strong hands. She remembered the tender way his palms cupped her face.

"I want my family to be proud of me, especially after I endangered Cairn and Branwen today."

She laid her gloved finger over his hands. "Your family is proud of you."

He raised his eyebrow. "They've resorted to telling me the wrong arrival time because I'm always late."

She shrugged. "You're enthusiastic about your

job. Give yourself some credit. You love what you do so much that you get carried away and lose track of time."

Since Sami had lived in Violet Ridge, she found that same joy every time she entered the Porcupine Suite. Every day brought a different customer with a new story. Getting updates from satisfied customers brought her joy. Just yesterday, her former client Betsy, a guest at the ranch earlier this month, had emailed her. A coworker had asked Betsy out but it was still too soon after Mark's death to entertain the offer. She had ended with, "Maybe next year."

What would the next year have in store for her and Crosby?

"We'd best get back to the lodge." Crosby lent a hand for her to disembark. "Everyone's waiting for us."

This was when his tendency to be late played in her favor. "They can wait another couple of minutes." In appreciation for today, she kissed him on his cheek, the slight stubble tickling her lips. "Thank you, Crosby. This has made…"

Before she could express this might have been her favorite experience ever, he let go of the reins and jumped down from the sleigh, pulling her into a tighter embrace. His lips crashed into hers. He smelled of pine and cinnamon and everything about the holidays. She reveled in his sweet taste, pouring a lifetime into this moment.

Crosby meant so much to her. His kindness. His thoughtfulness. His acceptance of her.

That was the best gift of all.

When they separated, the amber flecks in his brown eyes glowed with an intensity that he usually only reserved for his stories.

"Sami…"

She silenced him with another kiss. This wasn't a day for makeovers or long-term decisions. It wasn't about letting anyone down or any type of expectations; it was about living in the moment, something she did so well. That was the gift she wanted to give him today.

After another exceptional kiss, she stepped back. "Now we're late enough to be late, but not so late as to draw attention to ourselves."

Crosby stored the sleigh while she began grooming Cairn and Branwen. Crosby returned, and they worked in perfect harmony. Afterward, they went to the dining hall and enjoyed brunch with his siblings, their families and lodge guests.

After she enjoyed Ingrid's sausage casserole, she found herself at the coffee urn with Bridget. Sami caught the older woman staring at her left hand.

Why would she do that?

We'll be waiting for good news.

Sami gasped. Had Crosby's grandparents been expecting him to propose?

That was a little presumptuous considering

they were only friends and had never even been on a date.

Hadn't they?

What about that road trip to Pueblo? And then there were all of their fun Fridays where each dared the other to do something they'd never done before. But perhaps the moment that meant the most to her was the time he covered her with a blanket in her suite after she'd fallen asleep on him, watching a movie.

She could no longer lie to herself. This wasn't a crush or a mere passing fancy.

Somewhere along the way, she had fallen in love with her best friend. Her insides were shaking like a bowl full of Ingrid's chokecherry jelly.

She was in love with Crosby Virtue.

Her sister approached and filled a cup with hot apple cider. "Sami? Are you okay? You look like you just saw Marley's ghost."

Sami sputtered a sip of her coffee. She reached for a napkin on the nearby table, wiping her chin. It was almost a relief to have the hot liquid burn the inside of her mouth. "Just thinking." She started considering last Christmas when she was sitting in an office waiting to audition. "This is the first time in years I've had Christmas off. No beauty pageants, no traveling, no audition prep."

Amanda recoiled and then hugged Sami. "Mom put so much pressure on you. I'm glad you're here this Christmas."

Sami loved it at the dude ranch, where there was no pressure to be perfect all the time.

But had she projected that onto Crosby?

If so, no wonder he was behaving so strangely toward her. Who wanted to be around someone who wanted to change you? This was it. She had to tell him she loved him just the way he was. Together they could work out something about Asia and Mario. Maybe she could fulfill her contract with large gaps in between cruises, so she could return to Violet Ridge for regular visits.

She excused herself and found Crosby with Lily on his shoulders. His young niece reached for and snatched the last candy cane off the huge Christmas tree. "Thank you, Uncle Crosby! Now I'll have yummy minty hot cocoa like Rosie and Aspen."

Lily scampered away. Sami walked right up to Crosby. "I need to talk to you. Preferably in private."

"Sounds serious. Too much so for Christmas. What about tomorrow, before or after our shopping excursion?"

Crosby delivered a look that could have melted butter. Did he feel the same way about her? Sure, she could wait until tomorrow. Maybe she'd even email Mario and Asia tonight so she could start letting both of them down gently.

Jeremy made a beeline toward Sami and gave

her a dazzling smile. "Can I borrow you to start the sing-along?"

Jeremy reached for her hand and pulled her to the center of the room. From her vantage point, she saw Crosby approach Jeremy's aunt, offering her a cup of hot tea. Together, she and Jeremy led a chorus of Christmas carols, and her soprano blended in perfect harmony with his countertenor.

Afterward, several dude ranch guests came up and congratulated them, complimenting how well they performed as a duo. Jeremy insisted Sami have the lion's share of credit, but she demurred. Just then, Marilyn whispered something to Jeremy, and he wished everyone a Merry Christmas. They took their leave along with the guests. Then Seth and Jase began moving tables to the side while Crosby arranged folding chairs around the tree. Bridget tasked the children with distributing the presents, and Sami was shocked at the number of gifts at her feet.

Gathering all the members of the Virtue family together, Bridget took charge and explained everyone should unwrap one present in order of age, from youngest to oldest. Everyone sorted themselves according to age, and Sami found herself sitting next to Crosby. Fate seemed to be throwing them together this holiday season, and nothing would ever be the same now that she had admitted her true feelings for him.

Sami lost herself in the fun family time where

laughter and merriment reigned during the grand reveals. Even Hap and Trixie joined in and barked with delight at the excitement.

The triplets and Cassie's children were happy with their new toys and admired their new handmade blankets. Sami rubbed the scarf that Bridget had knitted just for her against her cheek. The angora wool was as soft as a kitten, the scarf was much softer than her current scratchy one.

After the last present was unwrapped, Crosby challenged the children to a foosball tournament in the rec center. A cheer erupted, but Sami wasn't sure if that was from his nephew and nieces or their parents.

Sami was about to tag along with them when Seth motioned for her and Amanda to follow him. Her curiosity overcame her desire to spend more time with Crosby.

Seth led her and Amanda into the library, where he handed each of them a wrapped present. Sami glanced at her sister, who shrugged before slipping her fingernail under the tape at one end, whereas Sami ripped off the paper. She found a walnut box carved with a tree on the top, almost identical to Amanda's.

Sami opened the lid and saw a number of her grandmother's Christmas cards. "Ben's brother-in-law's hobby is woodworking. When Grandma Bridget found the cards, I contacted Lucky about special memory boxes for the both of you. Sami's has a tree and Amanda's has a heart engraved on top. They are lined with felt, and there's room for more stuff." Seth tugged at the collar of his sweater as if uncomfortable at this type of sentimental expression.

Sami thanked Seth, her throat tight at such a lovely present. The Virtue family had opened up their hearts to her this holiday season, and she'd never experienced such love and affection. Amanda placed hers on the long table and hugged him while Sami traced the branches of the tree with her finger. Most trees like aspens and oaks had deep roots. Was she forming those types of roots here?

She'd always considered herself as someone who could pick up and go at a minute's notice.

But things seemed different now. What did she want for herself? More to the point, how could she leave all of this behind?

CHAPTER FOURTEEN

CROSBY STARED AT the window display. Larkspur and Linen was the men's clothing store that Valerie Kaminski had recently opened next door to Lavender and Lace, her successful upscale women's boutique. A male mannequin sported a deep red cashmere sweater and black wool pants while reclining next to a Christmas tree. Crosby looked down at the sliver of his chunky beige sweater, visible under his dark green puffer coat. His grandmother had kept a few of his father's clothes and mementos and had given him this sweater on Crosby's eighteenth birthday, saying he had the same lanky frame as his father had at that age.

This sweater was a link to Crosby's past, and he wouldn't part with it for anything.

Sami came running along the street, stopping to throw away a coffee cup in a recycling bin. Then she hurried and joined him.

"I'm surprised you moved up our meeting to the morning." She squinted and stared at him. "I know what you're thinking, and I'm not asking you to give up your favorite sweater."

Was he too set in his ways? Perhaps, but thanks to Sami, he had performed karaoke, went rock climbing and taken a yoga class with seniors.

He wouldn't have done any of that without her. Even once she left town, he vowed to keep stepping outside his comfort zone.

Crosby opened the door for Sami, and Valerie rose from her seat behind the register, looking somewhat surprised that customers had arrived this early.

"Are you returning something?" Valerie asked as she searched their sides for a package or bag. "Wrong size? Wrong color?"

"Crosby is giving the keynote on New Year's Eve." Crosby was taken aback at the pride in Sami's voice. "I want to buy him a new tie for the occasion. But he also needs new sweaters, pants, shirts, socks and whatever else you can think of."

Valerie escorted them to the neckwear table, telling them to come get her if they had any questions. Crosby looked down and scrunched his nose. Then he adjusted his glasses, glad to finally be free of the eyepatch. All the ties looked pretty much the same to him. "Maybe you should choose. You have such a good eye for color. That way it will be easier for both of us. I have to meet with Ben this afternoon to review Dominic's certification for working on historic buildings." Especially given that Gunther's numbers had doubled when confronted about the extent of the renovation.

"No way! It won't take too long. And I have my final fitting for my maid of honor dress at eleven. I thought you might be nice enough to buy me a snack for my effort before that, not that I should be able to eat anything after all the scrumptious food at your grandparents' ranch yesterday," she said, rubbing her stomach. "But Blue Skies only sells their cherry almond Kringle in December."

"Alright, well, we'd better get started." He glanced at a full-length mirror in the corner.

Sami plucked two ties and held them up to Crosby's chin with a critical eye.

"What color is your suit?" she asked.

"Black?" Or was it navy? "Gray?"

Maybe? Probably? Most likely. Who could concentrate on details like the color of a suit when he was stuck on the latest chapter of the book he was writing. Then there was City Hall and expediting Dominic's certification. But all of that took a backseat to Sami leaving soon.

"What about your shirt? White? Black? Light blue?" Sami's voice intruded into his reverie as she rattled off colors at amazing speed.

"Yes" was his one-word response.

She laughed and picked up a bolo tie and a traditional deep red silk tie with diagonal stripes of blue. "Hmm. Which do you like better? Bolo ties or traditional? I'm thinking you should go with a more formal look for the keynote. This one should match almost anything." Sami left his side for a second and returned with a shopping basket. She plucked out a solid black tie off the table and held it against him. "I suggest this as a backup."

Both ties went into the basket. From there, they moved over to the sweaters where she held up a light blue cashmere sweater and an Irish fisherman's knitted sweater, whose color resembled Crosby's favorite oatmeal. "Try these two on, for starters."

Crosby bristled but visited the changing room. It wasn't like he was going to buy either of these. Nothing could take the place of his father's sweater. He donned the oatmeal-colored sweater and paused. The fabric was soft and comfortable, so much so that he sat on the bench in the changing area and started thinking about Sami and the Midnight Express celebration.

Sami's voice surprised him. "Crosby? You've been in there for ten minutes. We're about to send in the fire brigade."

Where had the time gone? He exited the fitting room, the ties and his old sweater in hand. "I was lost in a train of thought."

She chuckled. "That pun is so you, but you might want to change into your own clothes. On second thought, this new look really brings out your eyes. Wear this one out of the store after we pay for it." Then she reached for the tag on the cuff and plucked it off before a deep blush came over her face. "I'm assuming you like it."

"It's much more comfortable than I expected." Sami was right about him needing to update his wardrobe. "In fact, I like this one enough to buy the same style in different colors."

She let out a deep breath that sounded a lot like relief. "I'm glad."

Almost as glad as he was that he could always be truthful with her. Well, except that he'd been holding back lately about how he felt about her. It was time to be open with her because if he let her leave without telling her how he felt? He'd regret that for the rest of his life. But Larkspur and Linen was no place to publicize his feelings for her. The Blue Skies Coffeehouse would be much more amenable to that type of discussion. "Sami..."

Jeremy entered the store, carrying a package. Sami waved hello and Crosby did the same.

"Sami! Crosby!" He stomped the snow from his feet, then rolled his eyes as he approached them. "Aunt Marilyn is wonderful, but she purchased a large when I'm a trim medium."

Of course he was.

Valerie escorted everyone to the register before leaving to find a size substitution for Jeremy's exchange. Sami dropped the basket with Crosby's purchases onto the counter. "Did your aunt enjoy the rest of Christmas Day?" she asked.

"She did, thanks for asking. She was quite tired, though, and had to have a nap in the afternoon. She's having lunch with her best friend so I'm on my own today." He glanced at Sami, then Crosby. "Care to join me at Blue Skies for a cup of good hot java?"

"We were just talking about their Kringle. We'd love to, wouldn't we, Crosby?" Sami accepted for the both of them.

Crosby nodded and pulled out his wallet. "Absolutely."

Jeremy grinned. "I had a few other invites, but I like hanging around with the both of you."

"Just our luck," Crosby muttered to himself.

Sami said something encouraging to Jeremy, while Crosby once again found himself on the periphery.

SAMI WAS STILL determined to help Crosby conquer his fear of public speaking. Being prepared for any last-minute pitfalls was a must, which brought them to the Wilshire Ski Resort.

She exited Crosby's car and took in the sight of the lodge, a mammoth modern glass affair that was the height of opulence.

To her surprise, she preferred the rustic charm of the Lazy River Dude Ranch.

Crosby joined her. He looked different in his ski

pants and jacket. In the past few weeks, there was a new air of confidence about him. She wasn't sure if she was projecting that onto him or not.

He winked at her before launching into a story about the history of the property, his hands gesturing with every word. She smiled. This was the Crosby she loved. The core of him would never change.

There it was again. That funny feeling inside her that was the proof she needed that this was love. The issue was that she had changed while Crosby was still the same wonderful man as always. If she stayed in Violet Ridge, she might slip and reveal these new feelings. Although she supposed she already had by kissing him like that.

Leaving would give her perspective about what she really wanted and allow Crosby a chance to find someone with whom he could build a lifetime of happiness. He deserved that.

Crosby tapped her arm, and she realized he was looking at her with concern. "Sami? You have the funniest expression on your face."

Before she could answer and launch into an explanation, Jeremy beckoned to them to join him in the rental shop, where they were outfitted with goggles, helmets and skis. Back outdoors, Sami turned toward Jeremy. "So, which way to the slopes?"

Jeremy gave her a dazzling smile. "Follow me, you two."

Juggling the skis and poles took a bit of effort, but Sami was proud of herself. She stood at the base of the mountain and said, "This is the last official part of Operation Crosby 2.0." An overwhelming success as far as his posture and projection of confidence were concerned. The true test of the changes, though, would come on New Year's Eve. "As I've mentioned, I've brought you skiing for the first time, so you'll be prepared for any contingency that happens on the night of your speech. It's my first time skiing, too."

"What do you mean? I've skied before."

Sami blinked and recalled their previous conversation. "But you said you've never skied before when Jeremy gave us the ski passes."

"I've never skied at this resort before." Crosby shifted his balance, carefully remaining upright. "Actually, I should have told you that Grandpa Martin is an expert cross-country skier. He taught all four of us how to ski."

She shouldn't have assumed Crosby couldn't ski, not when he lived in Colorado, even though he'd never eaten guacamole until she encouraged him to do so.

Sami then faced Jeremy, who shrugged. "My father won a bronze medal in the slalom. I started skiing when I was three."

Both were experienced skiers, and she was the only one trying something new. "Guess it's the bunny slopes for me. I'll meet you in a couple of hours." Disappointment welled as she had really wanted to do this with Crosby.

Crosby and Jeremy exchanged glances, and Crosby stepped toward Sami. "Grandpa Martin taught me cross-country skiing on flat terrain, but I've never conquered the resort slopes. I'll join you."

"Count me in, too." Jeremy grinned. "I'll be your ski instructor."

"Are you sure?" Even Sami knew how coveted this type of ski pass was. For the pair to give up their time on the slopes to teach her how to ski? Her heart soared as they all started for the beginner area together.

Hours later, she accepted high fives from Jeremy and Crosby at navigating the length of a football field on her skis.

"You did it!" Crosby said.

He hugged her, and she lingered in his embrace. Jeremy pointed toward the ski lift. "There's a basic hill to try, just waiting for us."

"I think I have the hang of it now." Sami held up her pole and smiled. "Let's do it!"

Crosby laughed. "Seems like you're hooked. Too bad you're leaving so soon." He winced as if regretting his words and adjusted his goggles.

It was only a short ride on the lift and soon the three of them were eyeing the bottom of what looked to her like Mount Everest. With seemingly no effort, Crosby and Jeremy began gliding toward the bottom. Keen to catch up to them, she started off too quickly and clattered to a stop, not far from them. She tried to stand but her legs wobbled, and her knees buckled. Sami stayed stuck in the snow.

Jeremy reached her before Crosby. Sami tried to stand again, but putting pressure on her right knee was near impossible.

"Ouch." She rubbed her knee and her gaze went to Crosby, who helped her remove her skis, murmuring words of support.

"This place has a terrific medical wing." Jeremy scooped up Sami as if she was a feather. "Dr. Velasquez is a marvel. You'll love her."

Over her protests, Jeremy carried her to the ski lift while Crosby gathered her poles and skis. Back at the base of the mountain, her cheeks flushed at everyone staring at her and Jeremy since he was carrying her. Once more, she started to lean into Jeremy, but she couldn't. The person she wanted to be by her side was Crosby, not Jeremy. The gentle soul with dark black hair was only a dear friend.

It was the man trailing behind who held her heart.

In the examination room, Jeremy and Crosby crowded around her until Dr. Velasquez, she supposed, entered. To Sami's delight, Jeremy looked smitten with the young doctor, but alas the doctor didn't seem to notice Jeremy in the slightest.

Dr. Velasquez asked the men to leave the room while she examined Sami's knee.

As long as she was here, Sami decided to take action. "I've known Jeremy ever since we met at an acting audition. He landed the gig for that fast-food restaurant and sang its jingle. You know, the really catchy one." Sami hummed a few bars of the famous tune.

Dr. Velasquez wrapped a blood pressure cuff around Sami's arm and nodded. "My daughter sings that at least once a day."

Sami checked the doctor's hands, but they were ring free. Dr. Velasquez took Sami's temperature and then prodded her knee.

"Jeremy is excellent with children." Sami kept up the praise on his behalf. "We were extras in a movie, and he kept the kids entertained between takes."

Dr. Velasquez removed the blood pressure cuff, her demeanor efficient and cool. "Can you bend your knee?"

Sami tried and winced. "Yes, but it hurts."

After removing an ACE bandage from a nearby drawer, Dr. Velasquez wrapped it around Sami's knee and went over care instructions in case of bruising and swelling. "Are you a guest at the lodge or are you a day skier?"

"Just here for the day," Sami answered and Dr. Velasquez called Crosby and Jeremy back into the room.

Dr. Velasquez faced Sami and repeated the instructions and began to leave. Jeremy pocketed his phone and let out a huge whoop of joy. "My aunt! She's in remission."

Jeremy hugged Crosby and then Sami, who winced. Then he hesitated in front of Dr. Velasquez. Sami saw the yearning in his eyes, but he stopped short of hugging her. "My aunt's been undergoing cancer treatments. I'm glad Sami and Crosby were with me in case the news had been different."

Dr. Velasquez paused for a second before she wrote something on a pad, tearing off the piece of paper. Sami went to accept what must be a prescription, only to find Dr. Velasquez handing it to Jeremy. "Since you and Sami are dating, make sure—"

"What?" Sami and Jeremy burst out their protests in unison.

Jeremy's eyes grew big as he implored Sami and Crosby for help.

"I'm leaving for San Diego next week. I'm not dating anyone," Sami confirmed, somewhat hoping for Crosby to contradict her.

But he didn't.

"Oh." Dr. Velasquez gave Sami the prescription and pointed toward the curtain. "I have another patient waiting."

"Harmony... I mean, Dr. Velasquez?" Sami had never heard Jeremy sound so humble, and from her boisterous friend, that was something. "Could we talk sometime? About what I can do to make sure my aunt stays healthy."

Dr. Velasquez hung her stethoscope around her neck and brought out her prescription pad once more. She scribbled on the slip of paper and passed it to Jeremy. "That's my personal cell. Text me, and we'll arrange a time to talk."

"Thank you." Jeremy carefully folded the paper and slipped it into his pocket. "Any chance we could talk tonight after my set?"

"Depends on my daughter." The doctor started for the curtain but continued, "I'll send you information on local caregiver groups. We can also discuss diet and fitness. I have some smoothie recipes that are quite healthy. For everyone."

Jeremy's eyes lit up even more. "Smoothies are my favorite."

Sami exchanged a look with Crosby to stop herself from giggling. It seemed Cupid's arrow had struck successfully. Dr. Velasquez left for her next patient. Meanwhile, Sami flexed her leg and turned toward Jeremy. "I'm so happy for your aunt." And for the prospect of him and Dr. Velasquez as a couple.

"Thank you both for your support," Jeremy said, his grin as broad as the Colorado skyline. "You're the best."

"I think you should ask the doctor to dinner," Sami said.

Jeremy scoffed. "She's the smartest person I know." He blushed and faced Crosby. "Present company excepted."

"Huh?" Crosby glanced at the curtain and then at Jeremy. "Oh! You like Dr. Velasquez."

Jeremy nodded. His phone chimed, and he read the screen. "My aunt is wondering if I can pick her up so she can come to my set tonight. Crosby, can you see Sami home?"

"As if you need to ask."

"And my knee already feels better in this brace." Sami flexed it again and shooed Jeremy away with a flick of her fingers. "Bring your aunt by the ranch tomorrow. I'll give her a facial and some special lotion for her skin."

Jeremy reached for the curtain. "She'd love that."

After he departed, Dr. Velasquez delivered Sami a cane to use for the rest of the day. "Just have Jeremy return it."

Sami tested the cane and blew out a breath. "Good thing you drove."

"Good thing there's no permanent damage." Crosby helped Sami into her coat and positioned her hat on her head. His hand brushed her hair, and he slipped his fingers over the long curly strands. "Seeing as you're leaving in a few days."

They stood there. She didn't move, and neither did he. It was as if they were taking in the other's presence and memorizing every detail. As if Sami didn't have Crosby imprinted in her head and heart already.

A nurse drew back the curtain and came inside the examination area. "I'm glad you're still here. Dr. Velasquez wants you to follow up with your primary care physician if you're having any trouble a week from now."

The moment was over, and they walked to his car. This wasn't how she'd intended this day to go, but it wasn't over yet.

CROSBY GLANCED AT SAMI, sound asleep in the passenger seat. When Sami had fallen and hurt herself, he'd felt his world collapse. Then Jeremy had taken charge, carrying her to the medical unit. For a minute, Crosby had fretted that he'd never be able to measure up to the other man. But he realized he didn't have to measure up to Jeremy or his own siblings or even his grandparents.

He only had to measure up to the standards he set for himself.

He was a pretty nice guy, if he did say so himself. Even so, he breathed a lot easier once Dr. Velasquez had relayed the all clear for Sami.

Crosby didn't want to wake her up, but he'd promised to lend her the book he had just finished reading. Suddenly, she stirred, saving him from having to disturb her.

She wet her lips and looked out the window. "Where are we?"

"Headed to my place, if that's okay with you? I wanted to get you that book. And I've been away longer than expected and I should feed Sundance." His voice held a note of apology.

"Seeing Sundance will do me a world of good." Sami straightened, moving her injured leg slowly. "Did he like his Christmas present from me?"

"He loves our matching hats, and so do I." Crosby wondered about the condition of his place when he'd left it this morning. Housekeeping wasn't one of his strengths. "It's too cold to wait out here. Best you come inside."

"No need to ask me twice. I need to use your bathroom and it's too cold to stay in here without a blanket." She pretended to shiver.

Crosby hurried to help her out of the car. "I should have taken you straight to the ranch. You'll be more comfortable there."

Then he handed her the cane and assisted her inside. "I'm glad you didn't. This way I can ease Amanda into what happened without her hovering around me." He waited until she was done in the bathroom before settling her on his couch, a hand-me-down from the lodge when Seth renovated the lobby. She accepted his offer of water and ibuprofen. "Please bring Sundance out to the living room. I'd love to see him."

Crosby brought his pet iguana for a brief visit, before he returned Sundance to his terrarium. After changing out of his ski gear, he thought about wearing his new sweater but slipped his familiar favorite over his long-sleeve black T-shirt. This was an afternoon for comfort.

Crosby made his way back to the living room, where Sami was snoring on the couch. He fetched one of his grandmother's cozy knitted blankets, trying to be as stealthy as possible while covering Sami.

She opened one eyelid. "I was just resting my eyes."

He still covered her with the blanket. "If your snoring was any indication, you were out cold."

She snorted. "I don't snore."

He raised an eyebrow. "Next time I'll record you so I'll have proof."

The full impact of *next time* crashed into him. She'd be leaving soon unless…

"Sami."

"Crosby."

They smiled at having spoken in unison. He bowed and waved his hand in her direction. "Ladies first."

"Can I put my foot on your coffee table?" He motioned for her to be his guest. "I'm really hungry. Please feed me lunch."

Just then, his stomach grumbled, and they burst out laughing. "With any luck, there'll be something in my cupboard other than cereal."

"You and your cereal," Sami said wistfully.

"But I'm so hungry I'll eat a whole box and be grateful for it."

He handed her the remote for the television and propped her leg on his coffee table, using a couple of his throw pillows. "Can you find a movie for us to watch? You can rest your knee and eat before I take you back to the ranch."

Crosby prepared a makeshift lunch of soup and grilled cheese sandwiches. He added some of the brownies that Ingrid had sent home and carried the full tray into the living room.

Sami rubbed her hands together with glee. "I could get spoiled by this treatment."

He handed her a sandwich and settled next to her, balancing his bowl of soup on his lap. The simple meal was perfect, especially with Sami by his side.

Halfway through the movie, she squirmed and Crosby jumped to his feet. "Do you need another dose of ibuprofen? Ice for your knee?"

He placed another throw pillow under her foot and was about to take away the tray when a single word stopped him cold. "Crosby."

"What do you need?" He wanted to do anything he could to make her comfortable. Happy.

"I'd really love to change." She plucked at her ski pants and two layers of thermal shirts. "This was great for keeping warm on the slope, but if we're going to watch the end of this movie, can I borrow some sweatpants and a shirt?"

Part of him had been hoping she'd say she needed him, but this request was easier to fulfill. A few minutes later, he returned with a pair of folded sweatpants and his college sweatshirt. "They have a drawstring," he said.

While she changed, he popped some popcorn. During the second half of the movie, a romantic suspense, he found it difficult to follow the simple thread of the plot with her so close. After a while, he gave up and simply savored this time with her.

At the point when it looked like the villain would get away with his scheme and foil the romantic relationship, Sami reached for him. "Aren't you scared?" she asked.

"Terrified." Of her leaving. Of falling into the same sedentary lifestyle he'd lived before she arrived in Violet Ridge. Of never committing to anyone like her.

She batted his arm. "You're making fun of me."

"Never." He shrugged and laughed. "Sometimes, a little. When the situation warrants."

Crosby winked at her, eager to keep everything on the same level until she left Violet Ridge. That was the only way to guard his heart. But hadn't he played it safe most of his life? As Mr. Hawk had so wisely mentioned on Christmas Eve, if something needed to be said, the time to say it was now.

"Sami."

"Hold on. I think the hero is about to save the

day." She shivered, and he shrugged out of his sweater, handing it to her. "I can't have the prettiest woman in town turning blue. I want you to have it. It'll look better on you, anyway."

Sami hesitated until he nodded. "But this was your father's." Then she wrapped it around her and rubbed her face against the collar. "It's softer than it looks."

"Now you know why I like wearing it." That and the fact that it created an ongoing connection between himself and his father. Still, he wanted her to have something of his, something to keep her warm, something meaningful. "I have a confession."

"I have something I have to get off my chest first." She nibbled her lip, and it took all of Crosby's control not to kiss her.

His admission could wait a few more minutes. "I'm always here for you." Crosby may never have spoken more honest words in his life.

Sami huddled in the sweater. "There are all sorts of reasons for a makeover, you know?"

Everywhere he turned, she always brought up his appearance. It tore him apart that they could never have had a solid relationship with her so focused on his physical image. His dreams shattered.

He clenched his jaw. "If you say so."

She clasped her hands in his. "A makeover isn't just about how you appear to others. It's also the confidence that comes from being authentic and true to yourself." She rubbed her thumb in the soft fleshy part of his hand before meeting his gaze. "And you, Crosby Virtue, are the most authentic person I've ever met. You didn't need contacts or a new outfit to know who you are. You're sweet and dorky in the best possible way, and you accept others just the way they are. You're perfectly imperfect, and I, for one, wouldn't like you to be otherwise."

She drew him to her, bringing her lips to meet his. This kiss seemed different from the others, deeper, richer, fuller. Crosby poured himself into the kiss, her light floral scent flooding him. She was part of his story, and he couldn't hold back any longer.

With confidence, he separated from her. "Sami."

His doorbell rang. He muttered under his breath as he opened his front door and found Amanda and Seth on the stoop. Amanda brushed past him and hurried into the living room. "Sami?"

Seth glared at him, and Crosby couldn't help but feel like he let his older brother down, first by allowing Sami to get hurt while skiing and then by kissing her.

Crosby closed his front door and offered to take their coats, but Seth refused with an arch of his eyebrow. "It's rather dark in here."

Crosby turned on all the lights while Amanda

helped Sami stand up. "We came as soon as we heard."

Sami blinked. "I'm fine. I thought I mentioned Crosby was bringing me home."

Amanda hugged her sister. "I had to see you for myself." Her gaze went to Sami's knee. "How bad is it?"

"It's already feeling better." Sami patted the knee brace. "This is more a precaution than anything else."

Seth glanced at Crosby again, his expression clearly telling Crosby how unhappy he was about Sami's injury. "It was an accident." Crosby's protest sounded weak even to himself.

Sami hobbled over and inserted herself between Seth and Crosby. "Crosby's a great ski instructor, and I'm fine."

Seth glanced over her shoulder, his face softening. "Sorry, little brother."

Crosby jammed his hands in his pockets. He'd always be the *little brother*. "Just as well that you're here. You saved me a trip out to the ranch."

Amanda and Seth helped Sami out to their car, and Crosby turned off the television. Some things would never change. He'd always be regarded as the youngest and least reliable Virtue, and he and Sami would always remain only the best of friends.

CHAPTER FIFTEEN

WITH FORTY-EIGHT HOURS until New Year's Eve, Crosby entered Timeless Tailors. He didn't have to wait long before the assistant called him back to the alteration room, where his suit for the celebration was hanging next to his tuxedo for Seth and Amanda's wedding.

Crosby lugged the tuxedo into the changing stall and returned to find his brother admiring his fancy suit in the ceiling-to-floor mirror. "My little brother cleans up well," Seth teased.

While Crosby didn't like to make waves, there was a time to put your foot down and this was one of them. Crosby stepped toward Seth.

"Today I'm your little brother, and yesterday you assumed I would let something bad happen to Sami because I wasn't paying attention or had my nose in a book." The grin left Seth's face, but Crosby continued. "I'm twenty-eight, Seth. Time for me to stop constantly being treated like a child by you, especially when I'm four inches taller than you."

Seth puffed out his chest. "I'll always be the oldest. I take my role seriously."

Especially after their parents died. Crosby was only too aware that Seth grew up faster than the rest of them that day. He went over and laid his hand on Seth's shoulder. "I know, but I'm tired of the three of you always thinking of me as the little brother."

"You'll always be the youngest." Seth seemed confused as though he was trying to comprehend Crosby's point but couldn't. "You can't change that."

Crosby raised his chin. "No, but times and people change. And it's past time that you all stopped treating me like less than, or someone who can't do anything right." He caught a glimpse of himself in the mirror. In the past few weeks, his posture was straighter from yoga, the contacts accentuated his brown eyes and the haircut showed off his long neck that was similar to his mother's if the pictures were any indication. A more confident man stared back at him. "I'll never be you or Jase or Daisy. The three of you are hard acts to follow."

"Hardly. I almost didn't finish high school." Seth fidgeted and then smoothed Crosby's lapel. "I did it for the three of you, so you'd all earn your diplomas."

"I know." Crosby was proud of how his brother

had taken the lead by being an example for his siblings.

"You should have told me this sooner," Seth reached for Crosby's bow tie and handed it to him.

Crosby placed the bow tie around his neck. "I'm telling you now."

Seth watched him, his eyes brimming with approval and something else Crosby couldn't identify. "And somehow you managed to capture the best of all of us. I'm proud to be your older brother, Dr. Virtue."

Seth had never said the words before, but Crosby had felt them in his heart. Still, it was nice to hear them aloud. His brother approached and started to tie Crosby's bow tie before stopping and stepping back. "Old habits die hard. You can do that for yourself."

"Thanks." Crosby tied his bow tie perfectly. "You're a great brother, Seth. Always there for all of us. I'm lucky to have you in my life."

Seth's nose twitched, and he swiped at the corner of his eye. "I suppose I should thank you for saying all of this today and not on my wedding day."

"You just did." Crosby dipped his head and wondered what was taking the tailor so long. It was almost as if he knew the brothers had so much to get off their chests.

Seth went over to the mirror and tied his own

bow tie, avoiding Crosby's gaze. "I talked to Jase last night."

"Glad to hear that two of the most stubborn, obstinate, loyal guys I know talk on occasion." Crosby cracked a grin, and then he realized why Seth wasn't looking him in the eye. Seth must have asked Jase to be his best man. "And Jase will make the perfect best man for you when you marry Amanda."

Seth faced Crosby, his frown too reminiscent of the gruff person he was before he met Amanda. "You're wrong. Jase and I agreed that we're still repairing our relationship, and there's someone else who's been an integral part of my life. I want you to be my best man."

This time it was Crosby who swiped at tears. "But I'm the little brother."

He met Seth's gaze, and they both laughed. "Who's taller by four inches." Seth threw Crosby's words back at him. "I'd be honored if you'd be my best man."

"The honor's mine." Crosby had been wrong about something else as well.

He'd been worried he'd fall apart once Sami left and there'd be no one to help pick up the pieces. That would never happen. His family would always be there for him.

Seth returned his focus to the mirror. "And Jase let something else slip."

Crosby smiled. "Are we going to be uncles to a new baby Virtue?"

Seth adjusted his gaze in the mirror, obviously watching Crosby. "He said he told you that we both know you're in love with Sami."

Crosby's chest heaved. "How long did you two talk?"

"Long enough for me to realize we need to get this out into the open." Seth pivoted until he looked Crosby in the eye. "Are you in love with Sami?"

How could he answer that? He weighed his words carefully. "I would think that if I was in love with Sami, she should hear the words first."

The door clicked open and closed, undoubtedly the tailor. At last. Crosby didn't know whether to be delighted that he was finally making an appearance or concerned that this conversation would now have to be continued later since there was no way Seth would let the subject drop without examining every angle.

Nobody entered the room, and Crosby returned his attention to Seth, who was tapping his foot as if waiting for Crosby to come clean. "I'll never do anything to make you and Amanda uncomfortable."

Seth rolled his eyes. "Your happiness is important, too. If you love Sami, don't hold back on my account. So far that's two excuses and no commitment to opening your heart to her. You need to tell her how you feel before she leaves Violet Ridge."

Every time Crosby had tried to do just that, something, or someone, got in the way. "I want her to have everything she wants and deserves."

No sooner had he said those words than the tailor finally showed up. Crosby knew from Seth's expression that they'd finish this conversation later, but as far as he was concerned, it was already done.

IN THE LAZY RIVER DUDE RANCH employee parking lot, Sami used the back of her palm to wipe away the tears on her cheeks. This couldn't be happening. *If I was in love with Sami.* Crosby's words that she'd overheard at Timeless Tailors echoed on repeat through her mind. If, if, if. She'd fallen for her best friend, and he didn't reciprocate her feelings.

An hour ago, she'd received a phone call from Mario asking if she could report immediately for a round trip to Hawaii, beginning on the third of January. Sami had thanked him but refused the offer, which had included a hefty signing bonus. Missing Crosby's speech was not an option. Knowing about his alteration appointment, she'd sought reassurance from him that she had done the right thing.

But his words made the answer to her dilemma crystal clear. How could she be around him when she was in love with him, and he didn't feel the same way?

Rifling through her purse, she found a manicure set, her favorite nail polish and one of Sundance's hats but no tissues. Where was a tissue when she needed one?

Sami stared at the tiny, knitted Santa hat. She figured Bridget must have made an extra one and slipped it into her purse. She wished she didn't know that, same as she wished she didn't know that Crosby wasn't in love with her. Leaving her car, she wandered around the ranch until she reached the frozen duck pond. One tear slipped down, then another. At least it was so cold outside that she wouldn't run into anyone she knew, especially her sister or Bridget. But the silent stillness was a bad antidote for the noisy thoughts penetrating her heart. She hurried to the canoe and kayak alcove and sat on the cold bench as the tears began falling in earnest.

"Sami?"

Amanda's voice penetrated through her sobs, and Sami regretted not going to her suite. She wiped her face with her coat sleeve, her mascara and rouge coming off on the white fabric, and then took long deep breaths so her voice wouldn't betray her heartbreak. "Amanda. What are you doing out here?"

"I could ask you the same." Amanda came over

and sat beside her, concern reflecting in her eyes. "What's wrong?"

Sami tried to smile but couldn't. "Nothing. Everything is great." Sami relayed the call she'd received but left out her refusal. "I'm leaving tonight."

Amanda laid her gloved hand on Sami's coat and frowned. "You've been crying way too much for this to be about the job offer. If you're that upset, maybe that's a sign you're supposed to stay here."

Sami sniffled, giving up the pretense everything was okay. "I have to follow through on my commitment."

Amanda's frown became more pronounced. "If that's what you truly want, I'll support you. But you don't have to search for something elusive when everything you want might be right here in Violet Ridge."

Amanda reached into her pocket and pulled out a bandanna, handing it to Sami. Sami's throat clogged, and she accepted the bandanna, wiping her cheeks. "But I never intended to stay."

"Would it be that awful?" Amanda asked, her voice soft, almost too soft to be heard even in the sheltered spot. "To stay?"

Sami blotted her eyes and then stuffed the bandanna in her pocket. "You know me. I'm always on the search for a new adventure."

Amanda reached out and rubbed Sami's shoulders. "Have you read all of Grandma Lou's letters?"

"I've read most of them, but I stopped." Even through the thickness of Sami's coat, Amanda's fingers worked wonders at comforting her. "I started feeling like I was invading someone's personal space."

Amanda stopped and waited until Sami faced her. Her frown finally softened into something more like a sad smile. "Promise me you'll read all of them."

Crosby would love the letters and photos. That type of private correspondence, a lifetime of exchanged stories and love, was right up his alley. A fresh wave of sadness overtook her, and Sami reached for the bandanna once more. "I promise. I wish you weren't seeing me at my worst."

Amanda gave Sami's hand a quick squeeze. "It's not fair that you're still beautiful even when you've been crying your eyes out. Besides, isn't that what sisters are for? To be there for each other in the ebbs and peaks." Amanda took the bandanna and wiped Sami's tears. "No matter where you are, I'll always be your older sister. I can't take back all the years I didn't protect you from Mom, but I can be here for you from now on."

Sami never thought of herself as a crier before, but she couldn't stem the flow of tears. After a few minutes, she finally composed herself. "And I'll always be your younger sister who'll never let you go and will always have your back. We're bonded at the hip now."

Amanda sniffled. "You're going to make me cry." She hugged Sami's side. "That connection will endure no matter where you are, but why are you really leaving? You're happy here. I heard it in your voice on Christmas Eve and saw it in your cheeks on Christmas Day. Can't this HR director find someone else?"

Sami stared at the frozen landscape, the bushes covered in snow and ice. It was hard trying to gain her mother's approval when no crown or sash was ever enough. It was harder to say goodbye to her sister.

But it was hardest to know Crosby didn't return her love.

Sami decided to confide the truth to Amanda. "After I received the offer from the HR director, I went to Timeless Tailors to talk to Crosby. He was speaking to Seth, and I overheard something I shouldn't have."

Amanda squeezed Sami's hand a second time. "Like how Crosby really feels about you? That's almost a relief seeing as how we've had to keep it a secret from you."

Sami bolted to her feet. "A relief?" Had she really known her sister at all? "To know someone will never return your love? That's cruel, and I can't stay under the circumstances."

Amanda's face crumbled. "So there's no chance?

I was hoping that the two of you might eventually feel the same way about each other."

Another tear fell. It was hard to admit the sparks were only felt at her end. She was hopelessly in love with Crosby, the man who fell asleep while eating cereal and researching some minute historical detail. This was a man who frolicked with his nephew and nieces while not being afraid to be silly with them. This same man had given her his most cherished possession, his father's sweater. And he thought of her as a friend.

"It takes two for a love story to blossom and flourish."

Now that everyone knew she was in love with Crosby, who didn't love her back, she was more resolved than ever to leave.

Sami drove to Violet Ridge to have dinner. She was unable to bear seeing any of the Virtue family. Upon her return, she snuck upstairs without running into anyone. *Whew!* Tomorrow morning, she'd leave at the break of dawn and spend the night in Utah before continuing to San Diego in time to greet the new year.

With the stealth of a Colorado mountain lion, Sami came along the hallway, only to find Crosby stationed outside her door. She gasped and placed her hand over her heart, which was threatening to escape her chest.

"What are you doing here?" Sami asked.

"I wanted to tell my best friend about something wonderful that's happened to me, but she's been avoiding me all day." Crosby pointed to her purse. "Did you forget to charge your phone? I've sent quite a few texts."

Best friend. Her heart cracked at his turn of phrase. That's all she was, and all she could ever be to him. Without a word, she slipped her hand into her purse and pulled out her phone, which she'd put on silent. Sure enough, there were at least fifteen texts from Crosby. She'd read them later, but first she drew on all of her acting lessons and pasted on her biggest beauty pageant smile. "I have news of my own—"

"When I didn't hear from you," Crosby interrupted, "I called Amanda. She said you're leaving for San Diego tomorrow, but that can't be right. You wouldn't miss the Midnight Express New Year's Eve Celebration."

He looked so hopeful and so firm in his conviction that her chest constricted. She'd do almost anything to spare him pain, but she couldn't be around him.

"Crosby... I've come to realize I'm holding you back." She unlocked her door and ushered him inside, where she made a beeline for her bedroom, stopping only to drag her set of luggage from the top shelf in her closet. She began throwing clothes haphazardly inside the first suitcase. "You won't be able to find the woman of your dreams if I'm around. You should invite Jasmine for tomorrow night."

"Sami." Crosby leaned against her doorframe, and she caught a glimpse of him in his new baby blue cashmere sweater.

She didn't want to notice how handsome he was, inside and out, any more than she could be around him. Not now. "My mind is made up. I'm leaving."

His jaw clenched before he crossed over to her, placing his hand on hers. He repeated her name until she looked at him. Her heart splintered into even more pieces. His piercing brown eyes contained the wealth of stories in them, and yet he couldn't be a part of her story. "You're really going before my speech?"

She wanted to hold his hand forever, but he wasn't hers. She removed her hand and instantly regretted it. "We both knew my time in Violet Ridge was limited. I want to see Saint Peter's Basilica, shop at the Grand Bazaar in Turkey and see Mount Kilimanjaro for myself."

She wished Crosby could have been by her side on her travels, pointing out the little details and making her laugh.

Yet his life was here. Sundance. His family. The Miners' Cottage. She'd never ask him to leave any of that for her even if he did feel the same way about her.

She opened her sock drawer and dumped every

pair on top of her other clothes. "And you're going to meet the woman of your dreams at the celebration. If you called her, I'm sure Jasmine would be more than happy to be your date."

"You're that certain Jasmine is my perfect holiday match?"

"I know you're going to make someone very happy." Her voice caught, the last word garbled. If only it were her. "I'll be back for Amanda's wedding."

Crosby stayed still as if intent on soaking up this time with her. "What about your gnomes?"

"Amanda's the homebody, not me." With that, Sami ran into the bathroom, shutting the door behind her.

Sami stared in the mirror. Could someone be two things at once: a world traveler and a homebody? The glass remained silent. Crosby would have an answer. Maybe it was time to ask if he wanted to see her favorite destinations with her. She plucked out several tissues from the box and dried her eyes.

By the time she opened the door, Crosby was gone.

CHAPTER SIXTEEN

WITH A GLANCE at Sundance, Crosby rearranged his stack of index cards one more time. "What do you think? Will I do my family proud?"

Sundance blinked at him, snatched a daffodil, a special New Year's Eve snack, out of his bowl and headed to the back of his terrarium once more. Crosby chuckled and practiced his speech again in the privacy of his living room. Yet there was something missing, a spark to catapult it from blah to great.

Or maybe it was more like someone was missing. Since yesterday, Crosby felt Sami's absence in every task, conversation and moment. She was really gone, setting off to do what she loved, same as he was doing what he loved here in Violet Ridge.

Why couldn't their two livelihoods be closer together?

Something nibbled at the back of his mind, and he relived that amazing road trip where he and Sami had detoured to historic sites where they tried on hats in the gift shop and chose souvenirs for his nieces and nephew. Later, at that roadside diner, they had scrunched their noses at their platters and happily switched. Laughing and chatting, they both tucked away the entire portion, preferring what the other had ordered. Before that trip, Crosby had always hunkered down at the Miners' Cottage, reading others' stories and diaries while researching the details for the different exhibits and his dissertation. It was only with Sami at his side that he discovered there was a whole world of stories and places out there for him to explore.

Crosby set the index cards on the table with Sundance's terrarium and glanced at his ancient pajamas, his most comfortable ones with a hole on the right sleeve. It was time to change. He ventured into his bedroom where the suit and tie that Sami had selected for tonight hung in his closet.

He caught a glimpse of himself in the mirror and noticed a bit of cereal on his stubble and another crumb on his sleeve. He ran his hands through his hair, trying to remember the last time he'd combed it. Yesterday, he'd confined himself to his house, using the excuse of finishing his speech to keep everyone at bay while nursing his heartache over Sami. Staring at his reflection, he remembered why Sami had really committed to this makeover experience. She wanted to have her best friend live up to his potential. He owed it to himself to let her efforts show tonight.

He straightened his shoulders and pulled himself to his full height, going through a couple of the yoga poses he'd been practicing. Despite his heartache, the exercise did him good. Then, he shaved, showered and remembered to apply the hair mousse that Sami had taught him how to use. After donning his new suit and tie, he stepped back. A little bit of self-care went a long way in presenting a revived Crosby to the world.

He owed all this to Sami, who had been so obstinate about thinking she was keeping him from meeting the woman of his dreams. Didn't she know she was that woman?

But how could she since he never told her? Never asked her if they could find a way to navigate their dreams together? For a while, it had seemed selfish on his part to interfere with her dreams of travel and just being herself, independent of her mother's schemes, Amanda and him. But what if he wasn't interfering and went alongside her?

His breath caught. There was a difference between standing in someone's way and sharing the journey. Since he hadn't expressed himself, Sami might not know he'd already met the woman of his dreams the day she'd arrived at the dude ranch. While he'd developed a crush for her on the spot, he hadn't truly fallen in love with her until these past few months. She was his Christmas match.

Crosby picked up his phone and snapped a close-up selfie, followed by a full-length version. How could he express his heart to her without coming off as possessive?

By being himself. Yes, that was the answer.

Finding the right words, Crosby forwarded the pictures to Sami.

Thought you might like to see the finished product.

He deliberated over the next message.

I'm a swan, but you know what they say about swans, right? When one commits to another, the two share an unbreakable bond. You're my swan and the woman of my dreams. Say the word and we'll talk about traveling the world together.

Crosby raised his chin and pressed Send. While he should have said this in person, this was the next best thing.

And if she didn't choose him?

His siblings would be there for him while he tried to mend his broken heart.

SITTING IN A diner two hundred miles from Violet Ridge wasn't how Sami had expected to spend her New Year's Eve. While she should already be nearing the San Diego city limits, something was holding her back. She had already notified Asia and the HR director that she was still in Colorado and would update them later.

Sami nodded at the server, who refilled Sami's coffee mug. She reached for the creamer and sugar at the end of the table and doctored her coffee until it was perfect. The steam and aroma tickled her nose, and she surveyed her surroundings. The Christmas tree in the corner was full of gnome ornaments. A longing for her cozy suite and the ranch overwhelmed her. Even worse, she was missing Crosby's speech. He'd put so much energy and effort into it, and she was letting her pride stand in the way of being there for him.

Crosby and the entire Virtue family had shown her something about love and community that her parents, particularly her mother, never had. Although Crosby had believed he needed to strive to measure up to them, he was an accepted and beloved member of the family. The triplets especially loved their uncle Crosby. In fact, the whole town loved Crosby, even Mr. Hawk.

If she loved him, and she did, shouldn't she be there for him even if it was the hardest thing she'd ever done?

Sami set her coffee down and took Seth's Christmas gift to her—the special wooden box—out of her purse. Within minutes, she was engrossed in the stories and anecdotes of her grandmother's trips with her grandfather. One paragraph jumped out at her. *Oh, Bridie. How lucky am I to have the best life. I teach for nine months and for the other three, Garrett and I travel the world together. Seeing such amazing treasures with the man I love by my side and then coming home to a job that I adore? Life doesn't get any better.*

Sami reread the Christmas letter and tapped it against the saucer. Grandma Lou wasn't just the homebody Amanda remembered from her summer visits. She was also a world traveler, who balanced her job and her home life.

Sami was more like her grandmother than she'd realized. Hadn't Sami already found a job she loved after a disappointing stint on the beauty pageant circuit and trying to act? Meeting a different slate of customers every week in her salon, each one with a fascinating story, kept her on her toes.

Then there was Violet Ridge, which had adopted her into its fold. How fun it had been helping the Thunderbolt volunteers with their hair and makeup. Surely there were other opportunities like that during the year. Nelda and Zelda had already offered her a chance to join in the spring event. Plus, there was Jeremy's aunt Marilyn, who was now in remission. Perhaps she could help cancer patients and survivors with a special spa day where she could offer free facials and special lotion to combat the skin dryness that was often a side effect of chemotherapy. She could give back to Violet Ridge as thanks for all it had given to her.

Had she been so intent on mapping out her future that she'd lost sight of what was right in front of her?

Sami took a sip of the coffee, now cold. How long had she been reading the letters? The diner was now empty, and the skies were growing darker with gray clouds. What time was it? She pulled out her phone and found several missed texts, including a couple from Amanda asking her to message when she arrived in San Diego.

She took a deep breath before opening Crosby's text. Her breath caught as she saw the photos of him in his new suit. He was going to wow the audience and Jasmine tonight.

Then she read his text, and her heart soared.

She was the woman of his dreams? How could that be? She heard him tell Seth that he wasn't in love with her. *I would think if I was in love with her, she should hear the words first.*

She couldn't have misunderstood him. After all, Amanda and she had talked about it. Her sister said everyone had kept Sami's feelings a secret from Crosby. Chills went through her. Did she have it backward? Had everyone been keeping Crosby's feelings about her a secret, while Sami had taken her sweet time realizing Crosby was her swan?

Sami groaned. If Crosby was in love with her

and she missed one of the most pivotal moments of his life, would her absence ruin any chance of them being together?

Sami did the math in her head. If she left now, she might arrive in time to hear his speech. At least she'd arrive by midnight. Maybe. She raised her hand. "Check, please."

The waitress came over and pointed out the window. "The snow's starting to come down harder. I heard they're closing the highway west of here. You might consider checking to see if the hotel has any vacancies."

No, no, no. This couldn't be happening. "What about conditions east of here?"

A truck driver was passing by their table. "Do you have four-wheel drive?" he asked.

Sami nodded.

"If you're heading toward Gunnison or Pueblo, you'd best leave now or hope there's room at the hotel."

Sami threw a twenty on the table. She had to make it to Violet Ridge tonight.

CHAPTER SEVENTEEN

SERVERS DISTRIBUTED DESSERT to the partygoers, and Crosby accepted his chocolate raspberry tart with a thank-you and a smile. The community center turned banquet hall had never looked more festive than for this Midnight Express New Year's Eve Celebration. This truly was the culmination of all the hard work in getting the Thunderbolt up and running again. Gold and silver balloons hung from the ceiling. Lanterns rested alongside antique clocks on each table adorned with gold-and-black tablecloths. The dance floor was currently empty but would soon be full of people celebrating the countdown to midnight.

He transferred his gaze to his grandparents, who were seated at the next table, surrounded by friends, and then focused once more on his siblings, who flanked Crosby.

Daisy sent a furtive look toward Ben, who shook his head. "Constance and Marshall are watching the triplets," he said. "You know they'd call if there were any issues."

Cassie exchanged a similar look with Jase, but Jase gave a reassuring nod and reached for his fiancée's hand. Cassie's mother, in town for the holidays, was babysitting Penny and Easton along with taking care of their two dogs.

Daisy's shoulders relaxed. "You're right." She sipped her water. "If anything, I should worry about Marshall slipping Pearl a treat that won't agree with her stomach."

Everyone chuckled, and Crosby could hardly blame Marshall for giving in to Pearl's soulful hound-dog expression.

Crosby slid his fork into the creamy tart, but his stomach rebelled. He wasn't particularly hungry. Dessert could wait until after his speech.

Seth sat on Crosby's left. His brother motioned for him to come closer until Crosby was next to him. "Speech or Sami?" Seth whispered low enough for Crosby's ears only.

Crosby patted his suit pocket. "I have the speech here, and I've practiced it so often Sundance could deliver it."

As for Sami? Crosby thumbed the little gnome in his pocket he had intended on giving her at midnight. It was a cute little thing with a black top hat and holding a pocket watch. Too bad he would never have a chance to give it to her considering she hadn't called or replied to his text.

Seth shifted in his seat. "I'm sorry it didn't work out for you both."

Not as sorry as Crosby.

Ben rose and placed his napkin over an empty plate before nodding at Crosby. "Introducing you is one of the perks of being the mayor."

Daisy delivered a thumbs-up to both of them before Ben climbed the steps to the dais. To Crosby's surprise, Sami's lessons were taking effect. A calmness overtook him that he wouldn't have had otherwise. He had her to thank for that, along with so much more. As his stomach settled, Crosby listened to the tail end of Ben's kind introduction. "...proud to introduce my brother-in-law Dr. Crosby Virtue."

The crowd delivered a warm round of applause. Ben patted Crosby on the back and rejoined Daisy and the others. With a deep breath, Crosby reached into his suit pocket and froze. The index cards weren't there. He kept his smile intact and patted his other suit pocket. They weren't there, either. Then he remembered. They were at home next to Sundance's terrarium.

Crosby glanced at the audience, his gaze narrowing in on Jeremy and his date, Dr. Velasquez, and then roving over Nelda and Zelda before landing on his grandparents. His grandmother beamed and winked at him.

Weeks ago, he would have panicked and folded on the spot. Instead, he raised his chin and remembered Sami insisting that her lessons were necessary in case of any last-minute complications. This was definitely a complication.

But Sami would be the first one here to tell him he could do this, with or without the index cards, with or without her. His resolve intact, he knew he could do this. The right words finally came to him.

"Happy New Year's Eve, everyone. Thank you to the committee for the honor of choosing me to speak to you tonight. I timed my speech this afternoon, and hopefully, the end will coincide with the start of the ten-second countdown for midnight."

The audience clapped and Crosby grinned. "Don't worry. I left that speech at home, and my iguana, Sundance, will be the only one who will ever have listened to it. Instead, I'm going to tell you a simple story."

This one he knew by heart. Crosby launched into the story of his great-grandfather, Grandma Bridget's father, Patrick Crosby, who had served in the military and arrived home via the Violet Ridge Thunderbolt on a long-ago New Year's Eve. There, on the train platform, Patrick reunited with the love of his life, Winsome, Crosby's great-grandmother. Crosby sailed into his conclusion, "The depot was the site of many a wartime reunion, and now it will be a landmark and tourist destination for stories for years to come. Thank you."

Crosby started to step off the dais when he caught sight of his grandmother wiping tears from her eyes. Then carefully and slowly, she rose to her feet. Soon others did the same, including his three siblings. Crosby inhaled a shaky breath as he walked down the steps to his table. He stopped and allowed himself the luxury of taking a long look at his siblings, all of whom were cheering for him. For him!

Crosby had relished defining career moments like receiving his doctoral hood at his graduation ceremony, but this reception topped that one. If only Sami had been here. He nodded as the crowd took their seats once more and the band began to play.

He was about to leave the stage when something else caught his eye. Someone stepped out of the shadows in the back, still clapping. Then his gaze met hers, and his heart almost stopped.

It was Sami! She was here and stunning in a gold evening dress and heels paired with, of all things, his father's sweater. She had a wrapped parcel tucked under her arm. His heart seemed to stop for a second before thumping harder than ever.

Was this a sign of good things to come?

PART OF SAMI felt like she was still on the highway. She didn't know how much of that was due to the three hours of nonstop driving with a quick detour to the ranch, where she changed before coming here, or her profound reaction to seeing Crosby. To think she almost missed his moving speech.

Crosby bypassed the table with his siblings and their significant others. They watched him as he made a beeline toward her. Amanda was the first to spot Sami. Her sister rose and gave her a thumbs-up, then took her seat once more.

"You came back." While they weren't the three words that had been on her heart for the past week, Sami savored hearing Crosby's voice.

"I could travel the world, but would it be worth it without you?" She shrugged, holding the package in her hands now. "Nowhere would be as vibrant, and the stories about each destination wouldn't be as meaningful."

Crosby closed the gap between them, looking most handsome in his new suit and tie. "I won't be the one to get in the way of your travels, but I'd be honored if you'd consider letting me accompany you."

Sami raised her chin in the same manner she'd seen Crosby do so often. "As my best friend?"

Crosby reached for the present she was holding and set it on a nearby table. "As something much more." He leaned in and whispered, "Much, much more. I love you."

Sami kissed him, his slight stubble tickling her chin, the taste of chocolate and raspberry lingering. This time the kiss was different because she knew he loved her. Just as his great-grandfather had come home on New Year's to the woman he'd marry, so, too, had she come home to the love of her life.

People started offering their congratulations, and Sami realized his audience was now their audience. Her cheeks heated at having so many from the town witness their reunion. Crosby reached up and cupped her face with his palms, his hands reassuring and strong. He bent down and kissed her again.

The world clicked into place. The decision to settle permanently in Violet Ridge was hers. She could still travel the world and fill her phone with pictures of famous landmarks with Crosby by her side.

Moments later, he broke their point of contact, but the connection still hummed between them. "Why aren't you in San Diego?"

Honesty was the only way to proceed. "I was at the tailor's and heard you say something to Seth, something along the lines of 'I would think if I was in love with her, she should hear the words first.'" She inhaled a deep breath. "I thought that meant you didn't love me, but now I know. I'm your swan, and I love you."

Crosby gently stroked her cheek. "I fell in love with you the minute you told me there was more to life than books." His smile lit up his face. "And you told me I'd meet the woman I was destined to spend my life with during this celebration. I have met her. It's you. It's always been you, Sami Fleming."

With that, they kissed again. She liked how this year was ending with every passing minute. After more kisses, she stepped away from him. "Do you think your grandparents will give me my old job back? I have great ideas. I want to dedicate an afternoon each month to Violet Ridge residents like Marilyn who are going through some health issues and need a little pampering."

He nodded. "They'll love that and support you."

Crosby reached into his pocket and handed her a New Year's gnome. She squealed with delight. "Is this for me?"

"You need something to put in the Porcupine Suite to look forward to seeing when we return from our travels. Where do you want to go first? Africa? Australia?"

She gazed at him. "Niagara Falls." She pecked his cheek, her lipstick leaving an imprint. "On our honeymoon. Then I'd like to come home to a reception like this. With all our friends and family."

She handed him her gift and watched as he unwrapped the house he'd chosen and she'd purchased for him at the holiday market. If only she'd realized sooner he was her perfect match, she might not have left.

But then she might have always doubted herself. Now she was sure. She was where she belonged.

People started approaching them. Folks admired Crosby's speech and seemed thrilled at this new romance. Sami basked in Amanda's welcome.

It was almost midnight, and Sami joined Crosby on the dance floor. She waved hello to Jeremy, who pointed to Dr. Velasquez with a smile. Happiness for her friend enveloped her as he had met his match in the good doctor.

Crosby swept Sami into his arms, and they danced until the band started the countdown. At the stroke of midnight, streamers and confetti fell from the ceiling. One gold streamer landed on Crosby's head while a silver one fell on her shoulder. Before she could brush them away, Crosby kissed her. This moment was the beginning of their adventures. It was the best New Year's yet.

EPILOGUE

Where had the time gone? Sixty years ago on Valentine's Day, Bridget had married her best friend, Martin, becoming Bridget Crosby Virtue. It was as if no time had passed from then until today when she'd soon witness the joining of her oldest grandson, Seth, in marriage to the lovely Amanda.

The central barn was decorated for the wedding and had never looked better. Bridget leaned on her cane and admired the delicate silver bracelet her granddaughter, Daisy, had made just for her. This morning, at their anniversary breakfast, Daisy had given her the bracelet and presented Martin with matching cuff links. Daisy's thoughtful present made today that much more special.

Inside the barn, ambient heaters provided warmth, allowing the guests to show off their wedding finery. Bridget let the heat seep into her bones. A few years ago, after her stroke, when all four of her grandchildren were single, she fretted she would pass away without any of them having a special someone. While Bridget understood there were people who enjoyed being single, she had been convinced there was someone out there for each of her four grandchildren. Today proved she was right.

Martin came over to her and pecked her cheek. She accepted his kiss and stood back, relishing the same twinkle that graced his eyes now, just as it had on their wedding day. He reached over and covered her hands on the cane with his. "I married the prettiest girl here."

She accepted his compliment, secure that he believed those words with his whole heart. That was why she loved Martin so much. He never committed to anything with less than his full self.

"We've been through so much in the past sixty years." She couldn't help but glance upward as she thought of her beloved son, Peter, and her delightful daughter-in-law, Rosemary, both lost in that tragic car accident. Hearing the police officer deliver the news was the worst moment in her life.

She had stayed strong for her four grandchildren until she found that same strength for herself again.

"Some days were harder than others, but we're still standing. Thank you for marrying me, Bridge." She still loved hearing his nickname for her as much now as the first time he'd used it.

"I'd do it all over again." Bridget smiled at her husband, the love of her life.

Jase, who was serving as an usher for Seth and Amanda, approached them. There was a lightness in his step that hadn't been there before he met Cassie. Thank goodness that her cowboy cop grandson had found his way back to them and fallen in love with not just Cassie but her sweet kids as well. Last month, the pair had surprised everyone with an impromptu ceremony, conducted by Ben, at Violet Ridge's City Hall, followed by a reception at Thistle Brook Farm. One look at Jase, and she knew his and Cassie's love would last a lifetime.

Jase escorted her to her seat in the front row of the groom's side.

Her happiness was overflowing at the sight of the floral arch gracing the area where Seth and Amanda would exchange their vows. Soft harp music filled the air, and Bridget turned to find Ben walking his sister, Lizzie Harper, and her husband, Lucky, to their seats.

Soon every chair in the barn was filled with friends and family waiting for Amanda. Silence descended before the harpist began the processional march.

Bridget's eyes brimmed with tears of joy as her three great-granddaughters walked down the aisle, each scattering flowers in their inimitable style. Rosie was dancing and throwing the petals with joyous abandon, while her sister, Lily, was serious, dropping each petal with measured care. In between them was Penny, who accepted her role as the mature oldest cousin in stride, alternating smiles with scrunching her face in concentration. They stood to one side of the arch and then Easton and Aspen rushed down the aisle, almost as if they were racing, their grins huge, until they met her gaze. They instantly slowed, and she winked at them as they passed.

Next came Ben and Daisy, and Bridget touched her new bracelet once more. There was something different about Daisy. Thankfully, Ben had come into her life and provided her with all the love she deserved. Come to think of it, during the champagne toast at the rehearsal dinner last night, Daisy had reached for one of the glasses of ginger ale that had been brought out for the children. Could it be? Would there be another great-grandchild blessing their family by Thanksgiving? Daisy floated past and Bridget tilted her head. Daisy blushed but nodded.

Seth and Crosby took their places at the front with Jase and Ben standing on the other side of Crosby. Bridget's heart was full at all of her handsome grandsons. The ranch was in good hands with Seth at the helm. Amanda was the perfect partner to see them through any contingency. To Seth's credit, he held his head high, beamed at his soon-to-be wife and showed no signs of nerves.

Then there was Crosby, who had found his

love at last. She was so proud of him becoming Dr. Virtue. Peter and Rosemary would have been ecstatic at his academic success but even more about his happiness with Sami. It had been a whirlwind few months for him, overseeing the historical renovations on the Miners' Cottage, aided by Dominic Martinelli and his construction company. Somehow in the midst of everything, he and Sami had flown to Paris for a long weekend where Crosby had proposed. Thankfully, Sami said yes. Martin had enjoyed taking care of Crosby's pet iguana, Sundance, a little too much and wanted one of his own. Needless to say, Bridget had put her foot down and refused while Sami consoled Martin by saying he'd be the first person on their iguana-sitting list.

Speaking of Crosby's fiancée, Bridget turned her attention to the back of the barn where her future granddaughter-in-law was processing down the aisle. Sami was gorgeous in her dark pink satin maid of honor dress. She blew a kiss at Marilyn Haralson, who had come to the ranch earlier in the week along with other cancer survivors for a full, free afternoon of beauty treatments. Then Sami produced a smile for Jeremy and his doctor girlfriend before stopping for a second. Her gaze fell on Crosby, and Bridget saw love reflected there. Theirs was a love story for the ages.

The wedding march began and everyone stood.

It took her longer to rise now than sixty years ago when she'd married Martin at the young age of nineteen, but rise she did. There had been so many beautiful brides since then: Rosemary, Daisy, Cassie. Now Amanda took her place among them and in Bridget's heart.

Amanda walked down the aisle on Martin's arm, her love for Seth reflected in her eyes. How Martin had glowed when Amanda had asked him to be her escort and how much Seth resembled Martin! *Sometimes it's like seeing double.* Martin answered the officiant's questions and then joined Bridget. Everyone sat and the officiant began the ceremony.

Martin reached over and kissed her cheek. "You're glowing."

Bridget squeezed his hand. "Daisy's pregnant. I'll be knitting a new stocking for Christmas."

The Virtue family was expanding, and Bridget's heart leaped with joy. Each grandchild had met the person who would stand by them in sickness and in health, for richer, for poorer, in the same way she and Martin had done for all these years. They had boosted each other in times of sorrow and rejoiced together when times were good.

Bridget took her seat with a grateful heart, thankful for this generation and the next. Mostly, she was thankful for the man who sat beside her. If her grandchildren were as fortunate as she was, they'd all have lives rich with unexpected twists and turns, along with support and love through every step of the journey.

* * * * *

For more small-town Violet Ridge romances by Tanya Agler, visit www.Harlequin.com today!

Get up to 4 Free Books!

We'll send you 2 free books from each series you try PLUS a free Mystery Gift.

FREE Value Over **$25**

Both the **Harlequin® Special Edition** and **Harlequin® Heartwarming™** series feature compelling novels filled with stories of love and strength where the bonds of friendship, family and community unite.

YES! Please send me 2 FREE novels from the Harlequin Special Edition or Harlequin Heartwarming series and my FREE Gift (gift is worth about $10 retail). After receiving them, if I don't wish to receive any more books, I can return the shipping statement marked "cancel." If I don't cancel, I will receive 6 brand-new Harlequin Special Edition books every month and be billed just $6.39 each in the U.S. or $7.19 each in Canada, or 4 brand-new Harlequin Heartwarming Larger-Print books every month and be billed just $7.19 each in the U.S. or $7.99 each in Canada, a savings of 20% off the cover price. It's quite a bargain! Shipping and handling is just 50¢ per book in the U.S. and $1.25 per book in Canada.* I understand that accepting the 2 free books and gift places me under no obligation to buy anything. I can always return a shipment and cancel at any time by calling the number below. The free books and gift are mine to keep no matter what I decide.

Choose one:
- ☐ **Harlequin Special Edition** (235/335 BPA G36Y)
- ☐ **Harlequin Heartwarming Larger-Print** (161/361 BPA G36Y)
- ☐ **Or Try Both!** (235/335 & 161/361 BPA G36Z)

Name (please print)

Address   Apt. #

City   State/Province   Zip/Postal Code

Email: Please check this box ☐ if you would like to receive newsletters and promotional emails from Harlequin Enterprises ULC and its affiliates. You can unsubscribe anytime.

Mail to the Harlequin Reader Service:
IN U.S.A.: P.O. Box 1341, Buffalo, NY 14240-8531
IN CANADA: P.O. Box 603, Fort Erie, Ontario L2A 5X3

Want to explore our other series or interested in ebooks? Visit www.ReaderService.com or call 1-800-873-8635.

---

*Terms and prices subject to change without notice. Prices do not include sales taxes, which will be charged (if applicable) based on your state or country of residence. Canadian residents will be charged applicable taxes. Offer not valid in Quebec. This offer is limited to one order per household. Books received may not be as shown. Not valid for current subscribers to the Harlequin Special Edition or Harlequin Heartwarming series. All orders subject to approval. Credit or debit balances in a customer's account(s) may be offset by any other outstanding balance owed by or to the customer. Please allow 4 to 6 weeks for delivery. Offer available while quantities last.

Your Privacy—Your information is being collected by Harlequin Enterprises ULC, operating as Harlequin Reader Service. For a complete summary of the information we collect, how we use this information and to whom it is disclosed, please visit our privacy notice located at https://corporate.harlequin.com/privacy-notice. Notice to California Residents – Under California law, you have specific rights to control and access your data. For more information on these rights and how to exercise them, visit https://corporate.harlequin.com/california-privacy. For additional information for residents of other U.S. states that provide their residents with certain rights with respect to personal data, visit https://corporate.harlequin.com/other-state-residents-privacy-rights/.

HSEHW25